Safe With Me

Book Five in the With Me in Seattle Series

By
Kristen Proby

SAFE WITH ME - Book Five in the With Me In Seattle Series
Kristen Proby

Cover Art:
Photographer: Molly Claridge of Be Still Photography
Graphic Artist: Renae Porter
Models: Michael Wilson and Steph Buzzell

This novel is dedicated to my own hero, my husband, Sgt. Alvin Proby. I love you, soldier.

Prologue

"Why do we have to go to daddy's house?" Maddie asks from the back seat of my SUV, her small arms crossed over her chest, holding her dolly tightly against her and her face scrunched in a scowl.

"Because it's Thanksgiving," I reply patiently. "Your daddy wants to see you for the holiday."

"I don't want to go," Josie joins in, mirroring her twin sister's pose, and I sigh deeply, scrubbing my hands over my face as I wait for the light to turn green.

"It's only until Saturday," I remind them while doing my best to ignore the pit in my stomach. I don't want them to go either. Their dad only sees them on holidays or their birthday, if he shows up at all. Of course they don't want to go stay with him.

They don't know him.

As I pull up to Jeff's small house in a suburb of Chicago, three men hurry out his front door and jump into a dark SUV parked in the circular driveway. Just before they pull off, one of the men glances back at us.

I cut the engine and frown as I watch the vehicle take off at a fast clip down the street. My flags are red and flying all over the place in my head.

I glance back at the girls. "Stay here for a second while I go make sure your dad is ready for you, okay?"

They both just frown at me, their dark brown eyes looking all forlorn and sad, and I frown back at them. "Stop being sad. Your dad loves you guys. You'll have fun."

They just shrug as I step out of the car and walk up to his front door. I glance over my shoulder, curious who was in that SUV.

They could be co-workers of Jeff's, but if that's the case, I'm not leaving the girls with him.

Jeff is an undercover cop, and the people he *works* with are unsavory to say the least.

I knock on the door, but there is no answer, and the house is still. I knock again and sigh deeply. If he's standing the girls up, *again,* I will kick his ass.

When there is still no answer, I try the knob and frown when the door opens easily. This is not Jeff's usual M.O. He always locks the doors, even when he's home.

"Jeff?" I call out as I walk inside, but there is no answer and the smell of something hot and metallic fills my nostrils.

I move into the living room and stop dead in my tracks. Jeff is lying on the floor, his eyes wide open, mouth gaping and a trickle of blood seeps from the single gunshot wound in his forehead.

Oh dear God.

My first thought is to run to him, to make sure he's okay, but I wasn't a cop's wife for five years for nothing, and I have my babies in the car.

I run back to the car, start the engine, throw it in gear and peel out of the driveway, heading in the opposite direction the SUV went in earlier.

Jeff is dead!

"Mommy, I thought we were going to daddy's house," Maddie has turned in her seat, trying to see out the rear window.

"Sit down, Mads," I order more harshly than I should, my eyes also pinned behind us.

I have to call the police.

"Where is daddy?" Josie asks, both girls are watching me carefully, and I know my shaking hands and sharp voice are scaring them, so I do my best to look and sound calm.

I'm sure it's not working.

"He had something come up with work," I lie and check the rearview for the hundredth time.

"Okay," Maddie replies and hugs her dolly close.

Shit, what am I going to do?

I pull into a gas station, grab my phone and step out of the car so the girls can't hear my conversation.

Jeff's partner answers on the second ring.

"Why are you calling this number?"

"Jeff's dead," I respond immediately. "I just found him in his house. I'm calling 911, but wanted to give you a heads up first."

"Sonofabitch," he mutters. "Did you witness anything?"

"I saw them leaving the house, but no, I didn't see them shoot him. I didn't even think to get the license plate number of the car. It's a dark SUV."

"That's no help, Bryn." His voice is sad and frustrated. Sully worked with Jeff for more than ten years.

"I know, I'm sorry. I didn't touch anything."

"I'll call it in. We will need an official statement. You know the drill."

I nod and then realize he can't see me. I'm shaking. It's hard to breathe.

"I think I'm going to leave town, Sul."

He sighs and clears his throat. "Where are you going?"

"Home. Seattle. My family is there. My cousin's brother-in-law is a cop with Seattle PD. Matt Montgomery. Can I give my statement to him?"

"I'm gonna need to get your statement before you leave. You know I can't let you go without it." It sounds like he's pulling his phone away from his face. "Bryn, hold on."

I pace by the car as I wait for Sully to come back. Jesus, is this really happening? Do I have time to go home and get some of the girls' things? I've wanted to move back to Seattle for years, but never dreamed it would be under these circumstances.

Suddenly, Sully is back on the line.

"I think it's a good idea that you go, Bryn. I can't tell you who that was, but you were seen at Jeff's house by the wrong people. Take the girls and get out of town. If you lay low, you should be fine, but I want you gone."

Fuck. Jeff, what have you gotten me into?

"What about my statement?" My voice sounds stronger than I feel.

"I'll meet you someplace with one of the other cops to get a statement. But I don't want you going back to your place. I'll take care of your stuff in a few days."

I scrub my hand through my hair and glance into the car to find the girls watching me.

"Okay, I have to get some things for me and the girls." I rattle off the location of the nearest discount department store and hear Sully sigh over the phone.

"Be careful. And text me Montgomery's number."

"Okay."

The line goes dead as I hop back into my car and smile reassuringly at the girls who are watching me with wide, scared eyes.

Kids are so much smarter than people give them credit for.

I scramble in my purse for my phone and text Stacy's husband, Isaac. The Montgomerys' will know what to do.

With shaking fingers I type: *Plz call me when ur alone.*

I dig in my purse again to make sure I have my wallet and all my necessities, and realization hits that I definitely can't to go back to our house to collect our things.

My phone rings, Isaac's name on the caller id and I answer it quickly.

"Isaac."

"Bryn? What's wrong?"

"I can't go into detail because the girls are in the car with me, but I have to come to Seattle right now."

"Bryn, slow down. Are you hurt?"

"No, we're all fine, but I don't think we're safe."

"What do you mean?" His voice has taken on a hard edge and it steadies me.

"I just saw something I shouldn't have. I'll explain when I get there. I just wanted to let you know that I'm driving home." I glance back to find the girls watching me with wide, somber eyes.

"You're driving?" He asks incredulously. "It's almost December, Bryn. The roads are going to be horrible."

"I know. I'll take my time. I'm going to have to stop at night for the girls anyway. It could take me a week to get there."

"I don't like this," he responds grimly.

"Me either." As the shock catches up with me, tears run unchecked down my cheeks.

"We'll be here, Bryn. Call me every day to let me know where you are. I'm going to talk to Matt."

"I'm going to need to talk to Matt as soon as I get there, Isaac. And a detective from Chicago should be calling him any time."

"Are you in trouble?" Isaac's voice is calm and cold, and I know he's thinking the worst.

"Not like you're thinking, but it's bad."

"Drive safely. Keep me informed."

"Okay," I agree, hang up and pull into a WalMart parking lot. "Come on girls, we need to grab a few things."

"Are we going to see grandma and grandpa in Seattle?" Josie asks.

They're so damn smart.

"Yes, sweetie, so we need to get some things to take with us."

"Yay, we get to see grandma and grandpa!" Maddie dances beside me as we walk into the store to buy necessities such as toothbrushes and underwear.

The girls have a few days worth of clothes packed with us, but all I have is my purse.

Maybe some hair dye for me.

I also pull my cell phone apart and throw it in the trash, adding a new cell to my list of things to buy.

I guess we're going back to Seattle sooner than I expected.

Chapter One

Bang! Bang! Bang!

My alarm shouldn't be going off yet.

Bang! Bang! Bang!

I wake with a start to the sound of someone trying to beat my door down, and my heart immediately slams into overdrive.

I jump from the bed, not bothering to throw anything on over my skimpy tank and panties and search madly for a weapon of any kind.

"Mommy?" Maddie asks sleepily from her bedroom doorway.

"Go back to bed, Mads." I usher her back into the bedroom and give her my best smile, which feels more like a grimace.

"Someone's at the door," Josie informs me and pulls her baby doll into her small arms.

"I know. I'm going to go answer it. Stay in your room." My voice is stern as I shut their door behind me and race down the stairs to the living room.

All of the blinds are still closed, so I can't see outside.

Bang! Bang! Bang!

I grab the screwdriver I was using yesterday to put a set of shelves together and open the door just a crack.

"Who is it?" I ask wearily.

"Bryn, it's just Caleb and me," Matt Montgomery answers, his handsome face grim.

I step back and open the door wide, sighing in relief.

"You scared the hell out of me!"

"What are you doing with the screw driver?" Matt asks and props his hands on his hips just as his younger brother, Caleb, scrowls at me.

"It's my weapon," I tell them both and raise my chin stubbornly.

"Right." Caleb steps forward and plucks the screwdriver out of my hand. "It's very effective."

"I could have stabbed you if you were a bad guy." I step back and push my hair off my face. "Why are you here at six in the damn morning?"

"Maybe you should put some clothes on," Matt suggests, and I squeal as I realize that I'm practically naked.

"Shit!"

"Mommy, you're not supposed to say that," Josie speaks up from the bottom steps of the staircase. "Maddie! Matt and Caleb are here!"

"Go put something on, sweetheart, we'll get the girls breakfast." Matt smiles at my girls and hugs them both, but Caleb is still quiet, watching me with sober blue eyes.

"Why are you here?" I ask them both again.

"We'll talk about that too," Caleb assures me, and finally offers me a half-smile, showing off the dimples in both of his cheeks as he lets his eyes wander down my half-naked body.

This man makes me quiver inside. Since I came home more than a year ago and got caught up in this big, loving family, Caleb has given me a permanent case of wet panties. Having him carry my drunk ass into the house after Jules' bachelorette party last year sealed the deal.

Even in my inebriated state, my body was on full hum while in his arms.

"I'll be right back," I murmur and run up the stairs, around the girls, trying not to think about the fact that both hot as hell Montgomery men just got a prime view of my mostly-naked ass, and that this is the most skin any man has seen of mine in close to five years.

Pathetic.

I can hear the girls loudly talking to the guys as I rush to pull on a hoodie and yoga pants, pull my hair up in a haphazard bun, and saunter back down the stairs.

"We are having Coco Puffs for breakfast," Maddie informs me.

"Okay, but have a banana with that."

"Oh, man!" Josie complains.

"You know the rule. You can have sugar cereal if you have fruit too." I kiss both of their heads as I walk past them to fill the coffee maker with water.

Matt grabs bananas and peels them for the kids. "You didn't tell me about this rule," he informs them with a mock glare.

"We didn't know about it," Maddie lies, trying to hold in a laugh.

"You know, I can take you to jail for lying to a police officer," Matt informs them with a grin.

"Nu uh!" Josie exclaims and giggles.

"Yep," he nods.

"We'll eat the banana," Maddie concedes and takes a big bite out of hers.

"That's better." Matt slides his hand down her ponytail from across the breakfast bar. "No jail for you today."

He's so good with kids.

All of the Montgomerys are.

Caleb is leaning against my kitchen counter, watching me carefully, his arms crossed over his chest. His hair has grown out a bit from his usual super short military cut, and his chin is covered in light strawberry-blonde stubble.

Those trademark Montgomery blue eyes follow me as I move about the kitchen, setting up the coffee and making sure the girls are set.

Just like every time I see him, electricity shoots down my spine and out my limbs and I just want to attach myself to him and devour him.

But instead I just smile and rub his bicep as I walk past.

"Coffee?" I ask him. His muscles flex at my touch, and my stomach clenches. Jesus, his arms are the size of my thigh.

"Please," he nods.

"Me, too," Matt agrees and steals a bite of Maddie's banana, making her laugh.

"So, what's up guys?" I ask as I hand them their mugs of fresh coffee.

"Girls, you finish breakfast, and we're gonna take your mom into the living room to talk, okay?" Caleb grins at the girls and kisses their cheeks. "Just yell if you need us."

"Okay!" Josie agrees and slurps up some Coco Puffs, dribbling now-chocolate milk all over the breakfast bar.

Maddie nods and takes another bite of banana.

I follow the guys into the living room, enjoying the view of their rear ends as I follow.

"Have a seat." Matt gestures to one of the chairs, but I just cross my arms over my chest and stay standing.

Have a seat my ass.

"Just tell me what this is about."

"Brynna, please sit down," Caleb murmurs softly and sits on the couch next to the chair they want me to occupy. I look back and forth between them, and realizing this is a losing battle, I sink down into the chair and sit on the edge of it.

"Okay, I'm sitting. Why are you both at my house at barely six in the morning, scaring the crap out of me?"

"I got a call yesterday at work," Matt begins and sighs deeply.

"At the precinct?" I ask.

"Yeah. It was a P.I., and he asked a bunch of questions about the family." He looks up at me, his eyes sober. "The whole family."

"Meaning, he asked questions about me," I murmur and feel a light sweat break out on my skin. "And if they've linked me to your family, I have to go…"

"You're not going anywhere," Caleb interrupts and takes my hand in his, holding it tightly.

"The investigator didn't specifically ask about you, but it raised some flags for me. I didn't like it." Matt shakes his head and stands to pace around the living room.

"It's been more than a year, Matt. Why now?" I try to keep my voice low so the girls can't hear me.

17

"I don't know." He turns back to us. "It might not have anything to do with what happened in Chicago."

"I don't think anyone can find me here," I tell them. "I don't own this house, I work for Isaac under the table, I haven't even switched my driver's license to Washington from Illinois. There's no reason for any flags to have gone up."

"I agree, and we'll continue to be careful, but we think it's in you and the girls' best interest to move in with either me or Caleb."

"Absolutely not." I pull my hand out of Caleb's and pace the living room.

"Why?" Caleb asks, his voice calm and low.

"Because, the girls have school. I have a job. We have a routine. I'm not disrupting that. They've been through enough." I continue to keep my voice low, but my entire body is taut and I want to scream. "We're finally at a place that we don't jump every time we hear a strange noise."

"Which is why you answered the door with a fucking screw driver as weapon?" Caleb asks with a cocked brow.

"I don't typically get visitors this early in the morning."

"We need to know you're safe," Matt insists and props his hands on his hips, staring at me.

"We are not moving out of this house." I cross my arms over my chest and stare Matt down.

"Fine, I'm moving in." Caleb stands and takes my shoulders in his big hands, his face fierce. "If you're going to be stubborn, fine, you and the girls will stay here, but I'm moving in."

"How is that possible?" I ask incredulously. "You get called out on a mission at a moment's notice. How is that going to help?"

Matt clears his throat and Caleb clenches his eyes shut for a moment and then pins me in his blue gaze once more. "Not anymore. My last mission was my final one."

"What?" I ask, my eyes wide, searching his handsome face. "Why?"

"It was time." He shakes his head and looks down before backing away from me and looking at Matt. "I'll stay with her."

"Sounds good to me."

"What am I supposed to tell the girls?" I ask, still trying to wrap my head around all of this. *Caleb is out of the Navy?*

"Are you not listening, Brynna?" Caleb asks. "You could be in danger. I'm not willing to take that chance. Until we know for sure what's going on, I'll be here. Starting today."

"Today's not good for me…" I begin.

"Starting today." Caleb's voice is very controlled and very low as he pushes his face close to mine. "This is what we do in this family, Brynna. We protect our own."

"I'm not…"

"Yes, you are." Matt responds before I can finish my sentence. "Stop being stubborn, and make the best of it."

I look back and forth between the two formidable men looming over me and I know I've lost this battle. I feel my shoulders droop and my lower lip quiver before I firm my jaw and blink quickly.

"What, you don't want me to cramp your style?" Caleb asks sarcastically, but his face is soft and his eyes are kind as he watches me carefully.

"No, I just want our lives to go back to normal, and it feels like that's never going to happen."

Before I know what's happening, Caleb has pulled me into his strong embrace, his hands sweep up and down my back and he murmurs into my ear, "You're going to be okay. I promise."

"You're sleeping on the couch, sailor," I mumble into his soft gray t-shirt, earning a chuckle from him.

"Deal."

***

"So what did you learn today?" I ask the girls as I set the table and walk back to the stove to check on the spaghetti sauce.

"I learned that Nelson eats his own boogers," Josie replies with a grimace. "Boys are gross."

"Who is Nelson?" I ask with a laugh and empty a package of angel hair pasta into a pot of boiling water.

"He's in her class," Maddie answers as she butters the garlic bread.

The front door opens and closes and seconds later, Caleb walks into the kitchen with a scowl on his face.

"Why was the front door unlocked?"

"Caleb," I sigh and shake my head, returning to the boiling pasta. "We're fine."

"Lock the damn door, Brynna."

"Caleb! You're not s'posed to swear." Josie frowns up at Caleb.

"Why do you have a bag? Are you spending the night?" Maddie asks, looking at the green duffle bag in Caleb's hand.

"I'm going to stay with you guys for a while," he responds and I clench my eyes shut.

Crap, I haven't talked to the girls yet!

"Why?" Josie asks.

"Because Caleb has some work being done on his place," I hurry to answer before Caleb can, and earn a look of surprise from him. "So he's going to stay here for a while."

"Okay," Maddie shrugs and grins widely at the tall man in my kitchen. "Can you sleep in my room?"

"No, I think I'll sack out on the couch."

"Will you read me bedtime stories?" She asks.

"I can do that," he confirms and grins down at her.

"Cool!"

"Mom usually reads to us," Josie cuts in with a scowl on her pretty little face.

Josie has always been the more guarded of the girls. She's not quick to trust, even with the Montgomerys, who have been a part of her life for over a year now.

She's also the moodier of the two.

"If you'd rather she do it, that's fine too." Caleb shrugs and sets his full bag down in the hallway.

"I want Caleb!" Maddie yells.

"I want Mommy!" Josie yells back.

"Enough!" I yell. "This is not a big deal, girls. Stop arguing and go wash your hands. Dinner is ready."

Both girls pout, their bottom lips sticking out and faces long, as they file out of the kitchen and into the small half bath in the hallway to wash their hands.

"If you keep your face like that for too long, it'll stick that way!" I call out to them and smile when I hear them giggle.

Caleb smiles as he approaches me, pulls the lid on the sauce off so he can smell the aromas of tomato and thyme, and then replaces it.

"Looks like I'm right on time."

"If you like spaghetti, yes you are." I pour the pasta into a colander and pull the garlic toast out of the oven. "I already set you a place at the table."

"Thank you."

I nod and turn away, but he grips my arm and pulls me back around to face him.

"Are you okay?"

"Fine."

"Having work done on my house, am I?" The dimples in his cheeks wink at me as he smiles.

"I didn't know what else to say. I don't want to scare them."

"My hands are clean!" Maddie announces as she dances back into the room.

"We'll talk later," Caleb whispers down to me and helps me get the rest of the dinner on the table. "This smells great."

"It's my favorite," Maddie tells him proudly. "I got to pick tonight because I got all the words right on my spelling test."

"Good job," Caleb commends her and holds their chairs out for them.

"Why are you doing that?" Josie asks with a scrunched up nose.

"Because that's what a gentleman does. He holds the chair out for a lady when she sits."

"I'm not a lady," Maddie giggles. "I'm a little girl."

"You're little ladies then." Caleb winks at them and stands patiently by my chair, waiting for me to set the large bowl of spaghetti on the table and take my seat.

"Thank you, sir," I say primly and sit in the chair.

When was the last time a man sat at our dinner table with us? Besides holidays with the family, never.

Never.

Caleb helps the girls dish up and then waits for me to fill my own plate before digging in himself. As he and the girls eat heartily, I sit back and watch the three of them, laughing and talking, and my heart catches.

Is this what *normal* is?

"…right mom?" Josie looks at me expectantly.

"I'm sorry, what?"

"We get ice cream for dessert tonight."

"Oh, sure." I nod and take a sip of my red wine.

For the rest of the meal, I watch Caleb interact easily with my kids. He is quick to laugh at their antics, and even Josie thaws to him, fighting Maddie to talk about her day.

God, he's so damn handsome. Like all of the Montgomery men, he's tall and broad. His hair is a dark blonde, but his eyes are ice blue and when he pins me in his stare, I swear he can see right into the heart of me.

He's in a gray t-shirt, tucked into faded blue jeans and black socks.

And I can't help but wonder what he looks like naked. For more than a year now, I've wanted to feel him over me, holding me.

Inside me.

And there have been moments when I know he felt the same way, but he's never crossed the line of friendship.

Damn him.

"Who's job is it to clean up?" Caleb asks when we've all finished our dinners. I've barely touched mine, but who can eat when Caleb "Hot Navy SEAL" Montgomery is sitting next to them?

Not me.

"We all help," Josie tells him. "You can sweep the floor."

"That's your job," I remind her. "It's her least favorite thing," I tell Caleb with a smile.

"Darn," she whispers and takes her plate to the sink.

"We all get KP duty," Caleb informs the girls.

"What's *cape* duty?" Maddie asks.

"K.P." Caleb scrapes the left overs into a plastic bowl. "It means kitchen patrol."

"We have to do it before we get ice cream." Josie scowls.

"Sounds fair to me," I laugh and begin to load the dishwasher as Caleb and the girls clear the table and wipe down the counter tops.

Before long the kitchen is clean and I've scooped everyone ice cream with chocolate sauce and sprinkles for the girls.

"Can we sit outside on the patio?" Maddie asks.

"No, Mads, it's winter," I remind her.

"I want summer. When will it be summer?" She asks.

"A few more months yet," Caleb answers and kisses her head as we all sit at the dining room table to eat our sweet treat.

"It's not raining," Josie points out.

"No, but the patio furniture is put away and it's cold outside."

"Dumb winter," Josie pouts and takes a bite of her ice cream.

***

"Are they in bed?" Caleb asks as I descend the stairs to the living room.

"Yes." I sigh and sit heavily on the couch next to him. "I love them, but dear God they're exhausting."

"They're beautiful," Caleb murmurs as he hands me a beer.

"We're drinking?" I ask with raised eyebrows.

"We're sharing this one."

"Okay." I take a pull on the brown bottle and then hand it back to him. "You know, you don't have to stay, Caleb. The girls and I are safe."

"Brynna, do you understand why I'm here?"

"Because someone asked a bunch of questions that weren't even about me. Caleb, we don't even know that anyone is looking for me."

"Look." Caleb scoots closer to me and wraps an arm around my shoulders. "I know we have the police keeping an eye out in Chicago, and we don't know for sure that anyone is looking for you, but Brynna, if there is even the slightest chance that you could be in danger, I need to be here." He kisses my temple, inhaling deeply. "If Matt's gut tells him something is off, then something is off."

"I don't like it."

"You don't have to." He takes my chin in his fingers and pulls my gaze to meet his own. "Keep telling the girls I need a place to stay. I'll stay out of your way as much as possible. Just keep the damn doors locked and your eyes open."

"I don't want our routine to be interrupted."

"Jesus, you're stubborn."

"You already know this about me," I remind him with a smile.

"You work for Isaac three days a week, right?"

"Right."

"Okay, you should be safe when you're there, with Isaac there, and all the other guys always coming in and out. I'll cut my work week down to three days a week so I'm here when you are."

"You're working already?" I ask, surprised.

"Yeah, I'm training civilian mercenaries just outside of Seattle." He shifts, as though he's uncomfortable talking about his new job, but I want to know more.

"What kind of training?" I ask.

"Weapons, mostly. Weapons were my specialty."

"What kind of weapons?" I ask, settling closer to him, leaning against his hard torso, enjoying the sound of his voice.

"You name it, I know about it."

"Hmm."

"In fact, I think I'll take you to learn to shoot tomorrow."

"Me?" I ask, and sit up straight. "Why?"

"Because you need to know how to protect yourself. You'll need a concealed weapons permit too."

"I already…"

"Stop." He pushes his fingers over my mouth, earning a vehement glare from me. "Let me teach you this, Bryn."

His arm is still around me, pulling me against his side, and his other hand is over my mouth, and all I can think about is the fact that his lips are inches away from my own.

Inches.

I drop my gaze to them and take a deep breath.

"No," he whispers and gently pulls his fingers away.

"What?" I whisper back, still looking at his lips, and my stomach flutters when he licks them.

"Don't look at me like that."

My eyes rise to his. "Like what?"

"Like you want me to kiss you."

"I do want you to kiss me."

There, I said it.

He sighs deeply, runs his thumb across my bottom lip and then gently wraps his arms around me, hugging me tightly.

"I can't do that. Go to bed, Brynna."

"But…"

He abruptly stands, pulls the beer bottle from my hand and walks away from me. "Go to bed."

Chapter Two

~Caleb~

What the fuck am I doing here?

The look on Brynna's gorgeous face as I told her I couldn't kiss her replays over and over in my head. It's two in the morning, and sleep is still far away. If it comes at all.

I don't sleep much these days.

The woman sleeping upstairs has been in my mind more than not for the better part of the last year. She and her two amazing daughters have me wrapped around their little fingers. Brynna is perhaps the most beautiful woman I've ever seen, with her long dark hair and deep brown eyes, and those lips of hers were made for kissing. Her legs go on for days, and her ass is round and would be perfect for my hands.

Incredible.

And her girls are just as beautiful with their long dark hair and their mother's brown eyes.

I rise from the couch and work my way around the inside of the house, for the third time tonight, making a sweep to make sure that everything is as it should be. Both the front and back doors are locked tight, along with all of the windows. The house is still, aside from the occasional creek or groan of normal house settling noises.

A single lamp is burning low in the living room, next to the couch. A red blanket and white sheet are folded neatly on one end, where Brynna left them earlier.

Satisfied that the house is safe for the night, I pull my shirt over my head and stuff it in my bag, unfasten the top button of my jeans and pull the 9 mm pistol from the waistband at the small of my back and set it on the table beside the couch.

Just as I reach for a clean tee and basketball shorts, someone lets out a soft cry upstairs.

Grabbing the pistol, I move quickly to the stairs, climb them swiftly, my back against the wall, and head for the girl's room, assuming the soft noise came from either Maddie or Josie, but as I cross by Brynna's bedroom, she lets out a louder, more urgent cry of distress.

I'll fucking kill who ever is hurting her.

Her door is partially ajar. I push it open carefully, my eyes quickly adjust to the dark, and I make a hasty sweep of the room, trying not to focus on the beautiful woman tossing and turning on the bed.

The room is empty.

"Don't you touch her!" Brynna cries out and flops onto her stomach.

I shove my pistol into the drawer of her bedside table and immediately climb onto the bed, leaning over her. I pull her damp, sweat-soaked hair off her forehead and cheek as she tosses herself onto her back once more and my heart stutters at the look of absolute anguish on her gorgeous face.

"Bryn," I call out to her softly, not wanting to scare the shit out of her.

"I won't let you get them," she shakes her head back and forth and tears leak out of the sides of her eyes and disappear into her hairline.

"Sweetheart, you're dreaming." I continue to caress her face gently. "Brynna, wake up."

Her eyes open wide and her gaze immediately finds mine. "Oh, my god."

She tries to pull away, but I ease her into my arms and pull her against me, tucking her sweet-smelling head under my chin and rock her back and forth as she softly cries.

"You're okay," I whisper and glide my hands up and down her back. I can feel her warmth through the light material of her little white tank top, and I want to rip it off her luscious body and feel her smooth skin. Her heart is hammering against my chest.

"I fucking hate nightmares," she whispers against my chest, her breath tickling my skin.

"You and me both," I agree. *So much so that I don't even sleep anymore.* "Wanna talk about it?"

"I haven't had it in a while," she murmurs and sniffles. The tears have stopped, thank God, because seeing Brynna cry is like having my heart ripped from my chest. I can't stand it.

"What is it about?" I ask and brush my fingers through her long, dark hair. The strands are soft and straight and fall all the way to the small of her back. I love it when she wears it down, whether she leaves it straight or puts those wavy curls in it, it doesn't matter.

"My girls," she whispers and buries her face in my chest once more and holds onto my sides with both hands as though the thought of what was tormenting her moments ago is too much to bear. "They were trying to hurt my girls."

"Baby," I whisper and tilt her head back until she's looking me in the face. "No one will ever hurt the girls. *Ever.*"

Tears well in her big brown eyes again and it's my undoing.

"Don't cry, Bryn." I brush my thumbs over her cheeks, wiping the tears away. "You're all safe."

"I'm so tired of being scared, Caleb."

"Hey," I whisper and run my knuckles down her smooth cheeks. "No need to be scared, baby. I've got you."

Her eyes fall to my lips, the same way they did earlier on her couch and my gut clenches just as my cock springs to life.

Get the fuck out of here, Montgomery.

"Caleb?" She asks softly.

"Yeah."

"Why won't you kiss me?"

I can't answer her. The truth fucking sucks, and I won't lie to her. Ever. Instead I brush my thumb over her lower lip, loving the way it feels against the pad of my thumb and wish with all my heart that things were different.

As my thumb reaches the center of that pouty lower lip, the tip of her tongue peeks out and brushes my skin and I lose it.

I cradle her cheek in my hand and sweep my lips over hers and then sink into her as she moans in happiness, wrapping those strong arms around me and pulling me closer to her.

Her mouth is pure fucking bliss. My other hand glides up her side, over the outside of her breast and up to cradle the other side of her face and I hold her to me as I feast on her mouth.

I've fucking wanted to taste her for months, and here she is, finally in my arms. Her light, exotic scent surrounds me, intoxicates me.

She sighs deeply as I slowly back away, kissing her nose and cheeks and finally pull all the way back, watching her carefully.

Her eyes are still closed as she pushes those amazing hands of hers up my chest, where she rests them, swallows hard, and opens her incredible dark eyes.

"I guess you will kiss me," she whispers.

"I couldn't help it." Sitting here with her, in the dark stillness of the middle of the night feels absolutely right.

"Okay," she murmurs and offers me a smile.

"You should get some sleep."

"Don't go." She grips onto my arms tightly, and her eyes are wide in fear. "Please? Not yet."

"Lie down."

"Caleb…"

"I'll stay, sweetheart. Just lie down."

She scoots down in the bed and lies back, moving over to her right to make more room for me in her bed.

My feet will most likely hang off the end.

I lie down on my side and pull her against me, kiss the crown of her head, and sigh deeply.

"I'm sorry I woke you," she mutters and nuzzles her nose against my sternum. I grin against her hair. She's so fucking sweet.

So fucking *good.*

"You didn't."

"You haven't been to sleep yet?" She asks and yawns.

"Not yet."

"Go to sleep, Caleb."

She wraps her arm around my waist and presses herself against me from head to feet, twining her legs with my own and damn if she doesn't fit me perfectly.

Her body is long. In the ankle-breaking heels she insists on wearing out with the girls, she's only a few inches shorter than my own six foot three.

"Caleb?" She asks sleepily.

"Yes, Bryn."

"Sleep. That's an order."

I chuckle and bury my nose in her hair, keeping the scent of her close.

"Yes ma'am."

And to my utter surprise, I fall into the most restful sleep I've had in years.

Chapter Three

~Brynna~

I wake slowly, lazily and stretch out like a fat, lazy cat. I purposely keep my eyes closed and smile softly, remembering Caleb coming to my bed to comfort me from my horrific nightmare. I know he's gone now because the bed around me is cold, but having him hold me, comfort me, in the middle of the night was just… amazing.

The man is incredible shirtless. In all the time I've spent with him, I've never seen him without a shirt, and even in the dark, it's a sight to behold.

Jesus, even his muscles have muscles.

I scrub my hands down my face and then open my eyes and frown.

It's light outside. Too light to still be before my alarm goes off. I whip my head around to look at the alarm clock and gasp when I see the time.

I'm late!

"Damn, damn, damn," I mutter and fling the covers off me. I race to the bathroom, yoga pants in-hand, to quickly pee, brush my teeth and throw my hair up in a messy bun.

"Girls!" I call out and briskly walk through my room and down the hall to theirs. "We overslept!"

I push their door open, but their beds are empty.

"Girls?" I call out again and jog down the stairs. Just before I turn the corner to the kitchen, I hear Caleb and the girls laughing so I stop short and listen.

"How old are you?" Josie asks.

"A lot older than you," Caleb answers. I can hear and smell bacon sizzling and my stomach growls.

"Are you older than mommy?" Maddie asks with her mouth full of something.

"Yes," he chuckles. "I'm a couple years older than her."

"Mommy is thirty," Josie informs him. "She's really, *really* old."

"Are you older than the Empire State Building?" Maddie asks with awe in her little voice and I cover my mouth so I don't laugh out loud.

"Uh, do I look older than the Empire State Building?" He asks.

"Maybe," Maddie responds.

"Do you have a dog?" Josie asks and slurps something. She must have talked him into another bowl of Coco Puffs.

"No," Caleb answers.

"Do you have a cat?" Maddie asks.

"Nope."

"Do you have an aldergator?" Josie asks loudly.

"You mean an alligator?" Caleb asks with a laugh.

"That's what I said."

"No, no pets. Especially not of the reptile variety."

Deciding to rescue him, I shuffle into the kitchen and my heart just stops. The girls are dressed, their long dark hair is brushed, and they are happily eating a hearty breakfast of pancakes, eggs and bacon. And, of course, Josie has her precious Coco Puffs.

He's taken care of my kids and let me sleep in.

The girls haven't seen me yet because their backs are to me, but Caleb looks up and offers me a soft smile. His eyes are warm and travel up and down the length of me, pausing at my legs.

"Sleep well?" He asks as I feel my cheeks warm.

"Too well," I confirm and join him in the kitchen. "I overslept. Did you turn my alarm off?"

"Yeah, I figured you could use a little extra sleep. The girls and I have things under control down here."

"Thank you." I stand on tip-toe and kiss his cheek, then walk around the breakfast bar to hug my girls.

"Mornin', mama," Josie throws her arms around my middle

and hugs me tight.

"Good morning, baby girl. Did you sleep well?"

"Yep!"

"Caleb made gross eggs," Maddie informs me and hugs me tight.

"He did?" I ask with a laugh and glance up at Caleb. "What kind of eggs were they?"

"Gross," Maddie shrugs and turns back to her food.

"Poached," Caleb informs me with a grin. "Not a big hit."

"Ah," I nod. "We're more the scrambled eggs type around here."

"So noted." He sets the girls dirty plates in the dishwasher and pulls a coffee mug down for me. "Coffee?"

"Yes, thanks, I'll get it."

"I can make you some eggs."

"I'm good." I shake my head and pour my coffee.

"Caleb, do you…" Maddie begins but I cut her off.

"Enough with the questions for this morning. Go upstairs and brush your teeth and get ready to go. The bus will be here in ten minutes."

"Mom, don't forget, today is dance class," Maddie reminds me.

"I know. Stacy is picking you girls up from school and taking you."

"Is this a once a week thing?" Caleb asks quietly.

"Yeah, Stace always picks them up and takes them. Sophie is in the same dance class."

He nods and scoops eggs, bacon and pancakes onto a plate and digs in. His jean-clad hips are leaning against the countertop and his bare feet are crossed. I watch in fascination as the muscles of his arms flex as he raises and lowers the fork to his mouth and feel my panties go wet and my nipples pucker.

Damn, he hasn't even touched me and I'm ready to strip naked and jump him.

"Mom, we're ready!" Josie calls and runs into the kitchen.

"Okay, good. I'll walk you to the bus."

"I'll walk you all to the bus," Caleb informs me and sets his half-eaten plate aside.

"Eat your breakfast, Caleb. We're fine."

"I'll walk you all to the bus," he repeats, winks at me, and moves with easy grace into the living room to pull on a green jacket and his shoes.

Once we're all bundled up, the girls pull their backpacks on and we walk up the long driveway to the road. Josie takes my hand in hers and Maddie reaches for Caleb. His handsome face looks surprised for a moment and then he smiles down at her as we walk.

Within minutes the bus pulls up and the girls climb aboard along with a few other neighborhood kids.

Caleb and I stand and wait for the bus to pull away before walking back to the house. As we start the walk down the drive, I shove my hands in my pockets, fighting off the chill in the air, and glance over at him. He's on high alert, his eyes scanning the house, the trees, the bushes.

"What are you looking for?" I ask and follow his gaze.

"Anything that doesn't seem to fit."

Everything looks normal to me.

"Aren't you guys being a little over cautious?" I ask and am met with an icy blue stare.

"No."

"Okay." I shrug and lead him back into the house. "Well, you survived your first Spanish Inquisition."

Caleb laughs and pulls his jacket off, hangs it on the tree by the door, and takes mine to do the same.

"They're really sweet girls, Bryn."

"Thank you," I nod. "But they ask a lot of questions."

"Yes, they do." Caleb shakes his head and laughs. "I almost think I'd rather be interrogated by the enemy. At least then all I have to give them is my name, rank and social security number."

"Don't say that," I mutter and hug him around the middle tightly, surprising him.

"Hey, what's this?"

"That's just not funny," I whisper and then back away, embarrassed. "I worried about you a lot."

"Why?" he asks with raised brows.

I roll my eyes at him and sigh deeply. "Oh, I don't know, Caleb. Maybe because you were constantly going God-knows-where, doing God-knows-what, and I knew it was dangerous, and I was on pins and needles until you came back home safely."

He flounders for a moment, and I realize I've just shocked the shit out of him.

Does he really not understand how much I care for him?

"Don't worry about it," I shake my head and turn away, walking briskly into the kitchen. "I'm happy you're safe. Just don't make jokes like that."

"Yes, ma'am," I hear him whisper behind me, making me grin as I load the rest of the dirty dishes into the dishwasher, put a tab of soap into the round compartment and start it.

"What do you have going on today?" He asks gruffly.

"I have errands to run this morning, then I don't have anything until the kids get home around six. I'll start dinner around five."

"Okay, well let's get ready to head out then. After your errands, we have someplace to go."

"Where?"

His face is still sober as he watches me. Something has changed in his eyes, in his posture. He looks… confused.

"You'll see," he mutters and turns to leave the room.

***

"I don't know about this," I mutter and watch as Caleb pushes a clip into his handgun with a loud *snick*.

"You need to learn," he reminds me for the thousandth time since we left the post office and he told me we were coming to the shooting range.

"Why? I don't like the idea of having a gun in the house with the girls."

"The girls won't be shooting it." He passes me a pair of clear shooting glasses and ear protection.

"Caleb, accidents happen."

"Number one," he begins, his voice hard, jaw locked and eyes cold. He's in military mode.

It's fucking scary as hell.

"Any weapon in your house will either be on our person or locked away. The girls will never have an opportunity to have an *accident.*" He cocks an eyebrow at me, waiting for me to respond.

I'll be damned if I will say *yes, sir.*

"Okay," I respond and lift my chin.

His lips twitch before he continues.

"Number two, you need to learn this so you can protect yourself. The people who may or may not be looking for you are dangerous, and they *will* have firearms. Your screwdriver can't compete with that."

"Hey," I begin, but he cuts me off.

"And number three," he leans in to whisper in my ear. "Don't be a pussy."

That does it. Just like that, I'm fucking pissed as hell.

Pussy? I'm no damn pussy.

I narrow my eyes at him and push my face up to his. "Bring it on, sailor."

"Good girl," he mutters and grins down at me proudly. "Have you ever held a handgun before?"

"No."

"Okay." He holds it up for me to inspect. "This is the safety. It's off because we're about to shoot it." He grins at me and I can tell he loves this. "This magazine has ten rounds in it. I have four more with me."

"Got it," I nod, staring at the black weapon in his hands, completely at a loss.

"Do you want me to go first?" he asks.

"Yes, please."

He nods, pushes his own glasses onto his face and sets his target. I glance around the range and take in the smell of gunpowder and male sweat. It's deserted right now, in the middle of a weekday. We are at the farthest window down, and are completely alone.

And Caleb is completely in his element.

"Stand back just a bit. I don't want one of these hot shells to hit you when it comes out of the pistol."

"Got it." I take my place, and when he's satisfied that I'm safe from getting hit, he turns to the target, raises the gun in both hands, his arms extended and muscles completely flexed and takes his first shot.

And I'm immediately wet and panting.

For the love of all that's holy this man is pure, unadulterated sex on a fucking stick.

He squeezes the trigger slowly for a couple of shots, and then empties the magazine quickly, not taking his eyes off the target.

When he looks back at me, he smiles smugly and pulls his target to him.

"You okay?" He asks.

"Fine." I clear my throat and feel my eyes widen when his target approaches. There is a cluster of small holes in the chest and another in the top of the head. "Nice shot."

He shrugs and replaces the target with a fresh one and sends it out. "Your turn."

"Maybe you should take another turn," I mention, trying to keep my voice light. I'm suddenly nervous as hell.

"Pussy," he whispers and laughs when I glare at him. He pulls out the empty clip and hands me a new, loaded one and the gun. "Load your magazine."

I do, clumsily.

"Relax, baby, you'll get the hang of it. You just need practice."

My heart stutters at *baby*.

"Now, face the target. Feel the weapon in your hands, Bryn. It's heavy. When it fires, it's going to have a bit of a recoil."

"Oh, goody," I murmur.

"You'll be fine."

I face the target and stare down at the weapon in my hand. How did I get here? How did my life come to this?

"Raise the gun."

I follow his order and stare hard at the target roughly twenty yards from me.

I squeeze the trigger and the first shot recoils harder than I expected, making me jump and stumble back a bit.

"Easy," Caleb murmurs behind me.

"I'm fine." Maybe if I keep saying it I'll start to believe it myself.

He moves up behind me and nudges my legs apart. "Widen your stance for balance."

I fire again, and my blood thickens as adrenaline pumps hard and fast through me.

It doesn't take a Navy SEAL to figure out how to line up the sights, and I squeeze the trigger, again and again, my body taught with aggression that I didn't even know I'd been holding.

Shooting is great therapy.

When the magazine is empty, Caleb wordlessly shows me how to switch it out, and I continue to throw the bullets down the range, clip after clip, until all four are spent.

I set the heavy gun on the shelf, pull my goggles and earmuffs off and step back. I have to lock my knees because my legs feel like Jell-O and I'm afraid I'll fall. My arms are humming, I'm panting, and I swear to God, I could run a marathon.

Suddenly, Caleb steps up behind me and presses the button to bring the target back to us.

"Take a deep breath," he whispers against my ear and I instinctively respond, pulling in a long, deep breath. He presses his chest against my back, his thighs against the back of my own, and pulls in a long breath of his own. "You smell so fucking good."

His cock stirs against my backside, through his jeans. He pulls his hands up my arms and down my sides to my hips, where he rests them as he runs his nose up the side of my neck.

With the noise and feel of the gun still in my head, my heart still pounding like crazy, I want him.

Now.

"You have no idea how fucking good you feel pressed up against me like this," he whispers, his voice rough and strained.

"I think I have an idea," I respond, surprised to hear the raw need in my own voice. Closing my eyes, I lean my head back on his shoulder and relish in the feel of his hands kneading my hips and his face pressed into my neck. My nipples are puckered and straining against my bra, and goosebumps have broken out up and down the length of my body.

I want him unlike anything or anyone I've ever wanted before.

"Caleb." His name is a whisper, a prayer.

"Smell so damn good."

"Touch me," I demand softly. His hands still. He kisses my neck softly, takes a long, deep breath, and then backs away.

I turn around in surprise and in full-blown anger.

"What kind of game are you playing?" I demand.

"I'm not playing a game." He crosses his arms over his chest.

"Caleb." I just stare at him for a long moment. Thirty seconds ago his hands were on me and he was whispering the sweetest things in my ear.

Now he's turned back into the drill sergeant.

And men say women are confusing.

Finally, he turns and pulls the target down.

"I'll be damned," he whispers.

"Let me see."

There are a few stray bullet holes around the white part of the target, but in the center of the chest and the top of the head are two good-sized holes where my bullets pierced the paper.

"You're a natural."

I shrug like it's no big thing, but inside I'm doing the mega happy-dance.

"Not so much a pussy, I guess."

Caleb laughs, long and loud and scoops me up into a long hug.

"Definitely not a pussy," he agrees as he pulls away from me.

"Caleb?" My heart is beating hard, and I'm still pissed at him. He's smiling down at my target, but when his eyes meet mine, he sobers.

"Yeah."

"Don't fucking touch me like that again unless you plan to finish what you start."

His eyes go hard and his jaw tightens. Before I can turn and walk away, he grabs my wrist and pulls me against him, pinning my arms between our bodies.

"Let's get this straight, Brynna. I want you so fucking bad my teeth ache. I've wanted you for months. But you're part of my family, and I'm supposed to be protecting you. Dropping my guard and fucking you into the mattress is not the way to keep any of you whole."

I gasp as his words sink in and I want to beg him to take me home do exactly that; fuck me into the mattress, but before I can speak, he lowers his forehead to mine and clenches his eyes closed as if in pain.

"I'm not going to fuck up our friendship, or make things weird for you with my family, just because I can't keep my damn hands off you. You mean too much for that."

I lean into him, wanting to comfort him, but he sighs, lifts his head and plants his lips on my forehead for a long few seconds and then backs away, turns his back on me, and loads the weapon and clips back into his locking gun box.

"I apologize. I won't touch you again."

Before I can argue, ask him to talk with me about this, he stalks off ahead of me.

"Let's go."

Chapter Four

~Caleb~

"My name starts with a 'c' and ends in a 't'. I'm hairy and round and squishy inside. What am I?" Jules doubles over in laughter in the couch across from me before taking another sip of her fruity drink.

"I need another beer," I mutter, grab my empty bottle and walk into Luke and Nat's kitchen that opens into the great room where we're playing this stupid game.

Of course, the girls chose it.

"A carrot?" Brynna asks in her sexy, low voice and pushes her dark hair behind her ear. Her eyes are a bit glassy from her drinks, and she's been smiling all evening. Coming here tonight was exactly what she needed, to spend time with friends and have fun.

But being so close to her is fucking killing me.

I've done a stellar job of keeping my hands off her since the other afternoon at the range. But all I want to do is pull her against me, under me, and lose myself in her for about a month.

It's ridiculous.

I've been with plenty of women over the years, but none of them had me tied up in knots, especially not before I'd actually fucked them.

"What kind of carrots have you been eating?" Leo asks Brynna, pointing at her and laughing his ass off.

"Ew. Yeah, never mind." Bryn shakes her head and takes a sip of her drink as I return to the room with my beer, sitting between her and Matt. The whole gang is here at Luke and Nat's tonight: Jules and Nate, Will and Meg, Sam and Leo and Matt. Even Isaac and Stace are here tonight. Luke's brother, Mark, also showed up.

The girls are freaking hilarious, and I pray with all my heart and soul that they don't start their orgasm talk bullshit.

If I have to sit here and listen to Bryn talk about getting off I'll lose my fucking mind.

"This is so fucking funny," Jules laughs.

"I know what it is," Will murmurs and grins down at Meg and runs his hand down her back to her hip. "Although yours isn't hairy."

Fuck me. I wonder if Bryn's is hairy.

"Yuck. Stop it," Sam scolds him with a scowl.

"What?" Will asks.

"For the love of all that's holy, Nat, stop fraternizing with the enemy!" Jules exclaims.

As per their usual, Luke and Nat are making out.

The man can't stop kissing the shit out of that woman. And now they have a second baby on the way.

I couldn't be happier for her. She deserves every happiness in the world. Luke is awesome to her.

"I'm married to him, Jules. He's hardly the enemy."

"Tonight he is. Girls against guys. Get your sexy ass over here with me." Jules scoots to the side, making room for Nat to join her.

"Are you going to kiss me?" Nat asks.

"After one more drink, yes."

"Definitely go over there with her," Nate quickly jumps in.

I scowl over at him.

Maybe McKenna has to die after all. Jules will get over it. Eventually.

Probably.

"Uh, they're our sisters, man." Matt reminds him with a frown.

"They're not my sisters," Nate responds.

I growl in my throat, ready to choke the fuck out of him with my bare hands.

"It's a coconut, you nasty people!" Jules yells and passes the cards down to Samantha.

I tune out the next question, aware of Brynna's thigh pressed against mine, how her hair smells, how her giggle makes my stomach clench in awareness.

If I keep this up, I'll have to have Matt come stay with her. I'm of no use to her if all I can think about is getting in her pants.

"You are all over-sexed." Samantha announces.

"Not all of us," Brynna pouts and scowls up at me.

Matt's head whips around and his eyes narrow on me.

Fuck.

"Don't start," I warn her, my voice low and hard. She crosses her arms over her black sweater, pulling it tight over her breasts and my cock stirs.

She's wearing a gray skirt that flows to her knees and mid-calf black fuck-me boots.

"What is it Sam?" Nat asks.

"It's gum."

"Here's one!" Will pulls his card from the *Dirty Minds* game box and laughs. "You stick your poles inside me, you tie me down to get me up and I get wet before you do."

I'm going to kill all of them.

"I like the tie me down talk, you know," Sam reminds us all, referring to her loud and explicit description of her sexual preferences after Jules' bachelorette party.

I didn't think I would survive that damn ride home.

Matt chokes on his beer as the others laugh at her. Leo stares down at her, dumbfounded.

"Seriously."

"Sure." Sam shrugs.

"It's a tent, people!" Will passes the box along.

"I haven't been wet in a while." Brynna announces.

Correction: I'm just going to kill her.

"How many drinks have you had?" Sam asks her.

"Too many," I respond for her. "Excuse us, we need to talk." I grip her arm in my hand and lead her out of the room, down the hallway that runs past the kitchen to Luke's office and slam the door behind us.

"What the fuck are you trying to do?" I ask her angrily, caging her in at the door. My palms are flat against the wood at either side of her head, and in the heels of her hot as hell boots, she's almost my height.

And fuck if that doesn't also just turn me the hell on.

"I don't know what you're talking about," she responds, meeting my gaze head-on.

"Bullshit." I can't help it. God help me, but I can't help but touch her. I lean in and rub my nose against hers, enjoying the way her eyes flutter closed.

"What do you want from me?" I whisper as my hands sink into her soft hair.

"I don't want anything from you," she answers and opens her eyes, pinning me in her chocolate brown gaze. "That's just it, Caleb. I just want *you.*"

I pull my lips up and down the soft skin of her throat. *Damn, she smells so fucking good.* I grip her shoulders in my hands with a growl and spin us around, push her to a leather chaise lounge sitting in the corner and guide her down on it, sinking to my knees before her.

"What are you doing?" she asks with wide eyes.

"How long has it been, sweetheart?" I ask her.

"How long has what been?" She shakes her head and frowns, as though she's trying to clear her fuzzy head.

"How long has it been since someone made you come?"

She stills, her hands gripped onto my shoulders, knees spread so I can kneel between them, and watches me carefully.

"Why?" she finally whispers.

"I thought this is what you wanted," I respond and raise up on my knees so our faces are level. I grip her hips in my hands and pull her closer to the edge of the seat. "I can smell how turned on you are."

Her mouth opens and closes twice, and her gaze falls to my lips. She licks her own, plump, gorgeous lips, and all rational thought goes right out the damn window.

I press my mouth to hers and she wraps her arms around my neck and I'm lost to her.

I need her.

44

I need to know what she feels like when she comes.

I kiss my way down her neck to her collarbone, nuzzle her breasts, and push her skirt up to her hips.

"Caleb."

She sinks her fingers into my short hair and pulls.

"Lay back."

"No. I want to watch."

Jesus, she's going to fucking kill me.

"Whatever you want, sweetheart." She's wearing small, lacy panties that are no match for me. I quickly rip them and toss them over my shoulder and spread her wide, gazing down at her in awe.

She's so damn beautiful.

"You shave," I murmur, surprised, and lean in to plant a soft kiss over the smooth skin of her pubis.

I can't fucking wait to taste her.

"Mmm," she murmurs.

"God, you're *so* turned on." I push a finger over her clit and down her lips and they are immediately soaked.

"You turn me on, sailor," she responds with a smile, her voice breathy as she pants.

She grips my wrist in her hand and pulls the finger dripping in her own juices into her mouth and sucks.

Hard.

And fuck me, I lose it.

I groan and bury my face in her pussy, licking and sucking on her small, tight lips, pushing my tongue inside her and swirling around, lapping up every drop of her sweet juices that I can.

"You have the sweetest little cunt," I whisper and move up to pull her clit between my lips, pushing the tip of my tongue against it quickly and plunge two fingers into her tight pussy.

My cock strains against my jeans, begging to sink inside her, but I have to make this quick.

The others will miss us.

And there is nothing more beautiful to me than watching Brynna come undone right now. She props those amazing legs on my shoulders, and I can feel the muscles tense around my ears as the force of her orgasm builds.

She bites her lip to keep from crying out and her muscles spasm, clenching my fingers like a vice and she pushes her pelvis against me as the orgasm consumes her.

As she settles, I pull my fingers out of her and lick them clean, watching her carefully as she pants and pushes her hair back from her flushed face.

She smiles dreamily, grips my face in her hands and pulls me up to kiss me deeply, pushing her tongue in my mouth, the taste of her on me not bothering her in the least.

"We have to get back," I whisper and pull away.

"But you…"

"I'm fine, sweetheart." I grin down at her and kiss her forehead.

"Later."

"No. There won't be a later." I stand and back away, giving her space to stand and set her clothes right.

"I told you before," she reminds me, her eyes bright with anger. I move in and hold her chin between my finger and thumb.

"I finished it. You came. End of story."

"You are so fucking infuriating!" she shrieks. I didn't know Brynna was capable of shrieking.

"Back at you, sweetheart. Let's go."

"I might kill you in your sleep," she threatens with a deep scowl as she pushes past me out the door of the office toward the laughter in the living room.

"It's a good thing I don't sleep," I mutter.

"I was expecting more than a *wham-bam-thank-you-ma'am*," she smirks over her shoulder, and that's all I can take.

I whirl her around and press her against the wall, pinning her hands above her head and devour her mouth, kissing and lapping, biting and pulling at her hungrily. She moans softly and rotates her hips against me, begging for more.

"Love the way I taste on you," she whispers. It's enough to make me almost come in my pants like a horny teenager.

She's so fucking sexy.

I pull away and release her hands and she raises them shakily to her mouth, watching me.

I swallow hard and run my hand over my mouth and I can still smell her on me.

Fuck it's going to be a long night.

"Let's go."

"I wanna see it!" Stacy is bouncing in her seat, clapping her hands.

"What do you wanna see?" Bryn asks as we resume our seats. I feel Matt's gaze on me, but I'll be damned if I'll meet it right now.

Or explain myself.

Fuck.

"I wanted a piercing," Meg shrugs as she climbs into Will's lap.

"Eyebrow, ear, nose, belly button." Leo is pointing passionately at each area as he shouts them out to her. "Are all acceptable piercings."

"Maybe I'll get my clit pierced," Brynna whispers, just for me.

I do my best to ignore her. She loves getting a rise out of me. Literally.

"That's not what I wanted," Meg responds with a grin.

"Jesus." He pulls his hand down his face and laughs. "I don't ever, *ever* need to know stuff like this about you."

"Hey." Will interrupts. "Don't knock it till you try it."

"So back to orgasms," Stacy begins and before I can stop myself, I jump to my feet, my arms slashing back and forth.

"No! No, no, no! No orgasm talk tonight."

"I could talk about orgasms," Mark offers.

"No! I'm serious." I glare about the room to all of the women. Any more talk about sex or orgasms tonight will be the end of me.

"Okay guys, we'll discuss the O during girls night." Sam smiles sweetly at me and I could kiss her.

"How are the living arrangements working out?" Matt asks as I sit back down.

"Fine." I shrug and take a sip of my now warm beer.

"He's nice to the girls," Brynna replies softly and offers me a warm smile, and for the first time in hours, *days,* my stomach settles. I grin down at her and rest my hand on her knee.

"They're easy to be nice to."

"No kid talk," Stacy announces. "We agreed. We're pretending we're young with no responsibilities."

Isaac kisses her cheek and wraps an arm around his wife.

"I am young with no responsibilities," Mark reminds us. "I recommend it."

"Right, 'cause you hate kids," Sam waves her youngest brother off. "You can't stand holding Livie."

"I love her. And then she goes home and I go find a warm body for the night." He winks at his sister smugly.

Sounds like Mark and I used to have a lot in common.

Now the idea of going out to find a quick lay makes me sick to my stomach.

Brynna's small hand covers my own on her knee as conversation continues to swirl around us, the girls laughing and teasing us guys.

I fucking love my family. They are my best friends, and Brynna is a part of this, not just because she's Stacy's cousin, but because she's become one of us.

I'll be damned if I'll screw this up for her. I'm too fucked up for anything long-term, and she deserves nothing less.

"Shit, now I want chocolate," Brynna mutters and bites her luscious lip.

I want to bite that lip.

"Do you have chocolate?" Jules asks Natalie.

"I live here, girls, and I'm pregnant. Of course there's chocolate! Follow me!"

All of the girls jump up eagerly and follow Nat into the kitchen.

"What is it about chocolate?" Nate asks and crosses his arms over his chest as he watches his wife stumble about Nat's kitchen.

"It's like crack to women, man." Matt checks his phone quickly and then shoves it back in his pocket.

"We have chocolate ice-cream, kisses, brownies and whipped cream."

I glance over at Luke and grin. He's got the goofiest smile on his face as he watches his wife disperse the chocolate amongst the women.

He's turned into such a pussy.

And why the fuck am I just a little jealous?

"I am so in love with you right now," Jules announces to Nat, "I want to lay you out on this countertop and eat this shit off of you."

"Don't mind us, we'll just watch," Nate calls out, earning a jab in the ribs from Matt.

"Dude," I exclaim, my eyes wide and hands out as if to say, "What the fuck?"

Nate just grins back at me smugly. "Not *my* sisters," he reminds me.

Fucker.

"Oh my God, so good," Bryn moans as she leans that perfect ass against the counter top and chews a bite of brownie.

Damn, that's what she'll sound like when I'm inside her.

I drop my face to my hands and scrub hard.

"I wish I had your boobs," I hear Sam announce and raise my head to see who she's talking to.

Of course, she's talking to Bryn.

"Right," she smirks and takes another bite of brownie.

"Dude, I do!" And just like that, Sam saunters across the room and cups Brynna's tit in her palm. "See? You have the perfect boobs. Stace, have you felt her boobs?"

Just kill me. Put a bullet in my head and end the agony.

"Oh yeah," Stacy waves her off. "She has great tits."

She has amazing tits.

"I wanna feel!" Jules bounces over and joins in.

"Give me more chocolate and you can touch all you want." Brynna laughs and then glances over at me. "This is the most action I've had in months."

"Motherfuckingsonofawhore." I grumble.

"Is Brynna single?" Mark asks Will.

"Keep your fucking hands off her," I growl at him before I know what's coming out of my mouth.

"Hey," he holds his hands up in surrender and laughs. "It was just an innocent question."

As the girls all quietly gossip and occasionally look our way, giving away the fact that they are most likely talking about us, Matt leans in and murmurs quietly, "What are you doing, man?"

"Don't worry about it," I respond and shake my head.

"You need to think long and hard about this. Brynna is special."

"You think I don't know that?" I laugh humorlessly and shake my head again, then look my older brother square in the eye. "She deserves much more than anything I can give her."

"I didn't say that." Matt's hands and jaw clench in frustration. "Just think about it before you start something."

I nod and look back over to the beautiful, tall woman laughing and nodding with Meg and Sam.

I would kill for her.

And her girls.

And not just because of the situation she's in.

God help me.

Suddenly, the girls are singing and dancing about the kitchen, catching all of our attention. They are a blur of arms and hair and bodies moving with the music, all about a girl asking who made someone the king of anything.

I don't know the song, but all of the girls seem to, as they know every single word.

Almost as though we're one person, all of us stand and gather in a semi-circle, watching our girls, all of us with those stupid grins back on our faces.

These women are incredible.

When the song ends, we applaud loudly, whistling and cat-calling, and the women laugh as they bow deeply, if a bit wobbly.

"Encore!" Mark yells out. "With less clothes. Except you, Sam, keep your shit on."

"We're a one-song show, guys. Sorry." Sam laughs.

The guys gather their women one at a time, making noise about it being late and needing to get home.

Our parents are babysitting all of the kids tonight, but it is getting late, and I need to make my late-night check of the house. I glance over to Brynna to find her watching me with wide, brown eyes. I hold my hand out for her, and she hesitantly joins me, linking her fingers through my own.

"Ready?" I ask.

She nods. "Yeah."

"We're out too," I announce as we make our goodbyes. Matt catches my gaze and raises a brow, gesturing down to our linked hands.

I pull Brynna toward the door and flip him off behind my back, earning a belly laugh from my brother.

Brynna and the girls live in Natalie's old house, just up the street from where Nat and Luke live now in the Alki neighborhood of Seattle. The drive is short, and quiet.

"I don't know why you're mad," I murmur, breaking the silence. "You got off."

To my utter shock, she reaches over the console and grips my cock firmly in her palm. "I'd be happy to return the favor, but you keep telling me no."

I pluck her hand off my crotch and return it to her own lap.

"The answer is going to stay no, Brynna."

"Fine." She raises her chin, but I can see a shimmer of a tear in her eye and my gut clenches. "I refuse to beg for sex ever again."

I pull up to her house and throw the car into park.

"Excuse me?"

"I'm going to take a shower." She slams out of my car and walks swiftly up to the house.

"I haven't checked…"

"Fuck it!" She turns back to me, her face furious, and then shakes her head, unlocks the door and steps inside. "It's fine. I need a shower. Stay away from me for a while, Caleb."

She disappears inside. I know I should chase after her, but I need a break. I take a deep breath of the crisp winter air and walk around the house, satisfied when all seems normal, and then go inside. I make my way around the house, checking locks and windows, and work my way upstairs. The girls' room is quiet and too still without them in their beds.

They've been gone for five damn hours and I already miss them.

What are they all doing to me?

Entering into the master bedroom, I can hear the shower running in the bathroom, and am surprised to hear Brynna singing.

I walk silently to the doorway and lean my shoulder against the jam, cross my arms and listen to her sweet, slightly off-key voice. The shower has glass doors, gone foggy from the steamy shower. I can see her body through the blurry glass, see her lean back and let the water run over her hair, her ass and breasts pushed out, and my dick is officially the hardest it's ever been in my life.

"I hate to break it to you babe, but I'm not drowning. There's no one here to save."

Oh, sweetheart. Someone is definitely drowning.

Me.

Chapter Five

~Brynna~

What is wrong with him?
What is wrong with me?
I just don't buy the whole, "You're too close to my family and I have to protect you" line he keeps giving me.

If he doesn't want me, he needs to just grow a pair and say so. I don't need his pity orgasms.

As I finish shaving one leg, I pause and stare at the tile.

Is that what it was in Luke's office? A pity orgasm? 'Cause if that's the case, I just want the floor to open up and swallow me whole.

Finishing the other leg, I rinse and lean back to wash my hair, absentmindedly humming.

Maybe I should just insist that he go. I can protect the girls, and I'm sure I could go stay with my parents if need be.

Although, if we really are in danger, I will do whatever it takes to make sure the danger stays as far away from them as possible.

Maybe Matt would come stay.

Just as I rinse the last of the soap from my hair, the glass door to the shower is flung open, and I'm pushed against the tile, Caleb pressed against me, still dressed.

He holds my face in his hands, panting, eyes on fire and looks like he's waging his own private war inside.

It tears my heart out.

"Caleb," I murmur and run my fingers through his hair as he slowly closes his eyes. "You're getting wet."

"Don't care." He leans his forehead against mine, his hands

glide from my face to my shoulders and down to cup my breasts, his thumbs brush over my nipples and I moan long and low.

"You're confusing me," I whisper and tilt my head back as his teeth scrape along my neck.

"Me too," he whispers back, then plants his lips on my ear and whispers, "but I want you, Brynna. I can't stop it."

"Stop trying," I urge him and try to tug the heavy, wet t-shirt off his back but he suddenly drops to his knees and pulls my leg up over his shoulder. I gasp and lean one hand against the adjacent wall to steady myself.

"Can't get enough of this," he murmurs against me and suddenly that talented mouth is sucking and pulling at my center and the world explodes in stars.

"Who knew that could feel so damn good?"

He stops and looks up at me, his face wet and dripping and incredulous.

"No one has ever done this to you before?"

I bite my lip and shake my head shyly.

His eyes clench closed and when he opens them, they're focused on my pussy.

"Your pussy is so beautiful, Bryn. I can't stop licking it." And just like that he leans in and runs his tongue from between my labia, up over my clit and back down again. "You are delicious."

"I want to taste you," I mutter and reach for him, but he pulls my hands into his and pins them to the wall at my hips.

"Later."

"Caleb," I pout, and feel him grin against my center.

"You can taste me later." He kisses my inner thigh, leaving bite marks as he does. "Love your legs. You have the longest fucking legs I've ever seen."

"Too long," I mutter and squeal when he sucks my clit into his mouth.

"Perfect," he corrects me and kisses up my body to my nipples, pulling and worshiping them with his tongue. "And Sam's right you know. You have amazing tits."

My giggle turns into a groan when he sinks a finger into me, my leg still propped on his forearm, keeping me open wide to him.

If he doesn't fuck me soon, I will lose my damn mind.

"Take your clothes off," I demand, but am met with deaf ears as he continues to assault my pussy with his hand and my breasts with his mouth. A warm pressure sets up camp at the base of my spine as I feel the orgasm build, just like it did earlier in Luke's office.

I've never had an orgasm like that in my life.

"Oh damn," I moan and thrust my pelvis harder against his hand. "Caleb!"

"Yes, baby, give it up."

I come apart as he sucks a nipple into his mouth hard and presses a second finger in to join the first. The only thing I hear is the pounding of my heart in my ears and the rush of blood leaving my head. We are both panting and needy, clinging onto each other.

"More," he growls and begins pumping those fingers in and out of me harder, faster, sending me directly into another long orgasm, making me scream out his name.

He pulls back and stands, shuts off the water and peels the wet clingy clothes off his hard body. When he turns to grab towels, I see a tattoo on his left shoulder blade, and another high on his right bicep.

And when he turns back to me, his cock is long and full, standing at full attention. I lick my lips at the idea of getting my hands, and lips, on his beautiful dick.

Every inch of him is just plain amazing.

He brusquely runs a towel over himself, wiping most of the water away, and then pulls me out of the shower and wraps me gently in a long bath blanket, running his hands up and down my body, letting the thick material soak up the water before he tosses it aside, lifts me in his arms, and sets off toward the bedroom.

"Round two." He smiles widely, his amazing dimples creasing in his cheeks and I kiss his cheek, inhaling his musky, male scent.

"My turn to drive you crazy?" I ask.

"Not yet." He kisses my forehead and lays me gently in the

middle of the bed.

"Caleb," I catch his hand in mine and kiss his knuckles, brushing over tiny white scars with my thumb. "I seriously think it's your turn to get off."

"Brynna," he murmurs and settles himself between my thighs, his naked pelvis resting against my own, and brushes wet strands of hair away from my face. "Watching you come is the sexiest fucking thing I've ever seen in my life."

He grins as I gasp.

"Trust me, I'm getting off on getting you off. We have all night. The kids won't be back until tomorrow afternoon, right?"

"Yeah," I nod.

"Let's enjoy each other, baby."

His voice is thick and hot with lust, and his eyes are bright as they stare into my own. How did I ever doubt that he wants me? It's written all over that incredible face of his.

"I do enjoy you," I tell him with a grin and run my fingertips down his back to his ass. "And your ass."

"My ass?" He asks with a laugh.

"Oh yeah, you have a great ass." The muscles flex under my palms as he lifts and begins to slide down my body.

"I'm glad you approve." He winks at me and sits back on his heels, dragging his hand from my sternum, down my cleavage to my belly. His face sobers as he watches himself touch me. "Your skin is so soft."

"As you can see, I have post-baby body," I inform him and smile when his eyes meet mine.

"Don't tell me you're self conscious."

"No," I wave him off and enjoy the way he's taking me in. "It is what it is. I had two babies in here." I rest my hands on my belly. "It took a toll. My body won't ever be what it was before them, but I'd do it all over again in a heartbeat."

"Don't cover yourself." He pulls my hands off my belly and kisses them both and then leans down and plants sweet kisses over my stomach and down to my pubis. "Your long body is sexy, Bryn. I love how tall you are."

I grin down at him. "I love how tall *you* are. It means I can wear heels when I'm around you and you're still taller than me."

"I fucking love it when you wear heels," he growls and settles down the bed so he can play with my pussy. "They make your legs look ten miles long."

"Caleb, if you go down on me again right now, my body will implode. I really want you inside me."

He ignores me, kissing the insides of my thighs and nuzzling my lips with his nose, making me squirm.

"Did you hear me?"

"I heard you."

"Well?" I ask but sigh when he shoves his hands under my ass and tilts my pelvis up, giving him better access to me.

"Brynna," he whispers against my core, making my pussy clench.

"What?"

"Give me just one more, baby. One more time."

He leans in close and pulls my lips into his mouth, hollows his cheeks and sucks gently, pushes his tongue inside me, always pulling my hips forward and harder against his face.

It's un-freaking-believable.

Suddenly, my thigh and stomach muscles begin to shake uncontrollably. I grip the sheets at my hips in my fists and plant my heels on his back, pushing my pussy against him harder as I come apart at the seams.

He lazily kisses my inner thighs, my hips and up to my breasts, where he pulls the nipples through his lips, leaving them hard and puckered. Finally, he climbs his way up to rest on his elbows beside my head and brushes his knuckles down my cheeks.

"Are you okay?" he murmurs.

"I don't think okay is the word," I respond with a grin and kiss him lightly.

"Better than okay?" he asks with a cocked eyebrow.

"Only one thing would make me feel better," I murmur against his lips just before he sinks down for a long, wet kiss.

"What?" he asks when he finally pulls away.

"What what?" I ask, my brain completely fried.

"What would make you feel better, baby?" He asks with a

chuckle.

A slow smile spreads across my lips as I circle my hips, nudging his cock with my pubis. "I think you already know."

"How long has it been for you, Bryn?" He pulls back and watches my face intently.

"Four years, seven months," I whisper and drop my eyes to his Adams apple, unable to meet his gaze.

"Look at me."

I shake my head no.

"Hey, baby, look at me." His voice is gentle and when I lift my eyes to his, they're possessive and hot.

Really fucking hot.

"You haven't had sex since you and Jeff divorced." It's not a question.

I nod.

"Damn," he whispers and kisses my forehead, down to my eyes and then my cheeks. "Bryn, I'm clean. I promise. I don't want a barrier between us. I've wanted you for far too long, forever it feels like, and I just want to feel you."

"I'm on the pill," I whisper against his lips and grin as I circle my hips again and he pulls back until the blunt head of his dick pushes against my entrance, and then slowly, inch-by-inch, he fills me.

"Holy Mary mother of God," he moans and stares down at me in awe. "You are so fucking tight."

"You are so fucking big," I counter.

"Am I hurting you?" He asks with a frown.

"No," I shake my head and glide my hands down his back to his ass and back up again.

"I have to move," he groans and begins to slowly push and pull inside me, allowing my body to adjust to him. "Wrap those amazing legs around me."

I comply, linking my ankles behind his back and wrap my arms around his neck, cradling him close. I love having his weight on me. I love feeling his breath against my neck. I love the way he smells and the noises he makes, like he just can't get enough of me.

"Oh, God," I murmur as he picks up the tempo and runs one big hand down my side to grip my hip and hold me steady as he begins to ride me hard.

Nothing has ever felt so damn good.

Reaching between us, I push my hand down to where we're joined and can feel the root of him as he disappears inside me, then slip my fingers up to circle around my clit.

"Oh, fuck yes, touch yourself," he mutters, watching my fingers make small circles around my nub. "God that's hot."

"Caleb," I gasp and tilt my pelvis. "Oh God, I'm gonna…"

"Yes, baby. Go on." He kisses me hard, his tongue slips between my lips to dance with my own and I feel that now-familiar pull low in my belly as my muscles clench around him and I buck beneath him, calling out as I fall over the edge.

"Brynna," Caleb whispers hoarsely as he buries his face in my neck and comes inside me, shuddering with his own climax.

After long minutes of laying like this, with Caleb still inside me, our breathing calms and he pulls out of me, rolls away and pushes my hair off my face as he says, "Stay here."

He walks into the bathroom, and I hear water running, and he comes back into the bedroom with a wet cloth and a towel.

"I can clean myself up," I remind him dryly.

"I know," he replies but continues to slowly clean between my legs, then dries me off.

"Can you please hand me my tank and yoga pants?" I ask.

"I prefer you naked," he frowns.

"I live in a house with two six-year-olds," I remind him with a smirk. "They jump into bed with me at the drop of a dime. No one sleeps naked around here."

"They aren't here," he reminds me and slides into the bed beside me as he pulls the covers up over us. "So maybe tonight can be an exception."

"Do you always get everything you want?" I ask and wrap a leg over his hip as I get closer to him.

"No," he shakes his head sadly, but before I can ask him to explain himself further, he smiles softly at me and kisses my lips gently. "But being here with you, naked and warm, is pretty awesome."

I can feel his dick stir against my belly and I look up at him in surprise. "Shouldn't we be getting some sleep?" I ask.

He pulls a hand down my bare back to my ass. "You are the best reason to lose sleep."

Suddenly, he pulls me on top of him, and lines my hips up with his and glides effortlessly inside me. We don't lose eye contact, or speak, as I ride him, hard and fast, until I press down hard, the friction from his pubic bone against my clit sends me into another tailspin, and I am lost.

He pulls me down to him, kisses me as his body goes taught and he comes. I lay on him, my cheek pressed to his sternum as I catch my breath and just as I'm about to fall into a deep sleep, I hear him whisper, "Sexiest damn thing."

Chapter Six

It's early when I wake the next morning and expect to be alone in my bed, but to my surprise, Caleb is sleeping peacefully next to me, on his back, one leg bent to the outside.

Even in sleep he's a force to be reckoned with. He is all defined muscle. I wonder what kind of exercise regimen he goes through to stay so fit?

I prop my head on my hand and let my eyes take a leisurely stroll down his hard body. The covers are bunched at his waist, giving me an excellent view of his abs. He doesn't have a six-pack.

If I'm counting correctly, he has a ten-pack.

The tattoo high on his bicep is an eagle, wings spread, holding something in its talon. The wings are colored like the American flag.

It must be a SEAL tattoo of some kind.

I lean over and gently kiss the ink.

Remembering how I wanted to taste him last night, and he never gave me the chance, I decide to take advantage of Caleb being knocked out and slowly ease my body down the bed, move under the covers to rest between his legs, and plant wet kisses over his hips, those amazing V lines that are sexy as all get-out, and over his lower abdomen.

His cock stirs, slowly lengthening in the early morning light. I run my tongue from his scrotum, up the underside of his gorgeous dick to the head, where I lap at it like an ice cream cone.

Glancing up to his face, I'm not surprised to find his eyes wide open and watching me intently, a half smile on his full lips.

Without saying anything, I sink down around him, pulling him fully into my mouth, sucking gently.

"Ah, hell," he whispers and lifts his arms to grip the pillow at either side of his head. His biceps and forearms flex, and my stomach clenches at the sight, knowing what it feels like to have those strong arms wrapped around me.

As I pull up his shaft, I use my hand to pump him slowly, firmly, and then sink down again, cupping his balls in my hand and rubbing that tender flesh just under his scrotum.

"Brynna!" he exclaims, surprised and turned on, and his cock hardens even more in my mouth.

With the next pass up his shaft, I barely graze him with the very edge of my teeth, just to tickle the sensitive skin, and suddenly I'm on my back beneath him and he's kissing me deeply, passionately, his hands roam up and down my skin, as though he's never touched me before.

"I wanted to make you come," I pout when he skims down to kiss my jawline and earlobe.

"You almost did." He bites the top of my shoulder and then glides his nose back up to my chin. "But you *always* come first, Legs. Fuck you smell good."

"I smell like sex," I laugh.

"Mmm," he agrees and gazes down at me, his ice blue eyes shining with lust and happiness. He positions himself and slowly pushes into me, all the way to the hilt. As he stills, he brushes his knuckles down my cheek and kisses me sweetly.

"How do you feel?" he whispers.

"Good," I reply and try to circle my hips, but he's pinning me, holding me still.

"Are we okay?" he asks, his eyes serious.

"We will be, as soon as you start moving your sexy ass."

He smiles, showing me his dimples, and glides in and out in one long, fluid motion.

"Better?"

"Oh yeah." I swallow hard. "Did you sleep?"

"Better than I have in years," he confirms with a slight frown and then moves his hips again. "God, you feel so good, baby."

He gathers both of my hands in his, laces our fingers and pulls them over my head, pinning them to the mattress as he begins to move faster and harder, watching me intently as he makes love to me.

I slide my legs up his thighs, and hitch them around his hips, opening myself up to him even more.

"Fuck, yes," he growls and loses himself in me, pushing and pulling, his breathing erratic, his hands gripping mine firmly, until he sinks in, hard, and comes violently, shuddering and growling, sending me over the edge with him.

As he recovers, he releases my hands and kisses my nose. "Well, good morning, Legs."

"Legs?" I ask with a giggle. "What is it with the legs?"

"Ah, baby, when you laugh when I'm inside you…" He shakes his head before resting his forehead against my own. "Have I mentioned that I love your legs?"

"Once or twice," I reply dryly. "But I don't mind being reminded."

***

"I want jellybeans!" Josie announces as we settle in the living room to watch a movie together.

"How often do you do movie night?" Caleb asks, sitting on the couch and passing Josie her package of jellybeans.

"I try to do it once a week."

"I want peanut butter cups!" Maddie grins up at Caleb and bats her eyelashes, making me giggle.

She is such a flirt.

"Coming right up," Caleb passes her the candy and grins as they lay on their bellies amid a plethora of blankets and pillows.

"What are we watching?" he asks.

"*Ivan The Incredible.*"

"Great," he grins and presses play on the remote, hands me the bowl of popcorn as he whispers, "I have no idea what that movie is."

"It's okay," I whisper back, "they'll fall asleep in an hour and finish it tomorrow."

"Do you want one of my peanut butter cups?" Maddie offers Caleb.

"No thanks, honey," Caleb smiles down at her.

"You don't like them?" she asks with a frown.

"Not really." He shrugs. "I'm not much of a peanut butter guy."

"You have to like them!" Josie jumps up and Maddie follows, mutiny in their eyes.

"I do?" he asks with a raised eyebrow, and I know what is about to happen.

"Yep! Here, eat it!" Maddie jumps up and throws herself in his lap, trusting that he'll catch her.

"You can't make me!" he shouts playfully, making a show of trying to fend them off as Josie joins in the fun.

"You must eat it!" Josie cries and begins to tickle his side.

"I'm not ticklish!"

"Yes you are!"

All I can do is sit back and giggle.

"Help! Brynna, get these little pests off me! I'm not strong enough!"

"You're a wimp!" Josie informs him with a loud giggle and continues to tickle him.

"Eat it, wimp!" Maddie laughs and continues to try to feed him the candy.

Finally, he opens his arms wide and gathers them against him, stands and proceeds to run about the room, yelling like a Spartan on that show on Starz, "Victory!"

He drops them, gently, onto their pile of pillows and blankets, not even panting. The girls are laughing with tears rolling down their faces.

"And you," Caleb points at me, a mock glare on his handsome face.

"What did I do?" I ask, eyes wide, feigning innocence.

"You were supposed to be my back-up."

"You handled things just fine," I grin and then am suddenly on my feet and over Caleb's shoulder, much to the delight of the girls who scream with laughter.

"I think I'll throw her in the garbage!" Caleb announces and heads for the kitchen.

"No, put her in the recycle bin," Josie giggles.

"You can't recycle mommies!" I call out and gently hit Caleb's back with my fists. "Let me go!"

"Traitor!" Caleb yells and circles back around to the living room and dumps me back onto the couch. "That was a warning, woman."

"So noted," I laugh, holding my sides. The girls continue to giggle and Maddie wraps her arms around Caleb's waist and hugs him tight.

"I love you, Caleb. Can we watch the movie now?"

His hand pauses on it's way to settle on her back and he blinks twice before answering gruffly, "Yeah, buttercup, let's watch it."

She grins up at him lovingly and then joins her sister, ready to watch the movie.

He sits beside me and pulls me to his side, tucking me against him as he kisses my head and grabs a handful of my popcorn out of the bowl and shoves it in his mouth, giving the movie his undivided attention.

Damn, this feels good. Having him here with us, playing with us, just feels right.

In less than an hour, the girls are passed out on the floor.

"Well, that didn't take as long as I thought it would," I whisper with a smile.

"Thank God," he mutters and tilts my head back to kiss me, sweeping his lips over mine gently before sinking in and pushing his tongue past my lips, holding my face in his palm. Finally, he pulls back and kisses my forehead. "Let's get them to bed, so I can get you to bed."

"Good plan."

***

"Mommy! Mommy!"

"Bryn." Caleb touches my arm.

"It's Josie," I cry out, immediately awake and springing from the bed to run down the hall to the girls' room. Caleb is right behind me.

"Mommy!"

"I'm here, baby girl. What's wrong?"

"She threw up," Maddie informs us and points to the side of Josie's bed.

"I'm sorry," Josie cries.

"Oh, baby, it's okay." I pull her into my arms, unaware that Caleb has left the room. I press my cheek against her forehead and gasp.

She's burning up.

"You have a fever, my friend. I'm going to take your temperature, okay?"

"Okay," she croaks and lays back just as Caleb returns with a large bowl and cleaning supplies.

"You take care of her, I've got the mess."

"You don't have to…"

"It's fine, Bryn. I've got it."

"Thank you." I kiss his cheek and bustle to the medicine cabinet for fever medicine and a thermometer and return to the bed just as Caleb is finishing with the mess on the floor.

"Mommy?" Maddie calls from her bed.

"Yes, baby," I respond and take Josie's temp in her ear.

One-oh-one. Damn.

"I don't feel good." Maddie sits up and wraps her arms around her waist.

"Come on, buttercup," Caleb scoops her up and carries her into the bathroom, where I hear her retching.

Josie hears it too, and it makes her throw up again. Thank God Caleb brought the bowl.

And so it goes for the next few hours, holding the girls while they throw up, cooling them down with wet cloths and finally, giving them fever medicine and praying it will stay down.

Caleb never falters. He never leaves us to go back to bed. He doesn't scowl and get grossed out by the amount of vomit coming out of these two little people.

He just quietly helps me, as we alternate between the girls, changing their clothes, helping them to the bathroom and comforting them.

I'm rocking Josie in the plush rocking chair in the corner, and Caleb is holding Maddie, sitting on her bed with his back against the wall.

"I don't know how to thank you," I whisper to him.

"You don't need to thank me, Brynna." He looks down into Mad's face and frowns. "Poor things are so sick."

"The flu is going around." I lean my head back on the cushion and close my eyes. "Samantha had it last week."

"What do we do now?" He asks.

"This is pretty much it," I respond with a grin. "Stay up and give them medicine, pray the hurling is over, and hold them."

"It's hard work," he remarks casually and watches me over Maddie's head.

"This is nothing," I laugh humorlessly. "When they were little, I never slept. They never wanted to sleep at the same time, no matter how hard I tried to get them on a schedule. They had to eat every two hours, both of them, so I felt like I was always feeding them."

I shake my head and smile over at him. "I think I went two weeks at one point without a shower."

"Why didn't you have help?" He asks.

"My mom came out for a few weeks when they were first born, but they were in the NICU because they were born early, and when it was time to bring them home, my mom had to go home, too."

"How early were they?"

"About three weeks," I reply.

"Where was Jeff?" He growls.

I laugh again and trace Josie's soft cheek with my fingertip.

"Working. Always working." I bite my lip, hating that I feel tears coming on. "He wasn't even there when they were born."

Caleb curses under his breath.

"He wasn't a bad man, Caleb." I take a deep breath and let it out slowly. "Honestly, he just shouldn't have ever started a family with anyone. I knew when I married him that the job was his priority. He never made that a secret."

Josie stirs, changing positions in my arms.

"I guess I thought he might change once the girls were born." I smile over at Caleb sadly. "But he didn't. And we realized early on that he shouldn't be with us."

"So you've been a single mom from day one." It's not a question.

"I have," I nod. "I love them so much. They are worth every hour of sleep lost, Caleb. But damn, it's exhausting and scary when they're sick. There are times that I've had one throwing up in the bathroom and one throwing up in her bed and I can only be with one of them. What am I supposed to do then?"

I look up at him and let the tears fall silently down my cheeks in frustration.

"Or when they're both crying for me, and I can only hold one of them at a time, especially now that they're so much bigger." I shake my head and wipe my cheeks. "I worry that I'm not enough for them."

"Stop, baby. You're such a great mom. They couldn't love you more."

I just nod and gaze over at Maddie resting peacefully in Caleb's strong arms, her cheeks still pink with fever.

"When I told them that their dad died," I whisper and swallow, rocking slowly, "I thought they'd be hysterical, but they just frowned and Maddy said, 'does that mean we won't see him again?'"

I turn my eyes back down to Josie and kiss the top of her head.

"What did you say?" he asks quietly.

"I just said yes, that was right. Neither of them cried, Caleb. They just frowned and hugged *me*, because they said I looked sad. They didn't mourn him because they didn't know him."

"It was his loss, Bryn, and his own doing."

"I know," I nod. "It just makes me so sad because they are so wonderful, and he missed out on knowing them."

Suddenly, Josie stirs again and cries before throwing up all over me.

"Here we go again."

***

Twenty hours later, we are all exhausted. At one point during the day, Meg brought us all soup and sandwiches, broth for the girls, and looked over them to make sure that it was indeed just the flu.

The past two hours have been relatively calm. The fevers are coming down, and they've managed to sleep relatively peacefully.

"I think we're about through the worst of it," I murmur and comb my fingers through Maddie's hair. I'm lying beside her, dozing in and out with her. Caleb is rocking Josie in the chair.

"She loves to rock," he murmurs with a soft smile.

"She's always been my rocker," I agree. "Maddie can sleep anywhere, anytime. Josie, not so much. But sit in a rocking chair with her, and she's a goner."

"I'm going to try to lay her down," he mutters and kisses her forehead. "Fevers are down, thank God. They scared me."

How can I resist a man who is so good to my girls?

I let my eyes drift closed, listening to him tuck Josie in her bed. I must doze for just a minute because the next thing I know, Caleb is lifting me off the bed.

"I can walk," I protest but wrap my arms around his neck. "I'm not a small woman like Jules."

"You're fine."

"I'm not feeling terribly sexy tonight," I murmur apologetically.

"I think I can control myself tonight," he replies with a laugh.

"I should stay with the girls. You go to bed."

"I grabbed the monitor," he holds it up for me to see. "So we'll hear them if they need us. For right now, I'm going to put you in a hot bath. You deserve it, sweetheart."

I'm shocked when he carries me into the bathroom to see that he's already filled the tub with steaming hot water and my lavender bath oil.

"How long was I out?" I ask.

"About fifteen minutes." He sets me down on the toilet seat, props the monitor by the sink and helps me out of my clothes and into the hot bath.

"Oh my, that feels good." I pull in a deep breath and let it out slow, then open my eyes and gaze up at the man standing next to the tub, his hands in his pockets. His eyes are tired. "This tub is big enough for two, you know."

"Nope, this is just for you, Legs. But do you mind if I jump in the shower while you soak?"

"Hmm…" I scrunch up my face like I thinking really hard. "Watch a sexy man get naked and take a shower while I lay here and be lazy? Sure, why not."

"Smart ass," he laughs and strips naked, completely comfortable in his own skin, and turns on the water in the shower.

I may be exhausted, but I'm not dead. Dear Jesus, the man is just *hot.*

"What is the tat on your back?" I ask. I can't read it from here, but it looks like four lines of script on his shoulder blade.

He drapes a green towel on the bar beside the shower and then backs up so I can get a closer look.

MONTGOMERY, CALEB J
990001212USN O NEG
CHRISTIAN

US CITIZEN

"What is it?" I ask, already knowing the answer.

"It's exactly what's on my dog tags, in case I was ever…"

"I get it," I interrupt him, not wanting to even contemplate the what-ifs. He looks over his shoulder at me and then frowns when he sees the look on my face.

"What's wrong?" He asks.

I shake my head and sink farther down into the water. "Thank

God you're safe."

He bends down to kiss my head and whispers, "I'm fine, baby." Then he walks into the shower.

Dear God, what if he'd ever been captured? Tortured? Killed?

A shudder wracks through my body, despite the hot water. I reach over to grab the soap, but it slips out of my hand, falling to the floor with a loud *thunk.*

"Are you okay?" Caleb shouts and throws the shower door open, his eyes wild and chest heaving as he pants.

"I'm fine. I just dropped the soap." He closes his eyes and shakes his head, and without a word, closes the shower door and finishes cleaning himself.

When he leaves the shower, he won't meet my eyes. He dries himself off, tying the towel around his hips and helps me out of the bath. When I reach for a towel, he takes it from me and dries me himself.

"Are you okay?" I whisper.

"Fine."

He continues to dry me off, then takes my hand in his and pulls me into the bedroom where he helps me into my pajamas and pulls on his own underwear and black basketball shorts.

"I'll sleep on the couch."

He starts to leave the room, but I stop him.

"Bullshit. You'll sleep in this bed with me, Caleb Montgomery."

He stops in the doorway and drops his head, as if in defeat and then turns to me, his eyes sad. "I shouldn't, Bryn. The girls are here."

"We're not naked. The girls will be fine. We'll probably be up before them anyway."

He props his hands on his hips and lowers his gaze.

"I'm afraid of hurting you in my sleep," he admits, his voice a hoarse whisper.

"What?" I ask and instinctively move to him, wrap my arms around his waist and pull him against me. "You'd never hurt me."

"Not intentionally, not ever." He cradles my face in his palms and gazes down at me intently. "But when the nightmares come, I get pretty violent, Bryn."

"I'll be fine."

He shakes his head but I hold on tight.

"If you abandon me now, after the battle we just went through together? I'll kick your ass."

His lips twitch before he rests them on my forehead and takes a deep breath.

"Are you sure?"

"Yeah, I'm sure."

He laces his fingers with mine and leads me over to the bed, tucks us both in, and pulls me against him, my back to his front.

"Thank you, Caleb. For everything."

I hear him sigh before he leans over and kisses the sensitive skin beneath my ear.

"Goodnight, Legs."

Chapter Seven

"Good morning!" Nat announces and kisses my cheek as she moves past me into my living room.

"Morning, sunshine," Meg grins and kisses my other cheek.

"You two are entirely too chipper for eight thirty in the morning." I shut and lock the door, as Caleb has instructed over and over again, and lead the girls into the kitchen.

"Oh good, you have creamer," Meg murmurs as she digs in my fridge.

"I bought it just for you." I grin over at the pretty auburn-haired woman and then hug Natalie, wrapping my arms around her shoulders and holding her tight. "How are you, little mama?"

"Good," she grins and hugs me back. "I'm hardly sick at all with this one." She covers her still flat belly with her hand and rubs in a clockwise circle.

"You could have brought Livie with you," I mention as we all fill our mugs and sit at the table. This is our weekly coffee date. I don't have to be to work until ten, so we usually meet for a quick cup of something hot and gossip. "Jules stuck at work?"

"Luke loves his mornings with Liv, so they're good," Nat waves me off. "And yes, Jules is in early morning meetings."

"Stacy is home with two sick kids." I grimace and take a sip of hot coffee, leaning my elbows on the table.

"How are yours?" Meg asks and joins us.

"Much better, thank God. They finally went back to school this morning." It's been a week since the girls were sick. "As much as I love them, I was about to put them up for adoption if they didn't go back to school soon."

"Good morning, ladies." Caleb saunters into the kitchen, wearing a dark blue Navy t-shirt and black shorts. He smiles at the girls and then turns that smile at me, his eyes warm and tender, as though he's remembering every little amazingly sexy thing he did to me this morning.

"Good morning," we all respond in unison.

"What are you up to?" Meg asks.

"I'm gonna work out for a while out back," he grins at Natalie. "Thanks for letting me install the equipment."

Natalie smiles and shrugs. "No problem."

Nat offered her Alki Beach house to the girls and me right after Jules moved out to live with Nate and I couldn't love her more for it. It meant that I didn't have to put my name on a lease anywhere and the girls and I don't have to live with my folks.

Caleb offers us a mock-salute and leaves through the back door to the fenced yard behind the house where he's set up all sorts of odd equipment to work out with.

"How are things with him?" Meg asks and gestures to the back door with her head.

"Fine," I shrug and take a sip of coffee.

"Are you sleeping with him yet?" Nat asks casually, and I gape at her.

"No," I lie and take another sip of coffee. "He's here to protect the girls and me."

"Right," Meg rolls her eyes and pushes out of her chair to refill our mugs. "That's why he looks at you like he wants to rip your clothes off and do you here on the kitchen table."

It's fun when he does me on the kitchen table.

But I don't voice the response aloud, I simply shake my head and laugh.

"Whatever."

"Deny it if you want to," Meg smirks and glances out the back window. "Damn," she whispers.

"What is it?" Nat asks and rises from the table to see what Meg is looking at. Her eyes widen and she glances back at me and then outside again. "Holy shit."

I know exactly what they're watching.

Or, who.

And yes, it is a sight to behold.

"How do you ever get anything done around here?" Meg asks as I rise and lean against the sliding glass door, coffee cradled in my hands, and watch the sexy man in my backyard. "I'd just stand around and watch him all day."

"Uh, Meg," I glance over at her and laugh. "You have one of these at home," I remind her, referring to Caleb's pro-football star brother, Will, who is also Meg's live-in boyfriend.

"And it's a good thing he's gone most of the day or I wouldn't get anything done either."

"It's starting to rain," Nat observes, but it doesn't seem to faze Caleb. He lifts two thick, heavy ropes in both of his hands. The ends are attached to Nat's photo studio out back. With a firm grip on the ropes, he begins to wave them up and down, quickly, the rain pounding down on him, causing his shirt to cling to every muscle as it flexes and moves with the motion of the exercise.

"Hot damn," Nat whispers and I silently agree. He continues to pump his arms furiously, effortlessly. "What does that exercise do?" Nat asks.

"Works his arms, back and abdomen, and it's cardio too," Meg responds and takes a sip of coffee.

Just then, Caleb drops the ropes, bends down to grab onto a medicine ball and lowers his tall body to the sit-up position.

"Maybe he'll bend over again," I murmur, earning giggles from the other two women.

"It's a good thing Jules isn't here," Nat mutters and licks her lips as her eyes watch Caleb hold the medicine ball in front of him, sit at a forty-five degree angle, and twist from his left to his right, over and over again. "She'd never let us watch him like this."

"Jesus, that medicine ball is fifty pounds," Meg whispers, amazed.

"Watch this part," I urge them as Caleb tosses the ball to the side like it's a beach ball and assumes the push-up position and begins to perfectly execute the push-ups, easily completing more than a hundred of them in two minutes.

"Why aren't you sleeping with him again?" Meg asks and I

choke on my coffee.

"I might be," I whisper and feel their astonished gazes on me, but I avoid them. "Don't you dare breathe a word of that to anyone."

"Who can blame you?" Nat asks just as Caleb stands and returns to the ropes. "Look at those back muscles."

"Look at that ass," Meg counters.

"You should see it naked," I respond and we all giggle again.

"Should I be grossed out by this?" Nat asks, tilting her head to the side. "He's practically my brother."

"But he's *not* your brother, Nat." I remind her with a grin. "And the Montgomery men are freaking hot."

"That's no lie," Meg agrees. "Aren't you going to be late for work?" She asks me.

"I have a few minutes," I murmur and feel the familiar pull low in my belly as I watch Caleb lay on the ground again and execute perfect sit-ups.

It would be the perfect position for me to ride him. I might have to suggest that tonight.

"He's hardly panting," I observe. "What kind of physical training must he go through to work that hard and have it hardly phase him?"

"Oh girl, you have no idea the rigorous training they go through to become SEALs. It's not natural." Nat shudders. "All of the boys have always been athletic."

"Obviously," I murmur sarcastically. "It's a bit intimidating."

"Caleb can be the scariest person on Earth if he's pissed off," Nat informs us, her eyes still glued to him. "He's just big and strong, and damn intimidating."

"You should see him with the girls." I grin, remembering our movie night last week. "He's funny and sweet."

I realize the room has gone dead silent. I look over to my friends to find them looking at each other and then staring over at me. "What?"

"You've got it bad," Nat remarks and snickers. "Welcome to the club."

"What club?"

"The 'I Love a Hot Man' club, sweetheart." Meg laughs and salutes me with her mug just as Caleb approaches the sliding door, frowning at me. I step back in surprise as the girls giggle.

"What's wrong?" Caleb asks, is hair and clothes soaked and a little muddy from the rain and grass.

"Nothing," I reply and shrug.

He narrows his eyes at me, watching me closely, and then turns his gaze to Nat and Meg.

"What's going on with you guys?"

"Nothing at all," Nat replies with a huge grin. "Just girl talk."

"Uh huh." He props his hands on his lean hips and watches all three of us for a moment and then shrugs and saunters to the fridge to pull out a cold bottle of water. "We have to leave soon," he reminds me.

"I know," I nod and watch as he saunters out of the room toward the stairway to go up and shower.

Natalie suddenly pulls me in for a long, hard hug. "Good luck," she whispers and then pulls back.

"Have a good day at the office, dear," Meg grins.

"Thanks."

***

I love my job. Not only because I'm good at it, but because it's fun and I feel like I'm part of a family.

Isaac Montgomery owns this construction business. He is married to Stacy, my first cousin, although she and I were really raised more like sisters. Since leaving Chicago, Isaac has not only looked out for me, but has given me this job in his office, paying me under the table to help in my need to disappear.

Thank God for them.

In the past year, I've not only cleaned up Isaac's accounts and maintained his billing and payroll, but have blended into the camaraderie of the guys who work for him.

Of course there is harmless flirting and teasing, but at the end of the day, I know the guys all have my back and they're fun to joke with when they come into my office with questions about their checks or benefits, or just to chat before they head out to a job site.

But there is a new guy, Levi Jackson, who creeps me the hell out.

He's never done anything inappropriate, but the way he watches me and the tone of his voice when he speaks to me gives me the shivers.

And not in a good way.

He's a good looking guy, and probably used to snagging any woman he sets his sights on, if she doesn't pick up on the creepy factor.

I have a sick feeling in my gut that he's set his sights on me.
So not gonna happen.

I find myself avoiding eye contact with him, walking past him quickly and generally avoiding him as much as possible. I'd tell him to fuck right off, but he hasn't done anything to warrant it.

Except give me the creeps.

Isaac shares the office with me, but is out with the crews most of the time, leaving the office duties to me, which suits us both just fine. He's outside instructing a crew on a new project, and I can hear his no-nonsense voice as I check company email.

The front door opens and closes, the hinges groaning loudly.

"We are a construction company," I remark loudly. "Can't you oil those damn hinges?"

"I think I'd have to have the boss approve that first."

My head snaps up in surprise. I was expecting Isaac, but instead, Levi is approaching my desk, a smirk on his face.

"Sorry, I thought you were Isaac," I respond politely. "What can I do for you?"

"I have a question about the insurance benefits," he replies and moves around my desk to lean a hip on my desk at my side.

Way too close for comfort.

"I explained the insurance to you last week, Levi."

He smiles and shrugs, crosses his arms over his chest and leans back a bit, watching me. "I'm slow."

"No, you're not."

"Maybe I just want to come in here and talk to a pretty lady." He smiles at me, like he's trying to pick me up in a bar, and it makes my stomach roll.

"Levi, I'm not interested. If you have questions about payroll or insurance, fine, but I'm too busy to chit chat and am not interested in your come ons."

I stand and try to move around him to the center of the office, but he blocks my path and deliberately brushes his arm against my breast.

"You know," he murmurs and reaches out to run the back of his index finger down my arm. "You don't look like you belong to a cop."

What the fuck? How does he know about Jeff? Who the hell is he?

I jerk away just as Isaac walks through the office door.

"I don't belong to a cop," I reply, my voice ice-cold.

"What the hell are you doing?" Isaac asks, his voice calm, but his blue eyes are pissed off.

"I was just asking Brynna some questions about my insurance."

"He was just leaving," I announce and glare up at Levi. "If you have any more questions, take them directly to Isaac."

He holds his hands up as if in surrender and backs away from me. "Sorry to bother you."

"Get to work," Isaac snarls.

"Yes, boss."

Levi hurries out the door, slamming it shut behind him and Isaac turns his cold gaze to me.

"What was that about?"

"Nothing I can't handle," I sigh as I sink down in my chair and return to my email, willing my rolling stomach to settle. Dear God, I just want to throw up. I feel like I need a long, hot shower to try to erase the feel of his finger on me.

"What was that about?" Isaac repeats as he braces his hands on my desk and leans down toward me. "And don't bullshit me."

"Levi came on to me," I shrug and offer Isaac what I hope is a confident smile, but it slips as I'm still shaking from his cop comment. "Except, why would he say that about me belonging to a cop?"

"He must have seen Matt pick you up yesterday," Isaac shrugs, as though that explains it all, and it does, thank God. I've never mentioned anything about my past before.

"Oh, you're right." I smile at him and shake my head. "No biggie."

"Are you sure? I'll fire the bastard."

"I'm sure," I shake my head and lean back in my chair as I push my hands through my hair and exhale deeply. "He's a bit creepy, but this was the first time he crossed a line."

"I'm going to be watching him. If anything like this happens again, you tell me right away and I'll kick that little asshole's ass, you understand me?"

"Yes, sir," I reply sarcastically.

"I mean it, Bryn."

"Okay," I respond.

He nods and settles behind his computer. Today is his office day.

"How are the kids feeling?" I ask.

"A little better. Stace and I were up with them all night."

He squeezes his eyes shut and pushes his thumb and forefinger over them.

"I know that feeling," I reply with sympathy. "Let me know if you guys need help."

"I think we're almost out of the woods. Stacey's mom is over helping her today."

"Good." I nod and switch to my payroll program to begin logging in hours worked by the guys. "I'll call her when I get home today."

"I'm serious, Brynna, if Levi pulls one more stunt…"

"Isaac, stop. I'm fine."

He watches me for a long minute and then exhales deeply. "Okay, I'll drop it."

He mutters under his breath something about Caleb killing him and hiding the body if he finds out about it, making me smirk.

"Caleb wouldn't do that," I tell him with a wide smile.

"Oh, honey, you clearly don't know my brother very well."

I know him very well.

***

"Where is Caleb?" Maddie asks and turns her big brown to me as she pushes her chicken nuggets around on her dinner plate.

"I told you earlier. He's having some fun with his brothers and his dad." After I finish slicing up some cantaloupe, I dish it out onto their plates and then return to cleaning up my mom and dad's kitchen.

"I miss him," Josie sighs dramatically.

"He just dropped us off an hour ago, girls," I remind them with a roll of the eyes.

"Hey! I'm not gonna watch this damn Nemo fish by myself!" My dad yells from the living room, making the girls giggle.

"Hurry up and eat so you can go watch Nemo with your grandpa."

After scarfing down their nuggets and fruit, they climb down from the stools at the breakfast bar and run to join my dad in front of the television.

"They seem to really like Caleb," my mom mentions casually as she walks into the room.

She's not fooling me.

"We all like Caleb," I tell her and grin. "He's family."

"Hmm," she replies non-commitally.

"What's your point?" I ask and prop my hands on my hips. Mom shakes her head and shrugs as she gathers brownie mix, eggs and oil, ready to make a treat for the girls.

"It was an observation."

"Mom," I begin but she interrupts.

"I'm happy that the kids like him," she murmurs as she opens the box. "He's a good man."

I frown and nod, watching her closely.

"And you've been alone for a long time."

"Mom," I try again but she turns to me with big tears in her eyes and I'm rooted where I stand.

"You've been alone for a long time," she repeats and swallows, blinking rapidly. "I wish you'd come home much sooner, and I'm sorry that you had to come under these circumstances. I'm so proud of you baby girl."

I move across the kitchen and wrap her in my arms, hugging her tightly. I get my height from my mom, along with my dark hair and eyes.

Eloise Quinn is a beautiful woman, inside and out.

"If he is who you and the girls want, I say go for it," she whispers in my ear and then steps back and smiles at me before returning to her brownies.

"Mom, I never said anything about feeling that way about Caleb," I reminder gently.

"I'm not blind or stupid, Brynna Marie."

She's got me there.

I fall silent and listen to the whirl of the electric mixer as she stirs the batter and get lost in my own thoughts.

Is Caleb who I want?

Oh, who am I kidding? Of course he is.

Chapter Eight

~Caleb~

"Well, ladies, you might as well just hand over your money now 'cause daddy's going home a winner." Will smirks at us and plops down in his chair as he passes everyone a fresh, ice-cold long-necked beer.

It's Thursday poker night at our parents' house, just us brothers and our Pop. We try to do this every month, and usually succeed, especially now that I'm no longer being called out on deployment at the drop of a dime.

"Big talker," Pop murmurs and studies his cards.

"You're losing bad, old man," Isaac taunts our father, his gaze on the small stack of chips before him.

"I'm about to hit my stride anytime now."

"It's okay, Pop, Will has a tendency to choke in the second half of the game anyway," Matt laughs and reaches over to ruffle Will's hair, who quickly evades.

"Whatever, jackass!" Will throws a kernel of popcorn at Matt, who smirks.

"You just can't stand to lose," Matt sneers at our younger brother.

"Dude, sports are my *job*. Of course I don't like to lose."

"This is poker, man. It's not a sport." I laugh and take a long sip of water as I lean back in my chair, one eye out for my mom. If she catches me leaning back in her dining room chair she'll kick my ass.

I'll always be afraid of that woman.

"You clearly don't play it right," Will mutters and throws his cards down on our mom's kitchen table. "I fold."

"Sucker," Pop taunts and pulls the pot toward him. "I've taught you everything you know, kids, but I haven't taught you everything *I* know."

We all laugh as we watch our father stack his chips and smile smugly as he takes a long sip of beer.

"How are things with Brynna and the girls?" Isaac asks me as he shuffles the deck.

"Good. I took Brynna to the range last week." I lean forward as my cock stirs at the memory of watching her with the gun in her hand. She's so fucking amazing. "Let her shoot my nine mil."

"Did it knock her on her ass?" Matt asks.

"Nope," I boast proudly. "She did great. Hit the target. Wasn't afraid." I shrug and take another sip of water. "I wouldn't want to be on the business end of her weapon."

"I know what kind of weapon you want to show her," Isaac smirks and examines his cards.

"Fuck you, man."

"He's just pissed because he's been married for so fucking long, he can't remember what a blow job feels like," Matt says, earning a glare from Isaac.

"I don't know that being married has anything to do with it," Pop says and stuffs some Doritos into his mouth. "Your mom and I have been married for almost forty years, and just the other night…"

"No! No! No!"

"Stop talking!"

"Oh my God!"

We all yell at the same time, begging our father to stop talking and he throws his head back and laughs his ass off.

"We may be old, boys, but we're not dead."

"I will murder you if you ever, *ever* imply that my mother has sex ever again," Isaac mutters as he cringes.

"Don't ever say 'mom' and 'sex' in the same sentence," Will says, his voice hard and strained.

"So is that why you don't want to get married?" Isaac asks Matt. "Afraid the sex will suck?"

"No," I butt in with a laugh, "Matt just doesn't like to be the one tied down."

"Or tied up for that matter," Will chuckles and then yells out in pain when Matt punches him in the arm.

"Dude, that's my fucking throwing arm!"

"Don't be a pussy," Matt smirks.

"I am not a pussy," Will counters and takes a pull on his beer. "And you clearly need to get laid."

"Who says I haven't been getting laid?" Matt asks.

"Who would fuck you? You're ugly as fuck," I respond, earning chuckles from my other brothers.

"He looks just like you," Pop responds and grins at me. "You're all a bunch of ugly shitheads."

"Stop calling my boys ugly!" Mom calls from upstairs. "And Caleb, stop leaning back in my chair!"

"How does she know?" I whisper and return my chair to all fours.

"She knows everything," Isaac reminds me. "Mom-radar."

"It scares me."

"It should," Pop smirks, his eyes trained on the stairway. Just then the house phone rings, and Pop stands to answer it. "Hello?"

He frowns. "Yes, this is Steven Montgomery." A pause. "Hello?"

He pulls the receiver away from his face and stares at it before replacing it.

"They hung up?" Matt asks and leans forward, his eyes narrowed.

"Yeah, just asked my name and hung up." He returns to his seat and we all stare at each other, frowning, our red flags not just up, but waving violently, and we are all on high alert.

"What the fuck?" I whisper and stand the pace about the room. "What is going on?"

"Why was he so freaked out at the idea of her being linked to a cop," Isaac whispers, and our heads whip around to focus on him.

"What did you say?" I ask.

He looks up at all of us and shakes his head as he scowls.

"What did you say," I repeat.

"There's a guy at work," he begins and takes a sip of his beer. "Levi Jackson. I've noticed him watching Bryn, making up excuses to talk to her."

"Why didn't you say anything before?" Matt demands.

"Let him finish," Pop interjects sternly.

"He's never crossed a line with her. Until yesterday."

He stops and rubs his hands through his hair in frustration. "When I came into the office, he had her cornered against her desk and I heard him say, 'You don't look like you belong to a cop.'"

"What the fuck!" I yell and stomp away from the table. "Why in the hell am I just now hearing about this?"

"Has she ever told the guys that she used to be married to a cop?" Matt asks.

"I don't think so," Isaac shakes his head. "She's really careful about what she tells them. Besides," he continues with a frown. "I don't think he was talking about Jeff. I think he saw her with you." He nods to Matt who scowls.

"Maybe it's just a coincidence?" Will asks. He's leaning back in his chair, arms crossed over his chest, deep in thought.

"That's quite a coincidence," Pop mentions.

"It's no coincidence," I growl. "Did he have his hands on her?"

Isaac grimaces and looks away, and that's all the answer I need.

"Sonofabitch! Why didn't she tell me?"

"Probably because she knew you'd react like this?" Matt asks. His eyes are hard and his face taut. He's in cop mode.

"Are she and the girls alone tonight?" Will asks.

"No, they're at her parent's house."

"I bet having a constant babysitter is starting to piss her off," Pop mutters.

"It is," I nod and rub my hand over my forehead. "But it's necessary. We don't know what the hell is going on." I focus on Isaac again, anger coursing through my body along with a touch of fear that makes me even angrier. "Don't you do back ground checks on your people?"

"Of course," he spits out. "He could just be a creepy kid who has a crush on her."

"Or he could be a fucking gangster who's trying to get close enough to kill her!" I shout back at him.

"Oh, I'm sorry, I didn't run the *are you a motherfucking gangster* report on him," Isaac bites out sarcastically.

"I'm going to kick your ass," I mutter and reach for my phone, needing to hear her voice, to assure that she and the girls are safe.

It rings four times and then goes to voice mail, so I leave a message asking her to call me and then text her.

Please call me back ASAP.

"No answer," I mutter.

"Call her parents' place," Matt suggests.

"Already dialing," I say and listen to their phone ring twice before her mother picks up.

"Hello?"

"Hi, Eloise, this is Caleb. Can I please speak with Brynna?"

"Oh, she and the girls left about an hour ago," she replies and all of the hairs on my body stand on end. "Her dad gave them a ride home."

"I told her to wait there for me and I'd pick them up on my way home."

Matt's eyes narrow and Isaac and Will lean forward as Pop stands and starts dialing his house phone.

"I'll try her cell again," he mutters.

"She said that the girls were tired, and she was fine, and they'd just wait for you at home."

"When did they leave?" I ask.

"About an hour ago," she repeats.

"Still no answer," Pop announces and hangs up the phone.

"Thanks, Eloise. I'll try her cell." I don't want to frighten Brynna's mom, so I keep my voice light and then end the call. "Shit."

"Where is she?" Will asks.

"Eloise says she took the girls home about an hour ago."

"But she's not answering her cell?" Matt asks.

"No, I'm leaving." I grab my coat. "I'm gonna go spank her ass," I mutter under my breath as I head for the door.

"Let us know when you find her," Pop demands.

I nod as I leave, intent on getting back to Bryn's as soon as I can. I swallow hard, trying to keep the fear at bay, and dial her cell again.

After the fourth ring it goes to her voice mail again, and this time my message isn't as calm.

"Answer your fucking phone, Brynna."

I hang up and toss the phone in the seat as I speed through Seattle back to the Alki neighborhood and to my girls.

My girls.

I slam out of my car and unlock the front door, punching in the code for the alarm system and move quickly through the downstairs to the kitchen. Brynna's purse is lying on the kitchen table, so I head for the stairs, climbing them three at a time. I stop by the twins' room first. Their door is slightly ajar and the nightlight is glowing. They are both sound asleep in their beds.

I pull their door closed quietly and march down to Brynna's room where the door is also slightly ajar, push my way inside and latch the door shut, locking it behind me.

"Brynna." My voice is hard, but not loud enough to carry down the hall to wake the girls.

She sits up abruptly, blinking at me. "Caleb?"

"What the fuck are you doing here?" I ask and cross my arms over my chest, looming over her.

"I live here." She frowns and reaches over to turn on the lamp on the bedside table.

"I told you to wait for me at your parents' house," I remind her, my teeth gritted. I want to throttle her and kiss the hell out of her all at once. She's tousled, her hair falling in waves around her face. Her skin is glowing, void of makeup.

She's stunning.

"Where is your cell?"

"In my purse."

I curse under my breath and pace about the room, unable to calm the hell down.

"I couldn't reach you."

"Caleb, I don't need a babysitter twenty-four-seven." She

scowls and sits up straighter. "We are fine."

"You don't fucking get it," I mutter and push my hands through my hair. "Someone could hurt you! All three of you!"

"Well they haven't!" She sets her chin and glares at me. Damn, I want to spank the hell out of her. She jumps out of bed and starts to move around me toward the door. "I need to check on my daughters."

"I already did." I grip her arm in my hand and pull her to a stop next to me. "They're sleeping."

"I don't think I want you to touch me right now." She pulls her arm away and backs up, glaring at me.

"But you apparently don't mind having Levi put his hands on you at work."

She scowls and retreats further, crossing her arms over her chest. "What the hell are you talking about?"

"Isaac told me all about Levi coming on to you."

"You have got to be kidding me." She closes her eyes and shakes her head. "Is this a damn pissing contest?"

"Why didn't you tell me?" I ask, ignoring her jab.

"Because it was nothing!" She gestures wildly with her hands and pushes them through her hair as she paces around the bedroom. "He's harmless."

"He clearly has an issue with cops, and he put his hands on you." My voice is low and hard and my hands are itching to reach out for her. "That's not harmless."

"He's nothing," she insists.

"I need to be able to trust you." Her eyes widen with surprise and hurt and my gut clenches.

Her jaw drops before she balls her hands into fists in frustration, whispers angrily under her breath and inhales sharply.

"You can trust me." She stops in front of me, inches from me, looking up at me in exasperation and hurt. "I'm not a child. I can take care of me and my kids."

"Do you understand what it would do to me if someone got to you?" I explode and grip her shoulders in my hands. "It would destroy me if you or those babies were hurt, Brynna. You are necessary to my survival, goddamn it, and I'll do whatever I have to do to keep you safe and whole, but I need you to talk to me when something feels wrong and I need you to do as you're damn well told!"

Her big brown eyes are round as she watches my face, her plump lips parted in surprise and I can't stand it anymore. I pull her against me, wrap my arms around her and hold on tight as my mouth claims hers, hard and possessive.

Fuck, she's *everything.*

I pull back and lean my forehead on hers, breathing her in, relieved that she and the girls are safe. My legs are shaky, and I feel rocked to my core now that the adrenaline from the potential threat is gone.

Like coming out of a mission alive.

"Let me do my job, baby. Talk to me. Please."

"I'm sorry, Caleb." Her voice is small. She grips onto my back firmly, pressing herself against me from her head to her pelvis. "I didn't know."

"Now you do." I swallow, staring down into her sweet face. "Besides, millionaires pay a lot of money for this kind of protection. You're getting it for free."

"Yeah?" She smiles sassily and drags her hands down my chest to my waistband. "What else can I get for free?"

"What do you want?" I ask and gasp when she unbuckles my belt, unfastens my jeans and sinks her hand under my boxers to my hard cock, gripping it firmly.

"Hmm…" She moves her head back and forth, like she's thinking really hard and then leans in to kiss my chest through my shirt, moving her way down my belly and kneels at my feet. "I think I'll just show you what I want."

After shimmying my jeans down around my knees, Brynna licks the tip of my cock, just like she would her favorite ice cream cone, and then sinks down over me, pulling me as far as she can into her hot, wet mouth and it's all I can do to keep my hips still.

"Fuck, Bryn."

She pulls up and licks down to my sack and licks that too, leaving no piece of skin untouched by that amazing tongue of hers. Watching her head bob and weave, her hand grip my cock at the base and those big chocolate eyes of hers stare up at me is the sexiest damn thing I've ever seen in my life.

Jesus, all she has to do is breathe and I can't wait to get inside her.

She cups a hand around my balls and sucks my cock, hard, making my spine tingle and stomach tighten, and I pull her up to her feet before I come in her mouth.

"You've really got to stop making me stop before I get the job done," she pouts, her eyes shining with laughter.

"Can't come yet," I growl and push her back to the bed, stripping her nightclothes and the rest of my own clothes off as we move. "Need to be inside you."

I guide her back onto the bed and follow her, bury my face in her neck and breathe in her fresh, clean scent.

"Smell so fucking good," I whisper as I settle my cock between her legs, nestled in her pussy, but not sinking inside her yet. I brace myself on my elbows and drag my teeth up the side of her neck to her ear, relishing in her strong hands gliding down my back to my ass and back up again.

"Caleb," she whispers, tilting her head to give me better access to her skin.

"Yes, baby."

"Make love to me, okay?"

The question is soft and sweet and I pull back to look down at her, brushing small strands of hair off her cheeks with my thumbs.

"In a minute," I whisper and glide my hand to her perfect, round breast and palm it in my hand, rubbing my thumb over her nipple.

She has great tits.

My hand pushes down to her sweet, hot pussy to find her wet and her clit already swollen and ready for me.

"You're so wet, Legs." Two fingers slip between her lips and my cock twitches and throbs at the way she clenches around them. "Does fighting with me turn you on?"

"Everything you do turns me on," she replies as she pants and writhes beneath me.

I grin against her neck and work my fingers fast, thumbing

that clit. Jesus, there's nothing like Brynna when she's turned on. She's so open and giving and so damn responsive.

"Caleb. Ah, babe, I'm gonna come."

"Do it," I whisper and push my nose up her neck.

"I want to come when you're inside me," she pouts with a groan.

"Oh trust me, Legs, you will." She tilts her pelvis against my hand, and bites her lip. "Let go, sweetheart."

And she does, moaning and hanging on to me tightly, riding out her orgasm. My hand is soaked as I pull it away and settle my throbbing cock against her again, slipping against her.

"Make love to me, Caleb."

"Happily." I grin at her and when she smiles back at me, with complete trust and love shining in her eyes, it's almost my undoing.

I grip my cock in my fist and guide it inside her, slowly, inch by inch, groaning her name as I sink in her wet heat.

"So fucking tight," I murmur through gritted teeth. "I'll never get enough of this, Bryn."

When I'm buried balls-deep, I tip my forehead to hers and brace myself here, seated inside her, surrounding her.

Shielding her.

Her pussy muscles squeeze and tug as she slowly circles her hips, and I can't help it, I begin moving in and out furiously, glorying in the way those tight muscles tug on my cock, milking it in the best way possible.

I push my hand between us and press my thumb against her hard clit and she clamps down on me even more, making me see stars.

"Ah, baby, you keep gripping me like this and I'm gonna lose it."

"Do it, Caleb." She pushes her hips faster, rocking and clenching, her hands kneading my ass, and I know it's only a matter of seconds.

"Come with me," I whisper and kiss her, press my thumb against that nub even harder and her legs spasm, hitch around my hips, opening her up to me even more and I can't hold it back any longer.

I have to bite my lip to keep from crying out as the orgasm gathers in my balls and explodes out of me, inside of this gorgeous woman.

Her hands grip my ass even tighter as she comes, pushing against me shamelessly and to my utter shock, she bites my shoulder.

Hard.

That's gonna leave a mark.

I grin down at her as I pant, exhausted. I rub my nose against hers, and then kiss her softly.

"You amaze me," I whisper.

"Back at you, sailor," she whispers back, her eyes still closed, making me chuckle.

Somehow, I find the strength to reverse our positions, cradling her on top of me. She drifts into sleep quickly, breathing deeply and draped over me.

This is where I lay for a long while, rhythmically combing my fingers through her long hair, listening to her breathe and the settling of the house.

How did she and girls come to mean so much to me in such a short time?

And what am I going to do when it's time to leave them?

Fuck, just the thought of it hurts more than any wound I ever received in the field.

Losing them will kill me.

Chapter Nine

"What is up with the early morning questions?" I ask the girls as I dish them up some scrambled eggs.

"They ask questions any time of day," Brynna informs me as she joins us in the kitchen, fresh from her shower. She stands next to me to grab a coffee mug and grins up at me. She smells like lavender and vanilla.

And my heart stumbles in my chest.

"You are beautiful," I whisper down at her. She lowers her gaze, a rosy blush tinting her cheeks. I lean over and kiss the top of her head, breathing her in. "Good morning."

"Good morning."

"Coco Puffs, please!" Josie calls out and grins sweetly.

"Are you made of Coco Puffs?" I ask Josie and pull a cereal bowl down from the cupboard.

"No, silly."

"I think you might be. You eat enough of them." I wink over at Maddie and dish up my own breakfast.

All this sex I've been having leaves me starving.

I'm not complaining.

"Eggs?" I ask Brynna, but she shakes her head and sips her coffee.

"Mommy doesn't like eggs," Josie informs me. "Only Coco Puffs."

"Uh, I don't think that's true," Brynna replies dryly. "Mommy just doesn't want anything to eat yet."

"Do you think your butt looks big in those jeans?" Maddie asks Brynna with a tilt to her head, and I almost choke on my bacon.

Brynna lets out a long, loud laugh and shakes her head. "Where did you hear that?"

"Mason at school said his mom always says her butt looks big in her jeans."

"Well, I am just not hungry yet," Brynna responds with a grin.

She better not think her ass is too big in anything. Her ass is perfect.

"I think we should get a dog," Maddie announces and munches on her bacon.

"We've had this conversation," Brynna begins.

"But mom," Maddie interrupts. "We need a dog."

"We do?" Josie asks, and Maddie elbows her in the side. "Yeah, we do! It would keep us safe and we would love it and feed it and you can pick up the poop!"

"I do *not* want to pick up any poop," Brynna laughs. "I told you we'd talk about it in the summer."

She looks up at me and shrugs. "They want a dog."

"I see."

"Who was the man at our house yesterday?" Josie asks and dribbles milk on the breakfast bar. I frown over at Bryn and back at the little girl.

"What man?" I ask her calmly, but my body is instantly on high alert. I set my plate aside and focus on Josie.

"The man who was looking in mommy's mailbox when we got home from school," Maddie responds.

"What?" Brynna lowers her mug. "There was a man looking in the mailbox?"

"Yeah. But we don't ever have mail in that mailbox, do we Mommy?"

I turn my eyes to Brynna, raising my brow in question. She shakes her head slowly.

"No, sweetie, we don't."

"With me. Now." I grip her hand in mine and pull her out of the kitchen to the living room. "Do you have a post office box?"

"Yes. That mailbox by the road never has anything in it. Even Nat and Jules' mail has stopped altogether."

"So it wasn't the mailman," I murmur and process everything

that's happened in the past twenty-four hours. "I need to get you three out of here."

"What are you talking about?"

"Brynna," I grip her hands in mine and pull her close. "I have Matt running a more intensive background check on that fucker at your job, but I don't trust him. My dad got a weird phone call last night…"

"That's why you freaked out," she whispers but I keep talking over her.

"And now we find out that the girls saw someone snooping around here. I don't like it."

"I don't love it either, but we can't just leave." Her brow is furrowed, and her hands shake as she holds on to mine.

"It's Friday, Bryn. Pull the girls out of school, and we will get away for the weekend." I lean in and kiss her forehead, trying to keep calm, to keep *her* calm, but my fight or flight instincts have kicked in and all I can think about is getting my girls as far away from here as possible.

As fast as possible.

"Okay," she whispers and pulls away. "When?"

"Now." My voice is hard. "The girls are dressed and ready. Run up and pack a bag for them and for you, and we'll go."

"Where are we going?" she asks.

"I know a place," I respond. "Hurry."

***

"Uh, Caleb?" Brynna asks dryly from the passenger side of my car.

"Yeah."

"We are less than ten minutes away from the other house." She frowns as I stop the car.

"Did you think I was whisking us all away on a European vacation?" I ask with a chuckle and push out of the car, opening the back doors for the girls to climb out.

"Is this your house?" Josie asks and holds her doll close to her chest.

"Yes, jellybean," I respond and usher them all to the door, carrying our bags.

"Why are we at your house?" Brynna asks.

"Because no one would expect to look for you here," I respond and pull the door closed behind us, locking it, as Brynna drops her purse on my couch and takes a circle about the living room.

"This is nice," she murmurs and smiles over at me.

I shrug and glance about the place. It's not messy because I'm never here long enough for it to get messy. The furnishings are practically brand new, although I bought them several years ago. There is nothing hanging on the walls.

It's not even close to being good enough for her and her daughters, but it's all I've got.

"It's small, only two bedrooms."

"That's all we need." She shrugs and flips her hair back over her shoulder. "How long have you lived here?"

"A couple years," I shrug. "I just rent it."

"It's definitely a guy place."

"A *guy* place?" I ask with a grin.

"Yep, no woman lives here, or has been here recently." She raises an eyebrow in my direction, and I know exactly what she's asking.

In the past I would have evaded the question like the plague, knowing that it was time to move along. But I am compelled to reassure her.

"Girls," I call out, my eyes still trained on Brynna's deep brown ones. "Why don't you take your bags to the bedroom with the green comforter on the bed and get your dollies settled?"

"Okay!" Maddie exclaims and jumps off the couch where she had been testing it out.

"Let's go!" Josie agrees and they are off. Their voices carry into the living room as they talk to their dolls, explaining where they are, and I grin at their beautiful mama.

She stays rooted in place as I move close to her and slide my hands up her arms, over her shoulders and pull my knuckles down her cheeks.

"I have never brought a woman here, Legs." Her eyes widen and I know she's about to tell me she doesn't care, but I lay my finger gently over her lips, stilling them. "You are the only woman I want here."

"Why?" She whispers from behind my finger and watches me closely.

I swallow and bend slightly to lay my forehead against hers.

"Because you're more than a quick lay, Bryn. Even without the sex, at the core of it, you're my friend. You're my family." She wraps her arms around my waist as I straighten and gaze down at her. I run my fingers through her soft hair and exhale slowly. "I can't lose that."

"I'm not going anywhere, Caleb."

"We'll see."

"I'm not…"

"Mom! Caleb has a TV in his room! It's really big. Come look!" Maddie hurries into the room and then stops cold, watching us carefully. "Why are you hugging Mommy like that?"

"I just needed a hug," Brynna replies with a bright smile. Maddie comes running over and loops her arms around both our waists, squeezing tight.

"I want to hug."

Running my hand down Maddie's back, I'm reminded how fragile she is, how tiny, and exactly what this mission is. Keep the girls safe.

Stop thinking with my dick.

I pull away and turn my back to them abruptly. "Go get settled, Bryn."

"I think we should…"

"Stay here," I interrupt and turn to face her but can't meet her eyes. "Do. Not. Leave. I have to go get food and other supplies. Get you and the girls settled and I'll be back."

"Caleb, we can't be holed up in your house for days! We'll all kill each other by tomorrow night." She props her hands on her hips and stares at me like I've gone mad.

"Do as I say," I respond and grab my keys. "And for Godsake, keep your phone on you."

And with that I leave, emotions I have no business having swirling around inside me. God help me, I'm falling in love with two amazing girls and their mother. And I'm exactly what they don't need. Broken. Hurt.

Another man who will end up leaving them, just like that pussy of an ex-husband of hers. What kind of a man lets his wife care for infant twins alone?

Yet here I am, knowing I can't be with them forever. They deserve so much more than a fucked up ex-SEAL.

But I'll be goddamned if I can stay away.

Chapter Ten

~Brynna~

"I don't want to!" Maddie screams.

"Stop touching her!" Josie wails back and tugs her doll out of Maddie's arms. "She's mine!"

"Girls!" I yell but am met with deaf ears as they start hitting each other, sobbing and crying. "HEY!" I roar and pull Josie away from Maddie.

"She started it!" Maddie yells between sobs and buries her face in her own doll.

"What the hell?" Caleb exclaims as he comes in from outside. "I could hear you all from the street." He's scowling at us all as he slams the front door and crosses his arms over his chest. "What is going on?"

"I hate you all!" Maddie yells and runs for the bedroom that she and Josie have been sharing in Caleb's house for the past two days.

"You're not s'posed to say hate!" Josie calls after her as she runs after her.

"Do *not* touch each other! Do you hear me?" I call after them and then square my shoulders and glare at the tall, too-handsome-for-his-own-good male standing before me.

"What did *I* do?" He asks.

"Caleb Montgomery, we have been in this house for more than two days. If we don't get out of here for some fresh air, it won't matter if there could be a homicidal drug lord trying to find us. I'll kill us all by lunchtime myself!"

His lips twitch and his clear blue eyes smile down at me. "I don't think you'll actually kill us."

"We can't take any more of this, babe." His eyes flare when I call him *babe*, just like they always do, and I soften a bit. "I know you're trying to keep us safe, but the girls are going stir-crazy. We can only watch so many movies, and if one of them says, 'she's touching me!' one more time I am going to poke my eyes out with a hot stick!"

"So, you're saying you want to get out of the house," he replies sarcastically and I ball my fist up and sock him right in the arm.

"Ouch," he mutters and rubs his bicep, scowling at me. "You're stronger than you look."

"Please, Caleb. It's not fair to them."

He exhales and shakes his head, eyes trained to the floor, and rubs his forehead with his fingertips.

"Have you and the girls been on that damn duck boat ride that goes through downtown?" He asks unexpectedly.

"No," I respond.

"I know the owner. There will be a small crowd, but it would be controlled and we can sit in the back so I can keep an eye on everyone around us."

"Okay!" I bounce on the balls of my feet as I wrap my arms around his neck and kiss him loudly on the cheek.

"Just a few hours," he clarifies and then softens. "I don't like seeing them so unhappy."

"They'll love this. It'll be perfect."

"Girls!" Caleb calls out and within a few seconds both girls come trudging out of their room, their faces long. "Get your coats. We're going out for a while."

"Yay!" Josie exclaims.

"I love you!" Maddie shouts and they both scurry to get ready to leave.

"See?" I kiss his cheek again and grin up at him. "Better already."

*   *   *

"Look, Mom! It's Jules and Nate's building!" Josie is pointing eagerly out the window of the duck boat, her yellow duckbill whistle in her mouth. When you get on the amphibious truck, you get a yellow duck whistle that makes quacking sounds.

It's incredibly annoying, and they will be "lost" by morning.

The truck drives all through downtown Seattle, by the famous Pike's Place market, through old Bell Town and then it drives right into the water of Lake Washington, and takes a tour about the lake, giving us a fantastic view of the Seattle skyline.

The girls are loving it.

"Yes, it is," I agree and smile at Josie. "But how do you know?"

"Because it's by the really good donut place," she grins. "I like the glazed ones."

"Ah, that's right," I nod and have a sudden craving for glazed donuts myself. "We went there the last time we stopped by to see Jules and Nate."

Josie giggles as I tug on one of her long pony-tails and I glance over at Caleb, who hasn't paid attention to one word the tour guide has said, but instead watches every person on the truck intently, his eyes narrowed. He and I are both seated on the aisle, giving the girls the window seats so they can see everything the tour guide is describing.

"Relax," I murmur over at him.

He doesn't even look my way.

I purse my duck call between my lips and blow it in his face.

He whips his head around and glares at me.

"Relax," I tell him again, with a grin. "This is fun."

His body is tense, every muscle flexed and ready to jump into action. His phone rings and he reaches for it and has it pressed to his ear before the second ring.

"Montgomery."

And suddenly, like magic, it's as though his body deflates like a balloon. "Thank God."

He listens and then chuckles. "Yeah, well, that's one less thing we need to worry about, but we're not out of the woods. Okay, later."

He hangs up and exhales, pushes his hand through his hair

and finally glances down at me. "I'll tell you when we get back to my place."

"Good news?" I ask.

"Yeah." He nods and scans the group again.

"They're the same people that were there twenty seconds ago. They haven't changed, Caleb."

"I don't like crowds," he murmurs as he shakes his head, his eyes trained on the exits, body still alert. I reach over and lace my fingers through his, anchoring him to me. I can't imagine what's going through his head right now. The girls are oblivious, loving the sights and sounds of the city, dancing along with the music and blowing into their duck calls.

"Thank you for this," I murmur to him and he nods once then breathes a sigh of relief when the vehicle stops back where we started and the passengers begin to dismount.

"Now what?" Maddie asks with a wide grin.

"Let's get ice cream!" Josie exclaims as we stand to be the last ones to leave.

"Let's go to the movies!" Maddie joins in.

Caleb swears under his breath and tugs one of each of the girls hands into his own as we walk past the Experience Music Project toward the parking garage.

We lucked out on the weather today. For February, it's relatively warm, and rain-free.

Thank God.

"Caleb! Look! Cotton candy!" Josie points at a red and white cart, laden with clouds of cotton candy in plastic bags, popcorn and slushy's.

"Okay, we can do cotton candy," Caleb grins down at the girls and leads us to the cart.

"I want pink!" Maddie and Josie exclaim at the same time.

"Two pink cotton candies," Caleb chuckles at the older woman working inside the cart. She smiles widely and hands them over, then collects the money for them from Caleb.

"Your family is beautiful," she winks. "And your girls clearly have you wrapped around their little fingers."

I tense for a moment, my eyes glued to Caleb's face. He continues to stare down at his wallet, a smile tugging on his lips, but then he frowns almost regretfully. Finally, he glances back up to the kind woman, offering her a fake smile.

"Thank you," he replies simply, accepts his change and hands the girls their sweets.

"What do you say?" I remind my girls.

"Thank you!" Their voice is a chorus of excitement as they dive into the sweet confection and nibble their treat.

"Thank you," I mutter to Caleb who meets my gaze with sad blue eyes.

"You're welcome."

***

"I want to stay here, Brynna." Caleb's hands are braced on the countertop at his hips as he leans against it and glares at me in exasperation.

"Absolutely not," I shake my head furiously, fold the dish towel in half length-wise and drape it over the cabinet door beneath the sink. "We have a life to get back to."

"Brynna, listen to me…"

"Caleb," I interrupt him, my voice calm and quiet and he stops talking and watches me carefully. "No. My girls need to go to school. I have a job. Yes, Levi is creepy, but…"

"Levi is no longer an issue." Caleb crosses his arms over his chest, drawing my gaze to his rippled biceps and I have to press my knees together from the zing of electricity that zooms through my pussy.

"What do you mean?" I ask.

"He's been fired."

I stand and watch him, waiting for him to explain further.

"That was Matt on the phone today." Caleb sighs and shakes his head. "The extensive background check came back. He has no violent history, which means he's just a creepy guy with a crush."

"So, he just figured Matt and I are together?" I ask and feel a light sweat break out on my forehead.

"Yeah." He chuckles and pulls me to him, as though he can't stand to be apart from me for one more second, even if we are arguing. "He thought Matt was your husband because he picks you up from work every day."

I close my eyes as I sigh and lean my forehead against his chest. "Thank God."

"He's still been fired. Even if he doesn't have a record, he was inappropriate with you. Isaac fired him before I showed up there and ripped his balls off."

I laugh and lift my head to gaze up into his eyes. "I handled him."

"I really think we're safer here, Legs."

My smile evaporates. "No."

He growls and pulls me against him more tightly, buries his face in my neck and takes a long, hard breath in. "You are so fucking stubborn," he murmurs against me, the words muffled, and I can't help but laugh at him.

"Back at you."

"If we are going back to your house tomorrow, I have some conditions."

"Wow, this sounds like a compromise," I reply dryly. He bites my neck, right where it meets my shoulder, before he pulls back and glares down at me.

"One, no school bus. Either Matt or myself will take them to and from school every day. I will not budge on this." He runs his hands soothingly up and down my back, but narrows his eyes at me, daring me to defy him.

"Yes, si-…" I catch myself and stutter, "Okay."

Caleb smiles down at me softly. "You can say 'yes, sir', you know. I hear it every day."

"Not in this lifetime," I mutter and chuckle. "No way."

"Okay, number two, we have the alarm system on the house expanded."

"I can't afford…"

"I know people, Brynna. This won't cost you a dime, and should have been done weeks ago. I want censors on the windows and motion censor lights outside." He stops and stares at me, waiting for me to acknowledge him, and I do with a nod.

"Number three, I want you to go to the range with me more often, and I'm leaving my nine mil with you at all times."

I begin shaking my head, but he leans in and rests his forehead against mine and rubs our noses together. "Please," he whispers, his voice rough, and I know it's taking everything in him to agree to letting us go home. He wants us all to be safe. How can I find fault in that?

"Okay," I acquiesce, and kiss his chin. "Anything else?"

"Yes, neither you nor the girls are ever to be alone. *Ever.*"

"Can we go to the bathroom alone?" I ask sarcastically.

"You are such a smart ass," he responds, but his lips are pulled back into a half-smile and his eyes are happy.

"I can live with this," I murmur and kiss his lips softly.

"Good."

"I'm sleepy." I yawn widely and then chuckle. "I think I'll head to bed."

"I'll be along soon." He kisses the tip of my nose before I move away from him toward the bedroom. "I have to call Matt and then I have a bit of reading to do."

"Okay." I grin and saunter into his bedroom, yawning once again.

***

"Holy fuck! Get down, get down! Retreat!"

Rat tat tat tat tat. Boom! Boom!

I jolt up in the bed and search frantically around, but Caleb isn't in the bedroom.

"Take cover, Goddamn it!"

I jump from the bed and run into the living room. The lights are still on, as is the television, turned to a military show on the History channel. Caleb is laying across the couch, where he must have fallen asleep while watching the show, but he's thrashing about, sweating and his breath is coming in hard, harsh pants.

I rush to his side and sink to my knees beside him.

What do I do? Do I touch him?

The television continues behind me. *Boom! Rat tat tat tat tat!*

I grab for the remote and snap the power off and then turn back to the terrorized man before me.

"Caleb," I murmur and gently lay my hand on his bicep, and before I know it he's rolled us both onto the floor, he's pinning me with his huge body and wrapped his hand around my throat, squeezing.

He's having one helluva nightmare.

And so am I.

"I said retreat, goddamn it!" He shouts and glares down at me, his eyes glazed and blank, as though he's not really there at all. It's the most terrifying thing I've ever seen in my life.

Holy fucking shit.

"Mommy! Mommy!" I hear the girls in the doorway, scared shitless and crying.

Dear God, don't let him choke me to death in front of my girls.

"I've got you, motherfucker!" Caleb growls in my ear, and a cold sweat breaks out all over my body. Jesus, if I were an insurgent, I would just lie down and die at the sound of this voice.

He wouldn't have to shoot me.

"Caleb," I try again, but he squeezes even harder. I wiggle my arms free and begin hitting him on the back and sides, over and over, trying to wake him but he just pins me harder with his legs and snarls down at me. The bright color of his eagle tattoo catches my eye and I watch his shoulder muscle flex as he tightens his grip on my throat.

"Stop hurting my mommy!" Josie cries just as the edges of my vision begin to darken and I see stars.

Just as Maddie lets out an ear-piercing scream, I knee the inside of his thigh, hard, and am suddenly freed and pushed away from him, rolled onto my stomach, gasping and wheezing.

I cover my throat with my hands and cough, pull myself up onto my knees and watch Caleb's eyes clear, the blankness replaced with horror and disgust. He scrambles away from me, in a backwards crab-crawl, until his back hits the wall.

The girls are huddled together in the doorway, clinging to each other with wide eyes, crying for me.

"Fuck me," Caleb whispers, and my head whips around to find his knees pulled up to his chest, arms wrapped around them, and his face in his hands. He's shaking violently.

"Caleb," I manage, my voice hoarse, but he cringes back away from my touch and shakes his head adamantly *no.*

I jump from the floor and run to my babies, pull them into my arms and carry them back into their bedroom, to the full sized bed they've been sharing.

"Why was Caleb hurting you?" Josie sniffles and buries her face against my chest as Maddie clings to me and buries her face in my neck.

"He didn't mean to," I reassure them, repeating it over and over again, while reassuring myself. I kiss their heads and breathe in their sweet baby shampoo smells, rocking them back and forth. "He was having a bad nightmare."

"He sounded scared," Maddie murmurs and sniffles.

"I think he's still scared," I whisper and kiss her forehead.

"Maybe we should hug him," Josie whispers, but cowers deeper into me.

My brave, sweet girls.

"I think Caleb needs to be alone for a little while, but you can give him lots of hugs in the morning, okay?"

They both nod. "Will you lay with us for a while?" Josie asks.

"Of course," I reply and tuck them in, then lay with them, smoothing their hair from their faces and murmuring to them. I brush the tears from their soft cheeks and kiss them both over and over again.

"I'm okay, babies."

"Love you, mama," Josie whispers as she falls back into sleep.

"Love you too, brave girl."

Maddie is already snoring softly, both of them have fallen into an exhausted sleep, and I leave them and prepare myself to confront Caleb.

Poor Caleb.

The lights are still on in the living room and I find him there, sitting on the couch, knees spread and elbows propped on his knees, his face in his hands.

"Caleb," I whisper and his head whips up, his face in utter anguish as his bright blue eyes find mine.

"I'm so damn sorry," he replies, his voice full of the anguish written all over his face.

"It's not your fault." I move to him, sit down next to him, but he pulls away.

"I shouldn't touch you."

"Caleb…"

"I could have *killed you.*" His voice breaks as he braces his face in his hands again. "Oh my God!"

"You weren't going to kill me, Caleb."

"Yes, I was! If I hadn't woken up, I could have choked you out, or broken your neck." He lowers his gaze to my throat and winces at the sight of what I can only imagine is bruises beginning to take shape. "God, baby, I'm so sorry."

"Caleb, this has never happened before. It's been an emotional weekend."

"It's never happened before *with you*," he corrects me. "I haven't slept with a woman in more than four years, Bryn. I can't risk it. My buddies have told me stories of the things I do in my sleep." He swallows hard and shakes his head. "But God, I love sleeping with you in my arms, and for the first time in as long as I can remember, I actually *sleep* when we're together."

He shakes his head in wonder and wipes his eyes and it breaks me that he's crying.

"I haven't had nightmares since our first night together." His voice is raw with emotion and I don't even feel my own tears running unchecked down my face. "But with you and the girls being in danger, and being on that fucking duck ride today, with all of those people, I guess it just caught up with me."

"Explain to me about the crowds." I sit back on the couch, facing him, and pull one leg up under me, careful not to touch him, but close enough that he can feel that I'm here.

"Crowds are the worst." He swallows hard again and scrubs his hand over his lips as he leans back on the couch, looking up.

"We are taught to always look for a choke point."

I cock my eyebrow at him. "English, please."

"Exit. Always know where your exits are. Crowds in Iraq are very dangerous. Those extremist fuckers will blow a whole crowd up, without hesitation."

My heart bleeds for him as he closes his eyes, and I don't even want to contemplate the horrors he's seeing behind his eyelids.

"I didn't realize you'd been in Iraq," I murmur.

"Not often, but enough."

He balls his hands into fists, and I can't stand it anymore. I reach over to sooth him, rubbing my hand up and down his arm but he flinches away from me, so I climb into his lap, leaving him no choice but to wrap his arms around me.

"Listen to me, very carefully." I pull my fingers down his face, never losing eye contact with him. "I'm okay, Caleb. You didn't kill me. You scared me."

"The girls…" he begins but I cut him off.

"The girls are worried about you and I had to stop them from coming to find you to hug you. The girls are fine, baby." I continue to calm him, push my fingers through his hair and down his cheek. "We're okay."

"I should start sleeping on the couch again," he murmurs and sighs as though he's resigning himself to the horrible idea. He watches my face carefully, as though looking for any fear or animosity. "But I don't want to."

"I don't want you to do that either," I shake my head and kiss his cheek. "I love having your arms around me at night. I've never had that before."

He clenches his eyes closed before gazing back at me. "Me neither. I would never hurt you, sweetheart. *Never.*"

"Caleb, you make me feel so safe. You didn't have this nightmare while sleeping with me. You were on the couch," I remind him and watch his eyes as he blinks several times before focusing on me again. "With a war show on the History channel."

"I've never had a nightmare while sleeping with you," he whispers.

I smile warmly and comb my fingers through his dark blonde

hair again. "I guess your couch-sleeping days are over, sailor."

He tightens his arms around my middle and presses his face to my neck, clinging to me as I twine my arms around his shoulders and kiss his temple tenderly.

"I'm so fucking sorry," he whispers again and I hold him close.

Tell him! Tell him you love him. My heart is so full of love for this intense, protective, broken man, but I'm confused too.

Am I in love with him, or do I just have a need to fix him?

"You're safe with me, babe," I respond and press my lips to his forehead. "Always."

Chapter Eleven

~Caleb~

I wake before the sun, alert and ready to start the day, despite only getting a couple hours sleep. We need to get an early start so we can get the girls to their school, Brynna to work, and I have to get to work myself.

We'll be back at Bryn's tonight.

I sigh and let my eyes travel over her face, down to her breast that's pressed firmly to my ribcage through her thin nightshirt and farther down to her waist. I can't seem to say no to her, even when it's for her own good, and I'm afraid that that will be my greatest mistake.

She is my weakness, but she strengthens me too. It's the damndest thing.

The reminder of last night's nightmare rocks through me and I clench my eyes closed and hug her tightly against me.

Jesus fucking Christ, I could have killed her. What is wrong with me? Yeah, war fucking sucks, but you come home and you get on with your life.

You don't jump like a pussy over every loud noise and you for damn sure don't try to choke out the woman that means more to you than life itself.

I press my lips and nose to her hair and inhale deeply, letting her sweet scent of vanilla and lavender fill my head and soothe me.

All I have to do is smell her and I'm calmer, yet I know I should pull away from her altogether. She and the girls need someone who's not so fucked up in the head. They deserve someone that doesn't lose his shit in crowds and have nightmares that make him want to shit the bed.

But the thought of someone else holding Brynna like this, or watching her two girls grow up into young women, makes me even more crazy in the head.

I pull back and look down into sleepy brown eyes. She's watching me lazily, and has begun to rub her hand up and down my side. She pushes one of those long legs between my own.

"'Mornin'," she mumbles.

"Good mornin', Legs." I kiss her forehead and pull my pelvis back as she drags her hand down from my side to my dick, enjoying my morning wood.

"Stop," I whisper and pull her hand up to my lips. "I can't."

"What do you mean?" She asks with a frown.

"Not yet." I shake my head and lace my fingers with hers, holding her hand close to my chest. "I need to say something."

"Okay," she mutters and settles against me, not letting me go, which is a good sign.

I couldn't bare it if she was afraid to be close to me.

"I just want to say something about last night," I begin and frown as I try to gather my thoughts. She just waits quietly, not moving, not tensing up. Just waiting for me. "I'm so sorry that I hurt you and scared all of you."

She opens her mouth to argue but I lean in and press my lips softly to hers, shutting her up.

"You are the strongest person I've ever met, Brynna," I whisper against her lips. "And I've met some damn strong people. You surprise me, and you humble me, and I'm grateful to be here with all of you."

Before she can respond, I kiss her again, more deeply now, and feel my cock harden in anticipation of sliding inside her.

Except, it's going to be disappointed to find that it'll be going without this morning.

Right now, this moment, is all about her.

I gently push her onto her back and pull away so I can examine the light purple marks around her neck.

"I'm fine," she murmurs, but I look up into her chocolate eyes with sadness and regret. "I'm. Fine."

I lower my gaze again and tip her chin up with my finger, gaining access to press light, tender kisses to her bruised skin. She purrs low in her throat and kneads the muscles of my shoulders as I move down her chest, licking and kissing her lazily. Her nipples pebble beneath her thin tank and I grip the hem and pull it up, exposing her perfect tits to my mouth. I suck and torment her, making her moan again.

"Caleb," she whispers.

"Shhh." I blow on the wet buds, making them pucker more and then continue on my quest down her slightly rounded stomach, kissing along the waistline to each hip, up each side, counting her ribs with my tongue. She boosts her hips up as I snag the hem of the shorts in my fingers and drag them, along with her panties, over her hips, down her long legs, and toss them onto the floor.

"Do we have time for this?" she breathes and clenches the sheets in her fists.

"Oh, I think so," I assure her and push her legs together and up, my hands pressed to the backs of her thighs, so her knees meet her chest. I lower my head and lick her, from her anus, through her sopping wet lips and to her already-swollen clit.

"God, you taste fucking amazing," I growl and repeat the motion again. She slaps her hands over mine, gripping me and pulling her legs even closer to her chest as I lap at her pussy.

I feel her start to quiver, and her legs begin to tremble beneath my hands. I release her and spread her wide, gazing up at her as I wrap my lips around her clit and suck rhythmically. Two fingers plunge inside her and she begins to buck beneath me, pushing her pussy against my hand and face, shaking her head back and forth on the pillow, her dark hair a riot around her sweet face, coming apart.

Her muscles squeeze me beautifully, and I want nothing more than to sink inside her and ride her hard until I come, but we definitely don't have time for that.

I continue to kiss her lips and clit gently, her thighs and pubis, as she pants and combs her fingers through my hair, scrubbing my scalp with her fingernails.

Before she can ask me to make love to her, I climb up her long body, kiss her deeply and then push away, sauntering to the bathroom with my shorts jutting out like a tent.

"Hey!" She exclaims.

"What?" I toss a smile over my shoulder.

"You're not done."

"I'm fine," I respond, pausing by the doorway to look back at her. I love seeing her on my bed, all rosy cheeked and satisfied. *My girl.*

"We have to get the girls up and leave soon." I sober and watch her silently for a moment. She sighs and pushes herself from the bed and walks to me, wrapping herself around me in a big hug.

"They'll be fine, Caleb. Just be honest with them." She grabs my hand and pulls me into the bathroom behind her. "We'll finish what you started in the shower. Conserve water, and all that."

I grin down into her happy eyes, cringing inside. What will I say to Maddie and Josie?

How do I explain what I don't understand myself?

"You go ahead, Legs. We'll conserve water another time."

She frowns up at me in confusion. Hell, I'm confused too. I just know that I'm not ready to make love to her again. Not yet.

"Another time," I repeat and kiss her hair before making a hasty retreat; before I lose my resolve and pull her into that hot shower and lose myself in her.

***

"Girls, wake up," I croon gently from the doorway, not wanting to startle them. Brynna is standing next to me, her hand on my low back. "You should wake them up," I whisper to her.

"Stop worrying," she whispers back with a small smile.

"Caleb!" Maddie jumps from the bed as soon as she opens her eyes and sees me. She runs over and wraps her arms around my waist, holding me tight.

I glance up at Josie and my heart stops. She's sitting straight up in bed, her brown eyes – the same as her mom's – wide and staring at me. She pulls her doll into her lap and hugs her tight.

She's scared.

"Good morning, buttercup," I murmur down to Maddie and squat down so I'm eye level with her. "How are you this morning?"

"I have to pee."

"Well then you should go," I chuckle at her and usher her through the door and turn to Josie. "Hey, jellybean."

She turns her wide eyes to her mom and then back to me and stays silent. Brynna crosses to her and sits on the bed with her, running her hand down Josie's long dark brown locks.

"Josie, it's okay, sweetie."

"You hurt my mom," she whispers and clasps her lips tightly together when they start to quiver.

"I didn't mean to, Josie, I swear." I walk closer to the bed but she flinches and cowers into Brynna's arms, so I stand where I am and shove my hands in my pockets, feeling like a complete asshole and out of my element.

Now what?

Maddie comes bouncing back in the room and climbs up on the bed, looking back and forth between Josie and me.

"Josie," Brynna murmurs softly. "It's okay, baby."

She shakes her head, frowning, clinging to her mom. She won't meet my eyes.

She's punishing me.

And she should. Fuck, I wouldn't trust me either.

"It's okay, Bryn," I mutter and smile reassuringly at the girls. "Let's get going. You all need to get to school and work, and so do I."

I turn and leave the room, my heart shattering into a million pieces.

***

"You don't have to walk me in," Brynna tells me with a roll of the eyes. "Isaac is right there."

"I don't care. I'm walking you to the door," I inform her and hold the car door open for her as she climbs out of my car.

We dropped the kids off at school ten minutes ago. Josie still won't speak to me, but Maddie made up for both of them, hardly stopping to take a breath all morning.

"What the hell happened to you?" Isaac asks as we walk into the office.

"Bite me," I respond and flip him the bird.

"You look like hell." He leans back in his chair and laces his fingers behind his head, scrutinizing me with narrowed eyes.

"Back at you," I reply and watch Bryn as she sets her bag in the bottom drawer of her desk and sits in her chair. She wore a turtle-neck top to hide the bruise on her neck, but when I look at her, they're like a shining beacon, reminding me what kind of monster I am. "Matt will pick you up at two thirty, and then the two of you will go get the kids from school."

"I work a job, Caleb," she reminds me, her eyes wide with frustration.

"I know your boss," I smirk and glance at Isaac. "She'll be getting off early to go get the girls and go home with Matt."

"Fine by me," he shrugs and leans forward, grabbing his coffee mug.

Brynna curses us both under her breath, making us both laugh hard.

She's fucking adorable.

"I gotta go to work myself," I wince when I check the time on my watch. "I'll see you this evening."

"Bye, dear," Isaac calls after me, and I throw him the bird again, slamming the door behind me.

As I slide into the driver's seat and start the car, I call up Matt's number through the blue-tooth and dial.

He needs a heads up.

"'lo?" He mutters, his voice gravely with sleep.

"Wake up, man."

"What's wrong?" He asks, his voice more alert and I can hear rustling in the background as it sounds like he sits up in bed.

"There's no emergency, I just need to give you a heads up because if Brynna doesn't say something to you this afternoon, one of the girls probably will, and I want you to hear it from me first."

Jesus, I'm babbling.

"You're a moron?" Matt asks dryly.

"No, asshole. I had a nightmare last night." I swallow hard, remembering coming to and Brynna pinned beneath me, her eyes bulging and red, gasping for breath.

Fuck me.

"Are you okay?" He asks softly.

"I'm fine, but I hurt Brynna and scared the girls."

"Damn," he mutters with a sigh. "What happened?"

As I explain the events, Matt quietly listens, never interrupting me to ask questions.

"And this morning, Brynna's acting like everything's perfectly normal. Maddie was fine too. Josie's not convinced. She was scared and isn't speaking to me." The thought of that still brings an ache the size of Montana to my chest.

"You know it's not your fault, right?" He asks.

"Whose fault is it then, Matt?" I ask angrily and absently rub my hand over my sternum. "I'm the one who had my hand around her neck. She has fucking *bruises!* If I were you I'd want to kick my ass."

"You were dead asleep, Caleb."

"That's no motherfucking excuse!" God, I'm just so angry. How could I do that to them? "How can she be so calm about it? How can she act like it's okay?"

"Have you asked her?" Matt asks calmly.

"No," I sigh.

"You two are so damn stupid," Matt laughs ruefully.

"What does that mean?"

"It's clear that she handled it so well because she's in love with you, Caleb. You two are crazy about each other. You have been for months."

"It doesn't matter."

"The hell it doesn't. I don't believe for a minute that you're having sex with her just because she's convenient."

Just the thought of that makes me want to punch him in the throat.

"I didn't say…"

"You deserve to be happy as much as anyone else, man," he interrupts, hitting the nail square on the head.

Leave it to Matt to voice what's going on in my head.

"And if you don't claim her and those little girls as yours, someone else will be more than happy to."

"Fuck you," I mutter without any real feeling behind it. He's right.

"Nah, you're not my type," he responds. "Thanks for the heads up, man. I'm gonna catch a few more hours sleep before I have to get Brynna and the girls."

"Okay. Thanks. I'll see you later."

I hang up and turn down the windy road that leads to the training compound that I now work out of.

The only good thing about getting out of the Navy is now being self-employed. I choose my hours with *Redwire,* the independent civilian company that works with the military in war-zones. I've been training their newbies in weaponry and marksmanship for a few months. They know that I'm one of the best in the field, which is why I make way more money now than I ever did as a SEAL.

Men and women in the military are pitifully underpaid.

Another bonus of this particular job is working with men who were either on my SEAL team, or were experts in other branches of the military.

Only the best of the best work here.

The training compound is twenty minutes south of Seattle in a remote area, away from businesses and residential homes. I park my car and walk into the main building to check my mail and check in with the owner.

"What's up, Mongtomery?" Jim Peterson nods from his office. He and I were on SEAL team five together ten years ago. He's a scary man when he wants to be, and knows his shit.

"Hey, man," I respond and shake his hand. "Sorry to leave you short handed."

He shrugs. "It's fine. Markinson is taking the classes on the days you're out. He's not as good as you, but we're muddling through."

"Thanks."

He nods once and points to the chair in front of his desk. "Have a seat."

"Why do I feel like I'm being called the principal's office?" I smirk as I sit in the chair and cross one ankle over the opposite knee.

"How are things?" He asks, his face serious.

"Fine."

"Bullshit," he counters.

I sigh deeply and scrub my hands over my face. "Do I look that bad?"

"Worse," he responds with a laugh. "I haven't seen you look this shitty since Columbia." His smile fades as we stare at each other, remembering the particularly dangerous mission in Columbia almost a decade ago, when we were supposed to rescue three American women who were being held hostage by the Columbian drug cartel.

The mission was FUBAR before we ever set boots on Columbian soil.

"Nightmares," I sigh and shrug and Peterson nods in understanding.

"There are people to talk to about that, you know."

I shrug and exhale. "I'm okay. I've been doing better. Last night was just rough."

He stares at me for along moment. "Okay. Have you talked to Kramer lately?" He asks, mercifully changing the subject. Kramer is another former teammate who also lives in the area and trains military working dogs for SEALs now.

"Not in a while. What's up?" I ask.

"He has to leave town for about a month for an assignment. He needs to find a place for Bix while he's gone."

"How is Bix?" I ask and grin as I think of the dog. Loyal, fearless and one of the best sailors I've had the pleasure of working with.

"He's good. He's not deployable." Peterson grimaces and shakes his head. "But he's good. Do you think you could take him for a few weeks?"

"I'll see what I can do. I'd better get out to the guys." I stand and shake his hand. "Thanks, sir."

"You're welcome, Sergeant."

***

~Brynna~

"Show me," Matt commands from behind the steering wheel as I settle in the passenger seat.

"Show you what?" I ask.

He cocks an eyebrow and watches me with those amazing Montgomery blue eyes, hands laced and resting in his lap.

"I won't ask again," he murmurs calmly and never breaks eye contact with me.

It's unnerving.

I cast my eyes down and pull my red turtle-neck away from my throat, showing him the bruise and then quickly replace it and pull my seatbelt on.

"How did you know?" I ask, not meeting his gaze.

He starts the car, throws it into gear, and zooms out of the parking lot with more force than I expect, given his calm demeanor.

"Caleb called me," he responds quietly and glances over at me. "Talk to me."

"I'm fine."

"Talk to me."

His voice is firm, not to be reckoned with. I sigh in defeat and sag in the seat, dropping my face in my hands.

"It was horrible," I whisper. "Scared me."

He rests his hand on my thigh and squeezes reassuringly. "Has he had nightmares with you before?"

"Never," I reply immediately, shaking my head adamantly. "He sleeps hard. Soundly."

"Really?" Matt asks, looking at me in surprise. "He hasn't slept well in a long time."

"He hasn't had an issue with me," I reply. "Until last night. But it was… different."

"Different how?" He asks.

"He had fallen asleep on the couch, watching war shows on the *History Channel*. When I woke up, I heard gunfire and cannons and Caleb was in the middle of the nightmare."

"So it didn't come on while he was in bed with you." He shifts his Jeep down as we turn onto the street where the girls go to school.

"No, he was on the couch."

"Interesting." I turn and watch Matt silently. He's in a white button-down and jeans, his pistol is resting in a holster on his hip. His light brown hair is in need of a haircut, and he didn't shave today, leaving a light stubble on his chin.

His left elbow is resting on the door and he's rubbing his fingers over his lips.

"How did you wake him up?" He asks.

"I kneed him in the thigh," I respond. He winces and chuckles ruefully.

"That'll do it." He grins over at me and then sobers. "How do you feel today?" He asks softly.

"My voice was a bit hoarse this morning, but other than that, I feel fine."

"Don't be obtuse, Bryn. How do you *feel*?"

He's just not going to cut me a break.

"Exhausted. Relieved." I swallow and stare down at my knees. "So in love with him I can't see straight," I whisper.

"Look at me."

My eyes find his as he offers me a gentle smile. "I think you'll be really good for each other. Give it time."

I nod just as the girls come running to the car.

"Hi mom!" Josie calls and scoots in to buckle her seatbelt.

"Hi Matt," Maddie grins as she joins her sister.

"Hi guys," I smile back at them as Matt pulls away from the school and heads toward home.

"How was your day?" Matt asks.

"Caleb hurt Mommy last night," Josie responds. I gasp and stare back at her with my jaw dropped.

"He did?" Matt asks and shakes his head slightly at me, telling me to not respond and let him handle it.

Just kill me now.

"Yeah, he wouldn't let her up off the floor," Josie responds.

"He didn't mean to!" Maddie jumps in to defend Caleb. "It was a bad dream."

Josie shakes her head stubbornly. "He hurt her."

"Do you think he did it on purpose?" Matt asks her calmly.

Josie shrugs and folds her arms over her chest stubbornly.

"Answer my question, please." Matt's voice is authoritative and strong.

Typical cop.

"I don't know," she replies with a frown. "It was scary."

"I'm sure it was, sweetheart," Matt murmurs. "Do you know what nightmares are, Josie?"

"Bad dreams?"

"Yes, they're really bad dreams." He affirms.

"Remember not very long ago when you came crying into my room because you had a dream that you couldn't find me, sweetie?" I ask her and watch her big brown eyes fill with tears.

"Yeah, I was really sad," she sniffs.

"Caleb was having a really bad dream like that, honey, except he thought he was in danger. He thought someone was trying to hurt him." Matt watches Josie in the rearview mirror closely.

"Who was trying to hurt him?"

"Bad people," Matt replies. "He used to have to go to places that had bad people in them who wanted to hurt him and his friends, so he could help people who needed him."

"So, that's what he was dreaming about?" Josie asks with wide, tear-filled eyes.

"Yes, honey," I reply and rub her leg with my palm.

"Oh," she whispers and looks down. "But I was scared that he was hurting you."

"Me too," Maddie admits. "But he was scared too."

"Damn," Matt whispers under his breath and shakes his head. "I'm so sorry you all had to see that."

"You wouldn't hug him today," Maddie accuses Josie.

"Hey, it's okay," I interrupt before a fight blows out of hand. "You can give him a hug tonight if you want."

Josie just nods and looks down at her hands as Matt pulls into our driveway.

"Looks like I don't need to stay long," he murmurs, eyes trained on Caleb just about to climb out of his own car. "He's home early."

"Yeah, he is. I wasn't expecting him home for another hour, at least."

Matt parks behind him and the girls climb out of the car with their backpacks. Caleb looks over at us hesitantly, and then opens the back door of the car and whistles.

A big, beautiful dog bounds out of the car, much to the delight of my daughters who begin jumping up and down and clapping their hands, wide smiles across their faces.

"And, that's my cue to leave." Matt smiles over at me, nods at Caleb, and leaves us all standing in the driveway.

"Sit," Caleb commands softly and the dog immediately sits at Caleb's side, not moving, looking up at him for his next command.

"Who is this?" I ask with one eyebrow raised.

"This is Sergeant Bix." Bix's tail wags once at the sound of his name. "He's a retired Navy SEAL and he needs a home for a few weeks while his handler is out on assignment."

"Can we pet him?" Maddie asks, her and Josie's bodies vibrating in anticipation. Bix glances longingly at my little girls and then back up at Caleb, waiting to be told what to do. "Please?"

"Sure," Caleb smiles. "Go ahead," he tells Bix, who happily jogs to the girls and they all collapse in a pile of elation, the girls rubbing him and talking to him as though they've known him for years.

"What happened to his eye?" Josie asks as she kisses his cheek. One of his eyes is permanently shut, like he's always winking, and the ear on the same side is slightly deformed.

Caleb looks up at me with serious eyes. "Bix was a dog that sniffed around for things that might blow up." He swallows and turns his gaze back to the dog. "He got injured while he was working and lost his eye and hurt his ear too, so he can't work anymore."

"Oh, poor Bix!" Maddie throws her arms around the dog and hugs him tightly. "Can he stay here, Mom?"

"This is sabotage," I hiss at Caleb. "You can't ask me if the most noble and adorable dog in the world can stay with us when my girls are already in love with him."

"What kind of dog is he?" Josie asks and giggles as Bix gives her doggie kisses on her cheek.

"He's a Belgian Shepherd. He's been trained to be a working dog since he was three days old."

"Wow!" Josie exclaims.

Caleb walks closer to me and drapes his arm across my shoulders.

"Taking on the responsibility of a dog is a lot right now, Caleb."

"He's the best trained dog you'll ever meet, Legs. He's fearless, obedient and one hundred percent professional."

I glance over and bust out laughing to find Bix flat on his back, paws in the air, tongue hanging out of his smiling mouth and relishing in a good belly rub from two eager six-year-olds.

"Yes, I can see that he's perfectly professional."

"He has to stay, Mom," Josie calls out. "He's a hero, like Caleb!"

Caleb looks shell-shocked as he turns me to face him. "He's an amazing dog, Bryn, and a helluva team member. It would make me feel better knowing he's here. Nothing will get to them with Bix watching."

"Sabotage," I whisper and grudgingly smile at the girls as they giggle and roll on the driveway with the big, fluffy canine. "I guess he can stay."

"Thank you, Mom!" Maddie calls out.

"Come," Caleb commands and Bix immediately jumps up and leaves the girls behind to stand next to Caleb. "Say hello to

Brynna."

He barks once and smiles at me, that tongue flopping out again.

"Hello," I murmur and pat his head and then give in and squat next to him and rub his face. "You're a sweet boy, aren't you?"

***

"But we aren't tired," Maddie protests as she yawns widely. Caleb throws a large dog bed on the floor between the girls' beds and points to it. Bix immediately lays on the bed, watching us with one raised ear and both his eyebrows moving up and down as he looks side to side at each of the girls.

"Why can't he sleep with us?" Josie asks and stares longingly at her new best friend.

"He sleeps on his own bed," Caleb replies and sits at her side. "Hey, jellybean, I'm sorry you're mad at me today. Maybe tomorrow will be a better day." I sit at Maddie's bedside and watch my daughter's internal struggle as Caleb watches her closely.

"Mom always says sweet dreams when it's time for bed," she tells Caleb softly. Bix lets out a long sigh as he lowers his head to his paws and Josie watches him with a smile. "I hope you have sweet dreams, Caleb, and no more scary ones."

I bite my lip and hug Maddie tightly, as Caleb silently holds his hands out to Josie. She climbs readily into his lap and hugs him, then scampers off to snuggle down into the covers.

"Good night, Mama," Maddie whispers.

"Good night, baby girl."

Bix raises his head and watches Caleb move to the doorway. He stops and looks back at Bix. "Stay, Bix. Stay with the girls."

With that, Bix lowers his head again and Caleb turns out the light, leaving only the light from the princess nightlight in the wall, and shuts the door behind us.

"I can't believe you talked me into a dog," I chuckle and lead the way down the stairs to the living room.

"He's already proven that he's well trained," he responds with a grin, referring to the numerous times he pressed his nose to the

126

sliding glass door, asking to be let out.

"Thank goodness," I agree and lower myself to the couch. Caleb sits beside me, but keeps at least two feet between us. "Oh, you wanna rub my feet? Here you go." I lay my feet in his lap and grin at him.

"I don't recall offering to do that," he mutters with a half smile, already digging his thumb into the arch of my foot, earning a moan of appreciation.

"Oh sweet Moses that feels good."

The heel of my foot is resting against his crotch and I feel his cock stir.

"Don't start," he warns.

"Why not?" I ask and rub the ridge in his pants with my foot.

"I'm not ready, Legs." He clenches my foot in his hand and then returns to rubbing it again.

"Uh, Caleb, we've been having sex for a few weeks now." I frown over at him and am shocked to see color spread up this cheeks. He stops rubbing my foot and turns his blue gaze to mine, his eyes ice blue and angry as hell.

Chapter Twelve

"What?" I ask and frown over at him.

"How can you be so normal?" He asks, staring at me with those amazing eyes.

"What are you talking about?" I ask and pull my feet away, tucking them under me.

"I could have *killed you* last night, Brynna."

I sigh and hang my head in my hands, so frustrated with him.

"Is this why you won't touch me?"

"Damn right," he confirms with a firm nod.

"Caleb, you're being ridiculous." I lower my hands and look up to find him watching me like I've just produced a second head.

"Brynna, I've snapped necks without giving it a second thought. I have that in me. I had my hand," he holds his large hand up for me to see, "wrapped around your tiny neck and was squeezing the life out of you, and all you've done today is be sweet and nice and fucking normal. Nothing about this is normal!"

"No, it's not normal, Caleb, but it wasn't on purpose, damn it!" I lean in and grip his forearm with my hand, holding onto him tightly. "You would never hurt me, babe."

"I'm capable of it." He shakes his head and sighs.

"No. You're. Not." He refuses to look me in the eye and he's really starting to irritate me. "Look at me."

He shakes his head no, staring down at my hand, and I don't know why but he just pisses me right off. I stand up and stomp away, up the stairs to my bedroom and into the bathroom. I have the urgent need to slam a door, but I don't want to wake the girls.

"Alright, Legs, why are you so pissed?" Caleb asks from the doorway of the bathroom, arms crossed over his chest, watching me.

"Because you're so damn stubborn!" I turn away from him and lean against the bathroom sink, head bowed. "I don't know what to say to you to make you understand that you didn't do it on purpose, and that I'm fine."

"I'm just so damn afraid of hurting you," he murmurs, making me whirl to face him.

"Not touching me hurts me." I lean my hips against the sink and cross my arms, mirroring him. "Not making love to me hurts me. Being tender and sweet to my girls and then backing away from *me,* hurts me."

"I want to touch you so fucking badly it's killing me," he whispers, his eyes closed and jaw clenched.

"I'm right here," I whisper back and slowly move to him. He's not going to make the first move, and I'll be damned if I'll go back to having a platonic relationship with him.

I love him.

I slowly wrap my arms around his waist and press myself against him, his arms still folded and pinned between us. Leaning in, I press a kiss to his sternum and nuzzle his chest through his soft t-shirt with my nose and look up to find his blue gaze watching me.

"You could never hurt me," I whisper and kiss his chin. "You love me."

His eyes widen for a fraction of a second and the next thing I know I'm in his arms, his hands are planted on my ass and he lifts me to him, kissing me ravenously.

"Are you sure?" He growls.

"If you don't get us over to that bed," I respond between kisses, "You'll have to worry about *me* hurting *you.*"

He chuckles and carries me to the bed, and I slide down him until my feet hit the floor and immediately begins stripping me out of my clothes.

Not one to feel left out, I return the favor, pull his black t-shirt up his chest and over his head, and let my hands glide down his smooth skin, over his nipples and down his muscular torso.

"You have abs for days," I murmur, watching my hands roam

up and down his stomach.

"We had to do a lot of sit ups," he mutters dryly and pulls me down onto the bed with him, and then, as if I weigh nothing at all, he flips me around, facing his feet, and lays on his back. "I've been dreaming of having your sweet cunt sitting on my face for months."

"I hate that word, you know," I tell him and balance myself with my hands flat on his stomach as he plants my knees beside his shoulders and spreads my core wide open.

"What?" He gently licks me, barely running his tongue along my lips, making me gasp. "You swear almost as much as Jules, except when the girls are around, of course."

"It just seems like a dirty word," I whisper and gasp again when I feel his tongue sweep from my clit down to my lips and back up again, harder now, pushing against my tender flesh. "Ah, God that feels good."

"I have the best view right now." He wraps his lips around my clit and gently pulls, making a smacking noise as he lets go and I can't help but move my hips in a circle over him, afraid of smothering him.

"That's right, baby," more smacking and pulling as he nibbles my clit and pussy lips over and over again. I clench my hands around his ribs and look down to see his very hard cock standing at attention and without giving it another moments thought, I reach down and circle him with my hand, pulling and pushing, up and down, stroking him firmly.

"Fuck!" His voice is low and hard and makes me dizzy knowing how much I turn him on. I continue to move my hips, brushing my pussy back and forth across his mouth and lean forward and take as much of his cock as I can into my mouth.

Which means I only get about half of him seated inside me because of his girth and length, but he almost jack-knifes off the bed.

"Damn, Bryn!"

"Mmm," I murmur in agreement and begin to suck him, keeping my lips firm against the velvety skin of his dick, loving the feel of the ridge of his head moving over my lips as he slips in and out.

He slips two fingers inside me, and I lose my concentration, having to sit up, still jacking him, and fucking his face.

Dear God, I'm going to come all over his face!

"Caleb, I have to move."

"Don't you dare," he growls against me, the vibrations of his voice pushing me even farther toward my release. I bear down on his fingers and feel the build up at the small of my back, my pussy clenches and I come against him, shamelessly grinding against his mouth and nose.

As my head clears, I lean down again and pull his throbbing cock into my mouth, sucking him harder and faster, jacking my hand up and down his shaft, until I can't stand it anymore.

I need him inside me.

Now.

I pull my pussy away from his face and climb down his long torso, dragging my wetness along his chest as I go. My hips rise as I hold his dick at the root and guide him inside me, settle my knees beside his hips and ride him backwards.

"Jesus fucking Christ, Brynna." His hands glide down my back, on either side of my spine, to my ass and hold onto my hips as I ride him ferociously, gripping and pulling on him with my muscles. I brace myself on one hand between his knees and cup his scrotum in my other hand, gently kneading and pulling on his tender balls. His hands fall from my hips to my calves and slide to my feet where he holds on, bucking up into me, meeting me with every thrust of my hips, and massages my feet with his big hands.

I'm getting a fucking foot massage while I fuck him senseless!

And it's fan-fucking-tastic.

His right hand abandons my foot and I feel him caress the globe of my right ass cheek before he spreads me open and circles the tight rim of my anus, wet from his mouth and my own juices.

"Holy shit!" I cry out, but push back against him. The feeling is foreign and odd, and maybe a little taboo. He doesn't push it inside me, just continues to rub against me.

"You are so fucking beautiful," he groans and I know he's close. His sack tightens in my hand and his cock hardens even more inside me. I clench around him and sink down, succumbing to my own orgasm, rocking and shivering over him.

"Oh my god!" I call out as he lets go and comes hard inside me.

Holy shit. I had no idea sex like this existed.

We're both panting and sweaty and I'm pretty sure I lost the feeling in my legs about ten minutes ago. I pull forward, allowing him to slide slowly out of me, and before I know it, Caleb pulls me back to him and settles me against him, tucked to his side.

"You are trying to kill me," he mutters and kisses my forehead. "Holy fuck, Legs."

"I couldn't help myself," I chuckle. "You're just so… *hot.*"

He laughs and smiles down at me, those dimples of his on full-blast.

"See?" I ask and cup his face in my hand. "This is who we are, Caleb. Don't forget that."

He sobers and searches my eyes for a long moment before he pulls me into a strong hug, his nose pressed against my hair.

"You are the best part of my life, Bryn. Don't *you* forget *that.*"

I smile softly and kiss his chest, my eyes heavy with fatigue.

Right back at you.

***

"That outfit you got for the concert is smokin' hot," Jules informs me and grins as we walk through the mall in downtown Seattle. "Oh, look! *Michael Kors!*"

"You need another handbag like you need another hole in your head," Nate chuckles and kisses her temple.

"A woman can never have too many handbags, ace," Jules informs him.

I am shopping today with Jules and Nate, Nat and Luke and Stacy. It was supposed to be a girl's day out, but Caleb insisted we take the men along for protection and he and Matt and Isaac stayed home with the kids.

I think we got the better end of the stick.

Natalie and Luke are walking ahead of us, Luke pushing Olivia's stroller and Nat has her arm around Luke's waist, her hand planted firmly in the back pocket of his blue jeans.

"Hot guys pushing a stroller are really hot," Stacy leans over and whispers to me.

"*Luke Williams* pushing a stroller is hot," I respond and we giggle, shoving each other's shoulders.

"We can hear you," Nat calls back to us sarcastically, causing Stacy and I to fall into a fit of laughter.

"I didn't whisper!" I call back.

"If you're gonna marry a hot movie star," Jules taunts Nat from behind us, holding her own hot husband's hand, "you have to know that people are gonna ogle his hot ass."

"He does have a nice ass," Nat agrees and pats it with a smirk.

"I'm glad you approve, baby," Luke murmurs down to Nat and kisses her softly.

"Gag," Jules mutters, making me grin. "Hey guys, I have to use the little girls' room."

"Do you need to go to the doctor?" Nate asks. "That's the fourth time since we've been in the mall."

"No," she waves him off. "I've been drinking a lot of water."

"No, you haven't, Julianne." I look over my shoulder to see Nate glaring down at her.

I'm sandwiched between two of the hottest men on the planet.

The others are at my house right now.

"Come on, girls. Y'all need to freshen your lipstick." Jules leads the way to the public restroom, leaving Nate, Luke and Livie behind.

"I don't wear lipstick," Stacy reminds us as we follow the petite blonde. She's stunning today, just like every day, in a maxi dress with a denim jacket over it and black heels that click along the floor as she walks.

Jules is the only woman I know who wears heels all day shopping without needing a foot transplant by the end of it. If I didn't adore her, I'd despise her.

When we all get in the bathroom, Jules looks under the stalls to be sure we're the only ones there.

"This isn't high school, Jules," Stacy reminds her with a smirk.

"I need you two to keep Nate busy for a while," She informs Stacy and me, her eyes wide with excitement.

"Why?" I ask. "Where are you going?"

"She and I are going lingerie shopping so she can wear something hot when…" Natalie begins but is cut off by Jules as she jumps up and down and claps her hands excitedly.

"When I tell him I'm knocked up!"

"Holy fuck!" Stacy exclaims.

"Wow!" I agree, and we both rush her and hug her close, rocking back and forth.

"Oh, let me in there," Natalie says and wraps her arms around all of us.

"This family is suddenly swarming with babies," Stacy murmurs and wipes tears from her eyes.

"Oh my God, can you imagine how beautiful their baby is going to be?" I ask and hug Jules tightly again. "This gene pool is seriously impressive."

"I'm so excited for you," Nat tells her and squeezes her hand. Jules looks at each of us and sighs with a big smile on her face.

"I know it's soon. We just got married a few months ago, but…" She shrugs and flips her hair back over her shoulder. "Ready or not, here it comes."

"Nate is going to be beside himself," Natalie says with a grin.

"So you're gonna get all sexed up and then tell him?" I ask with a smile.

That's so Jules.

"Hell yes I am." She nods and then her eyes go wide. "Wait. I really do have to pee again. Why didn't anyone ever tell me that you pee all the time when you're prego?"

"I did tell you," Nat calls to her through the stall door. "You never listen to me."

"So what's the plan?" I ask.

"Why don't you two take Nate and go get a table at that Italian place across the street, and Jules and Luke and I will meet you there in a few?" Natalie suggests as Jules comes out of the stall and washes her hands.

"Sounds good," Stacy nods. "I could go for some lasagna."

"Okay," Jules grins and we follow her back out to the guys. "Hey, ace, would you go with Bryn and Stace to get us a table at the Italian place across the street while Nat and Luke and I go buy a some baby shit for Olivia?" She smiles sweetly and rubs her fingers over his chest. He narrows his gray eyes down at her for a moment, as though he knows she's lying and trying to decide if he should call her out on it or not.

Finally he shrugs and simply says, "Sure."

"Bye bye!" Livie calls from her stroller, smiling and clenching her tiny fist in and out, doing the toddler wave.

"Bye bye," we call back and wave to her, leading Nate out of the mall.

"What is she really buying?" He asks us as soon as we're out of ear-shot.

"Baby stuff," I reply with a shrug and Stacy nods in agreement, but neither of us can look him in the eye.

"Women always stick together," he mumbles under his breath. I giggle and loop my arm through his.

"Yep. Glad you're finally catching on to that."

We push through the glass doors of the high-end Italian restaurant and Nate approaches the hostess to request a table, just as Steven and Gail Montgomery are leaving the restaurant, laughing with a tall, very handsome strange man.

Steven sees the three of us and his eyes go wide and face immediately loses all of his color.

"Hi, guys." Stacy smiles, happy to see her parents-in-law.

"Oh my goodness! Hello!" Gail pulls us all in for a hug and turns to the tall man who has stepped back and folded his arms over his chest, watching us all with narrowed bright blue eyes.

He has dark, perfectly styled hair and an olive complexion, broad shoulders under a cable-knit sweater, and just a hint of a dark five o'clock shadow dusting his chin.

"Dominic," Gail addresses him and turns to us. "This is Brynna,

Stacy and Nate." She turns back to us. "This is Dom Salvadore."

"Hello," he nods and offers us a half smile, and I do believe my girly parts just came awake.

Who the hell is this guy, and why are Caleb's parents having lunch with him?

"I think Jules and Natalie will be along in a moment with Luke and the baby, if you'd like to say hi," Nate offers, his eyes glued to Dom, watching him carefully.

"We would, but I do believe we need to go," Steven responds quickly, ushering Gail out ahead of him. "Kiss Liv for us."

They wave and quickly exit, leaving the three of us looking back and forth between us with puzzled expressions.

"Weird," I finally remark.

"Definitely," Stacy agrees.

Nate pulls his phone out of his pocket and wakes it up. "She said his name is Dominic Salvadore?" He asks.

"Yeah. What are you doing?" I ask.

"Making a note." He tucks his phone back in his pocket and winks at me and I melt. Nate is seriously hot, but more than that, he's kind and strong and so good for Jules. We all adore him.

"You could kick his ass," Stacy offers and smirks at him.

"Of course I could, sweetheart. That was never in question."

He raises an eyebrow and scoffs.

"Did I mention that you have an ego the size of the Space Needle?" I ask.

Nate laughs, a full out belly laugh and drapes his arm around my shoulders, hugging me to his hard side, as the hostess motions for us to follow her to our table.

"Ego or not, honey, I could kick his ass."

***

"I shouldn't have had that slice of tiramisu," I mumble and rub my belly as Stacy pulls her minivan into my driveway.

"Who is that behind us?" Nat asks and then giggles. "It's Will and Meg."

"What are you doing here?" I ask as I gather my purchases from the back of the van.

"Isaac sent out an S.O.S.," Will informs us with a laugh.

"What? Why?" Stacy's voice is surprised, her eyes wide with worry.

"He's got a cop and a SEAL in the same room with him," Luke replies with a laugh and lifts Olivia into his arms, pulling her out of her car seat. She laughs with him, as though she knows what he's talking about. "What could possibly be going on in there?"

Us girls all look at each other and immediately make a beeline for the front door. Jules pulls her phone out and has it pointed out like she's about to take a picture.

"What are you doing?" Luke asks her as I unlock the door.

"I'm ready to document whatever is on the other side of that door."

Never, in a million-billion years, am I expecting what we find inside.

"Holy shit," Nate mutters under his breath. "Hey, Jules, is it wrong that I suddenly find your brothers smokin' hot?"

"Mommy!" Sophie exclaims and runs over to Stacy, hugging her around the knees.

"That's a great color on you, man," Luke taunts Caleb who scowls. No one in the room has moved besides Sophie and Jules has hit *record* on her phone.

The guys are sitting on the floor, around the girls' small craft table. Josie and Maddie have set up a tea party with what look to be brand new *American Girl* dolls – holy crap, that must have cost them a fortune – and they all, every last one of them, are wearing tiaras.

Tiaras.

Even Sgt. Bix is seated dutifully between Josie and Maddie, sporting a princess tiara on his head, his bad ear flopping over the side. His eyebrows move up and down as he surveys the scene.

"Wow, you're so pretty, Matt," I mutter, not able to hold it in anymore.

"Okay, tea party is over," Caleb announces and pulls the pink tiara from his head and hands it to Maddie.

"But you only had one cup," she complains.

"That was plenty," he mutters with a scowl and pulls himself up off the floor.

"Isaac, are you wearing a necklace?" Will asks, howling in laughter and pointing at his brothers.

"Sophie wanted me to wear it," Isaac responds, puffing his chest out. "Just you wait," he points to Luke. "Liv will do the same to you."

"This is so going on *YouTube*," Jules mutters and continues to film.

"Turn that off now, Jules," Matt instructs her, his voice hard.

"Not a chance in the world," she shakes her head and giggles. "This is awesome."

"Give me your phone!" Caleb lunges for her and she throws the phone to Meg.

"Take it!" She shouts.

Meg easily catches it and continues to film, moving quickly about the room. As Isaac is about to pull the phone from her hand, she throws it to me.

"Legs, I swear to you, if you don't give me that phone…" Caleb stomps toward me, glowering at me.

"You'll do what? Spank me?" I smile sweetly and pull the phone out of his reach.

"What is wrong with these women?" Matt asks the room at large. Luke, Will and Nate are laughing so hard they're holding their stomachs.

"Oh man, this is the best day of my life," Will sputters as he tries to pull air into his lungs. "I'm so glad we caught it on video."

"I'm going to break all of your legs," Caleb promises. "And what is up with your kids being little extortionists?" He asks me.

"What are you talking about?" I ask and look immediately at my girls, who refuse to look up and meet my gaze.

"They talked us into going to the American Girl doll store," Matts begins. "We figure, sure, we'll get them a doll. It'll keep them busy."

"Seven. Hundred. Dollars." Isaac stomps his foot with every

word. "For three little girls to get a doll and a whole wardrobe for said doll."

"Why did you buy them so much?" I ask, my eyes wide in shock.

"They lie to you there," Matt responds with a sigh. "The tags have numbers on them, which we thought were the prices."

"But no," Caleb joins in as the rest of us stand in the living room, watching them in awe as they tell their story. "No, it's a code number that tells you how to find the price on a chart. A chart!"

"So instead of that outfit being eight dollars like we thought, it was forty damn dollars!" Isaac exclaims, pointing to Sophie's doll.

"Forty dollars for a doll outfit?" Meg asks with wide eyes. "Holy crap."

During this whole exchange the three little darlings in question have been silently playing with their dolls, as though they're the only ones in the room.

"And then when we check out, these three smile up at us with the most innocent looks on their faces." Matt shakes his head in disgust.

"They're not innocent," Caleb grumbles. "They're freaking extortionists."

"Nate?" Josie has walked over to the tall, dark man and taps his arm to get his attention.

"Yes, beautiful girl," he replies and squats so he's eye-level with her.

"Can I have a ride on your motorcycle when it's sunny outside?" She asks and twirls her hair around her finger, her brown eyes wide and flirty, and if I'm not mistaken, she actually bats her lashes at him.

"Of course you can," Nate replies with a smile and taps her nose gently with his forefinger.

"Thank you!" She wraps her arms around his shoulders and hugs him and then returns to her doll.

"If she's already hitting on the guy in the leather jacket with a bike," Will remarks with a laugh, "You're going to have your hands full with that one."

Caleb curses under his breath as the rest of us laugh.

"That, right there, is why we're only having boys," Nate tells Jules as he points to Josie.

"I guess we'd better hope this one's a boy then," she replies with a grin, watching Nate's face.

"That's fine, I just… Wait." He turns on her and grips her shoulders in his hands, watching her face intently. "What did you just say?"

"I wanted to tell you later when we're alone, but I can't keep secrets, and most of our family is here anyway, so…" Jules shrugs and bites her lip, her eyes glistening with unshed tears. "We're gonna have a baby, ace."

He leans in and cups her face in his hands, pulls his fingers down her cheeks and rests his forehead against hers, and the room is completely still as we wait to hear what he has to say.

"Am I dreaming?" He asks, his voice raw.

She shakes her head no and wraps her arms around him. "No."

He kisses her then, long and hard, like I've never seen him do in public before, not even at their wedding. He finally pulls back and gazes down at her with so much love in his eyes, it feels wrong to be watching it, like we're intruding.

Caleb reaches down and links his fingers with mine and squeezes tightly. All of the Montgomery men are quiet.

This is their baby sister.

"I love you so much, Julianne." Nate finally speaks and brushes the tears off her cheeks with his thumbs. "Thank you," he whispers.

He scoops her up into a big hug and twirls her in a circle before setting her down and turning to the rest of us. "We're gonna have a baby!"

"Congratulations!" We descend on them, hugging and laughing and then hugging each other, celebrating and rejoicing in the new life that is about to join our family.

"Mommy," Maddie tugs on my hand to get my attention. "Can Sophie stay with us tonight?"

"No sweetheart," I lift her in my arms and kiss her cheek.

She's almost too heavy to hold like this now. "Not tonight."

"Why not?" Josie asks.

"Sophie has to go home and sleep in her own bed," Stacy tells them with a smile.

"She can sleep in our bed, like Caleb sleeps in Mommy's bed," Maddie replies and once again the room goes dead silent. My eyes go wide and I look around the room, looking for Caleb, who is standing next to Nate, also with the deer in the headlights look on his handsome face.

Isaac laughs, and everyone joins him, and I just close my eyes and lean my head against Maddie's shoulder.

Just shoot me.

Chapter Thirteen

~Caleb~

"So, did you bring me here to remind me how out of shape I am?" Brynna plants her hands on her hips and glares at me after we enter through the non-descript front doors of Rich McKenna's gym in downtown Seattle.

"No," I chuckle and hold my hand out for her jacket.

"I'm not taking my jacket off," she pouts.

"You're adorable. Give me the fucking coat."

She glares at me some more just as Jules yells from behind us, "There you are!"

"Jules is here?" Brynna asks with wide brown eyes. Before I can answer, Jules runs to us and catches Brynna up in a big hug.

"I've been trying to talk Nate into letting me do some pull-ups, but he won't let me do *anything.*" Jules rolls her eyes and then grins. "I'm going to get so fat."

"I don't think that's possible," Brynna replies while shaking her head. "Besides, he's right. Unless you're doing yoga, you shouldn't be doing anything in this gym."

"That's what I keep telling her," Nate responds as he joins us. "This is a sparring gym. We don't do yoga." Nate wraps an arm around my sister's shoulders and kisses her temple.

"It's great to see you guys," Brynna begins and glances at me. "But, what am I doing here?"

"Caleb didn't tell you?" Jules asks.

She shakes her head and Nate smiles reassuringly.

"Nate is going to show you some self-defense techniques," I inform her and take her hand in mine, squeezing it firmly.

"Why?" She asks and stares at Nate.

"Because he kicks ass," Jules replies proudly, making Nate laugh and shake his head.

"Can't you show me?" Brynna asks me quietly.

Sure, if you don't mind me getting distracted every ten seconds and turning a self-defense class into crazy hot sex.

"I could, but Nate has actual fighting experience," I reply instead.

She turns her eyes to Nate and frowns. "I am perhaps the most out of shape woman in this family. You know that, right? Instead of treadmills and weights, I spend my time chasing and lifting twins."

"You don't have to be an athlete to protect yourself, Brynna." Nate winks at Bryn, kisses Jules once more and then pulls away, holding his hand out for Brynna to join him. "Come on. It'll be fun."

"Tell my kids I loved them," she pleads as she tosses a look to me over her shoulder. "And I want to be cremated, please."

I laugh and shake my head as I pause beside the big ring in the middle of the room next to my baby sister. Nate leads Brynna up into the ring and begins murmuring to her, demonstrating with his hands as he speaks.

"Damn, he's fucking hot," Jules whispers beside me.

"Really?" I ask and scowl down at her.

"What?" She grins innocently then leans her head against my arm. "He's mine. I get to say stuff like that."

"Not around me." I sigh and watch the tall, lean woman in the ring.

"She's beautiful," Jules murmurs.

"She is," I confirm and sigh again. *She's so fucking beautiful she takes my breath away.*

I don't know why she insists that she's out of shape. She's tall and curvy, with just the right sized ass and breasts. Her thighs are solid, probably from chasing after the girls. And her brown eyes destroy me, whether they're happy or scared or glowing with lust.

"And according to the girls, you're sleeping in her bed." I can feel her smile against my arm and I narrow my eyes as I watch

Nate wrap his arm around Brynna's throat, as though he's approaching her from behind.

"I am." What else is there to say?

"So how is it going?" Jules asks and pulls away so she can look up at my face.

I keep my eyes on the ring.

"Fine."

"Jesus, you're so difficult!" She punches me in the shoulder and then shakes her hand with a scowl. "Ow."

I smirk and glance down at her. "I'm not telling you about my sex life. Ever."

"I just want to know how things are going," she pouts.

"We're fine," I repeat.

"Are you guys going to the Nash concert tomorrow night?" Jules asks with a grin.

"Yeah," I nod and sigh and pull my hand down my face.

God, I don't want to go to that concert.

"Are you sure that's a good idea?" she asks softly.

I shrug nonchalantly. "Bryn wants to go. She doesn't go anywhere without me, so that means we're going."

"You don't have to babysit her every minute of the day, Caleb." She rolls her eyes and shakes her head. "What, are you worried that she'll get hit on?"

"You don't know dick about it," I reply tightly.

"Well, if you guys would tell the rest of us what's going on, I'd know *dick* about it!" She responds and then sighs heavily. "There will be a lot of people at the concert." I glance down at her briefly, registering the concern on her pretty face and I square my shoulders and look away.

Too many fucking people.

I give her a jerky nod and she swears under her breath.

"Hey, Craig! Come up here and help me out!" Nate calls out to a muscle-bound guy at the other side of the ring. Craig jumps up through the ropes and joins Nate and Brynna with a grin.

"What can I do?" he asks, looking Brynna up and down, and I feel my hands clench into fists.

"Craig's a nice guy," Jules mentions deceptively casually.

144

"Hmm," I grunt.

"They'd make a cute couple." She taps her lip with her finger. "I should set them up."

"I should kick your ass," I growl.

She turns her gaze to mine and a wide, knowing smile spreads across her face.

"You're not setting her up with anyone, Jules," I warn her.

"You don't seem to want to claim her," she shrugs.

"I've claimed her," I mutter and swear under my breath.

The little brat won't stop until I spill my guts.

Jules whips her head around to watch me, her blue eyes wide and mouth dropped open.

"You love her," she whispers.

More than anything.

"I can't have her," I whisper back and push a hand through my hair.

"Why?"

"She deserves so much better, J." I shake my head, watching the amazing woman up in the ring with my brother-in-law and a muscle-head who would give his left nut to fuck her.

"What in the hell are you talking about?" She's keeping her voice down, but I can tell she's pissed as hell.

"I'll end up hurting her. Physically. Emotionally." I shrug again and glance down into Jules' angry eyes.

"So, what? You'll fuck her while you're staying with her and then ride off into the sunset when it's all said and done?" She glares up at me with her arms crossed over her chest and I feel like an asshole.

Because when she puts it like that, I *am* an asshole.

"I don't know," I respond and suck in a quick breath when Nate pushes Brynna onto the ground, knocking the wind out of her. Both Nate and Craig squat beside her, helping her up. "I just don't want to bring my baggage into her and the girls' lives."

I feel Jules' eyes on me, so I glance down to find tears in them.

"Caleb, life is too short for this. She and the girls love you. You love them. Be happy." She wraps her arms around my waist and holds onto me, pressing her cheek against my chest. "Just be happy. All of those guys whose lives you saved, and even those who lost their lives beside you, would want that for you."

How does she know? I don't deserve what Brynna and her girls are offering me. I couldn't protect my guys to ensure they had the kind of life I can see myself having with these amazing girls.

Instead, they got a pine box and an American flag.

"Be happy," Jules whispers. "Enjoy her. If she can't handle it, she'll tell you. Christ, Caleb, Brynna is one of the strongest women I've ever met. She can handle just about anything you throw at her."

I frown as I watch Nate and Craig with Brynna. Her scowl as she concentrates on what they're trying to teach her. Her smile when she gets it right. Her exasperated sigh when she gets it wrong and ends up on her magnificent ass.

She's mine.

Craig whispers something into her ear, making her laugh up at him, her eyes shining, a light sheen of sweat covers her face and chest, and my breath catches.

And then the bastard does what any red-blooded American man would do while that close to a woman like Brynna.

He tucks a piece of her hair behind her ear.

And I see red.

***

~Brynna~

How in the hell am I supposed to concentrate on not getting my ass kicked when I'm in the ring with Nate McKenna?

I know he's married. To one of my best friends. And I'm in love with his brother-in-law. But for the love of all that's holy, he's in a black tank that shows off perfectly toned muscles that stretch beneath that delicious tattoo that runs down the length of his arm. His hair is pulled back at the nape of his neck, showing off his square jaw and bright gray eyes.

146

Everything about this man screams sex.

Screams. Sex.

And it doesn't hurt that he's one of the sweetest men I've ever met, and to top it all off, he's completely in love with his wife.

Is there anything sexier than a hot man in love with his wife? No.

"Remember, if they manage to get their arm around your neck, you pull your arm up and jab down, *hard.*" Nate murmurs in my ear from behind me. His arm is wrapped around my neck, as if he's surprised me from behind.

"Right," I confirm, not sure that I'll ever remember any of this later.

"Okay, I want to show you some fighting techniques." Nate smiles reassuringly and turns to the side of the ring. "Hey Craig! Come up here and help me out!"

The man named Craig easily pulls himself up the side of the ring and through the ropes and walks confidently to our side.

"What can I do?" he asks with a grin. He's handsome, in a boy-ish kind of way. His body is hard and bulked up, but he has a young face. I bet he was called baby-face all through school.

He's good looking, but not what I want.

What I want is standing at the edge of the ring with his sister.

I glance over to find Caleb scowling down at Jules who has her arms wrapped around his waist and is hugging him close. I wonder what they're talking about.

"Pay attention, Bryn," Nate calls me to attention and motions for Craig to move behind me and show me how to place my feet and hands. We go through several minutes of instructions, with both Nate and Craig laying their hands on me, showing me how to hold my arms, spread my feet, tilt my hips.

"Okay, are you ready for me to hit you?" Nate asks.

"I'm gonna die," I whisper, earning a laugh from Craig behind me.

"I won't let him kill you," he murmurs into my ear. "Besides, you know how to deflect this. Just remember what he told you."

Nate comes at me, and just when I think I've outmaneuvered him, he sneaks in with another jab, and I'm flat on my back with the wind knocked out of me.

"Shit!" Nate and Craig both squat beside me and take my hands in theirs, helping me up to a sitting position.

"You okay, sweetheart?" Nate asks.

I nod and drag air into my lungs. "Knocked the wind out of me."

Nate steps back, but Craig smiles gently down at me and tucks my hair behind my ear and glides his knuckle down my jawline, sending goosebumps down my arms. "Nothing sexier than a sweaty woman," he mutters.

"Sweaty women are not sexy," I respond with a wrinkled nose, smiling up at him and then quickly glance guiltily around for Caleb.

"I think that's enough for today," Caleb announces as he bounds into the ring, his face tight with anger. He glares at Craig who immediately backs away and takes my hand in his, helping me to my feet. "Are you okay?" He asks me.

"I'm fine. I can keep going."

"No, that's enough for today." He shakes Nate's hand. "Thanks, man."

"Anytime."

"I want to play too!" Jules announces as she pulls herself into the ring. "C'mon, Bryn, I'll spar with you."

"No!" Both Nate and Caleb yell at once.

"She won't hit me hard," Jules mutters with a pout.

"I'm not hitting you at all. You're pregnant for Godsake." I shake my head at her and laugh. "You can go nine months without kicking ass, Jules."

"Nine months." Her eyes go wide before they land on Nate. "You'd better get ready for lots of verbal ass kickings if I can't kick your ass in the ring."

"Yeah, you scare me." Nate smirks and pulls her into his arms.

"You're sweaty," Jules complains and tries to squirm away, but Nate holds strong.

"C'mere," he mutters and buries his face in her neck, making her giggle.

"I'm out of here," Caleb announces.

"Hold up," Nate calls out and kisses Jules' head before sauntering over to Caleb. "If you have time, I'd like some one-on-one time with you in the ring. You look like you could use something to take a swing at."

I look up in surprise to see Caleb considering Nate's invitation. He glances down at me with hot blue eyes and then back at Nate.

"Yeah, I've got time."

"Don't hurt him too much, ace," Jules grins and kisses Nate's cheek before taking my hand and leading me to the side of the ring.

"Have they done this before?" I ask her.

"I don't know," Jules shrugs. "I don't think so, but Caleb comes to this gym when he's in town, so they might have."

"Helmets?" Nate asks.

Caleb shakes his head no and reaches over his shoulder, grips his t-shirt and pulls it over his head and tosses it my way.

"Damn," I whisper at the sight of him. Every time I see his bare skin is like the first time.

A crowd has gathered around the ring to watch the two athletes go at each other. They circle each other, both the same height, broad-shouldered, but where Nate is dark, Caleb is fair.

It's quite possibly illegal to have two amazingly hot men in the same ring together.

Suddenly, Nate leans in and jabs, and it's on. For several minutes, they punch and deflect, kick and push and throw each other on the floor, only to bounce right back up.

Their faces are feral, eyes hot and trained on the other, and it's the hottest damn thing I've ever seen in my life.

"They're going to kill each other," I mutter in awe.

"Maybe," Jules nods. "Jesus, look at them!"

Nate takes a swing at Caleb's face, but he grips Nate's fist in his hands and twirls, picks him up on his back and slams him to the ground, his elbow in Nate's throat.

Nate kicks out of the hold and they continue, heaving and sweating. Bleeding.

Nate has a trickle of blood coming from his nose, and Caleb is bleeding near his left eye.

And neither looks ready to stop.

Finally, after Nate kicks Caleb in the ribs and follows up with an elbow between his shoulder blades, Nate's dad rings the bell.

I didn't even notice that he was here.

"Enough!" Mr. McKenna yells out. "If you have more aggression to get out, take it up with a bag. Not each other."

Nate and Caleb are both bent at the waist, panting and sweating, catching their breath. Jules and I are both holding ours.

"What the hell was that all about?" I ask.

"Testosterone?" Jules asks with a bewildered shrug. "It was kind of hot though."

I nod in agreement and watch as Nate stands upright and approaches Caleb, shakes his hand and pulls him in for a man-hug. He talks low for a few moments and Caleb's eyes narrow before he pulls back and nods, offers Nate a half-smile and pats him hard on the shoulder.

They both come down off the ring and smile at us.

"Feel better?" Jules asks.

"Yeah," Nate shrugs and offers her a cocky smile. "I could have taken him down."

"In your dreams, McKenna. I was going easy on you," Caleb retorts and pushes his arms through his shirt and pulls it over his head.

Oh, don't put the sweaty muscles away yet!

"We should go," I murmur and smile at Caleb. He's still a bit reserved and quiet, and I can't figure out what's wrong with him.

"We should go too," Nate agrees and pulls Jules to him, knowing how sweaty and grimy he is.

"See you tomorrow night!" Jules waves at us, laughing and half-heartedly trying to fight Nate off.

Caleb leads me to the car, opens the door for me without saying a word and then climbs into the driver's side. After driving for more than ten minutes in complete silence, I decide to clear the air.

"I didn't flirt back," I blurt out.

"What?" He asks, barely sparing me a glance.

"With Craig. He flirted with me, but I didn't flirt back." I cross my arms over my chest and look out the window, not paying any attention to the sights of downtown Seattle, or the rain as it rolls down the window in ribbons.

"I don't give a shit about that guy," Caleb mutters and turns down my street.

"Then what's wrong?" I ask with a frown.

He swallows and glances at me, rubs his fingers over his lips and looks like he's going to say something, but changes his mind.

"Nothing."

He's lying.

"Caleb…"

"I'm fine," he cuts me off and shoves the car into park when we reach my house. "Don't worry about it."

When we get inside the house and Caleb checks the alarm and the windows and doors, he stops in the kitchen, not meeting my gaze. Bix greets us, happy to see us, and enjoys scratches on the head from Caleb, who is still sweaty and dirty from his vigorous workout with Nate.

"Do you want to join me in the shower?" I ask.

He shakes his head and gestures toward the back yard. "I'm going to go out back and work out. Call me if you need me."

And with that, he marches out back, dog in tow, and straight to the ropes attached to Natalie's studio, working them vigorously. By the time he stops, his muscles have to be singing in protest, but he moves straight over to the bar he had installed for pull-ups, jumps up and immediately begins raising and lowering himself on the bar.

Bix lays on the deck, keeping watch.

What the hell is going on his head?

"Mommy! Mommy!" The girls come racing through the front door, coats and backpacks on, excited to be home from school. Matt grins from the doorway.

"Did you have fun at the gym today?" He asks.

"Don't make me hurt you," I respond with a chuckle. "I can do that now."

"Good to hear." He nods and then frowns. "Where is Caleb?"

"Out back. He's cranky," I reply with a sigh and relieve the girls of their backpacks.

"In that case, I'll go. See you all later." Matt waves and leaves and I kiss the girls in turn.

"Did you have a good day?" I ask them.

"Yeah," Maddie responds. "Why is Caleb cranky?"

"I don't know."

"Let's go work out with him," Josie suggests to Maddie who grins and they both make a beeline for the door before I can tell them to leave him be.

I put their bags away and pull the ingredients for dinner out of the fridge just as I hear high-pitched squeals of laughter coming from the girls in the backyard.

I look out the sliding glass door to find Caleb holding onto Maddie's waist, holding her up to his pull-up bar, helping her raise and lower herself in pull-up form. She tries to look over her shoulder at him, a huge smile on her face, full of trust and love, as Josie and Bix run circles around them, laughing and barking.

"Let me down!" Maddie calls out and Caleb complies, lowering her to her feet and then tackles both girls in his arms, falling to the ground, making sure the girls fall on top of him, while Bix barks and bounces around them, smiling his doggie smile with his tongue flopping out of his mouth.

It's the sweetest picture I've ever seen in my life.

Chapter Fourteen

"The show was ah-mazing!" Stacy exclaims as she settles into Isaac's side, drink in-hand, smiling widely.

My cousin is well on her way to getting her drunk on.

"It was," I nod and grin and can't help but gaze over at Will and Meg who are wrapped up in each other on a couch nearby. "Will," I call to him, "that was quite possibly the most romantic proposal I've ever seen."

We are all at the after party for Nash's first concert in their *Sunshine Tour*, where Will surprised us all by taking the stage and asking Meg to marry him in front of thousands of screaming fans.

"I'm a romantic guy." He shrugs and grins.

"You're a lot of things, babe," Meg responds with a loud laugh, "but romantic isn't one of them. Did Luke give you pointers?"

"Hey! I have my romantic moments!" Will frowns at her and then whispers something completely inappropriate in her ear, making her blush furiously.

"Oh yeah, that's right."

"I don't want to know," Matt shakes his head with a laugh and then glances at Caleb, who hasn't commented all evening, or even looked my way twice. I wore this sexy outfit, and he hasn't even noticed. Instead, his body is tense, and his eyes are narrowed, watching the room, the people around us, and just generally pissing me off.

I know he's trying to keep me safe, but for the love of Jesus, I have more muscle surrounding me right now than the president.

"You okay, man?" Matt asks him.

"Fine," Caleb answers with a nod.

"Are you sure?" I ask, resting my hand on his arm. He doesn't spare me a glance, just tightens his jaw even more, if that's possible.

"I'm fine," he repeats, his voice hard and firm.

"Hey, Sam." Jules approaches Sam from across the room. "Leo was just looking for you a few minutes ago. You must have been in the restroom."

Samantha is dating Leo, the lead singer of Nash, and I couldn't be happier for her. They make a great couple. Leo is all tall and tattooed and sexy as all get-out, but Sam keeps him grounded and isn't afraid to cut him down to size when his ego gets a bit out of hand.

Not that it does often, I think Sam just likes flipping him shit.

"Do you know which way he went?" Sam asks.

"Out into the hallway," Jules points toward the door and Sam leaves, off to find her man.

"I bet she's gonna get orgasms later," Stacy whispers over to me, making me smirk.

"Definitely," I confirm and smile to myself.

"Where are the kids and Bix tonight?" Isaac asks.

"They're all at my mom and dads," I reply with a grin.

"You two need to get a room," Jules scowls at Will and Meg who are currently necking on the couch.

"Dude, they just got engaged," Nat waves Jules off. "Let them have fun."

"You don't care because you'll be joining them any second now," Jules accuses her with narrowed eyes.

"Good idea," Luke smirks and dips Nat low, kissing her deeply, earning a loud groan from Jules.

"Yuck," she murmurs and sips her water. "Meg, I want to see your ring again."

Meg happily holds out her left hand for Jules to inspect, grinning proudly.

"Did you pick it out by yourself?" Matt asks Will.

"Yep," Will nods.

"He did good," Natalie murmurs and smiles warmly. "You have good taste."

"Of course I do," Will chuckles and kisses Meg's cheek.

"And he's so modest," Meg shakes her head and pushes her fingers through his hair.

"Were you surprised?" Will asks her, his voice soft and all trace of his arrogance gone.

"Completely," Meg assures him and kisses him soundly. "Best surprise ever."

"Brynna, you look beautiful tonight," Luke comments before raising his drink to his mouth, surprising me.

"Thanks," I murmur and feel my cheeks heat. "I'm glad somebody noticed," I mumble and look away from the group, scanning the crowd. The girls exchange looks and then watch Caleb and I, thinking they're sneaky. Thanks to my girls announcing our sleeping arrangements last week and me finally confiding in them while we got ready for tonight's concert, they all know that Caleb and I are having sex. But I told them that it's just sex and nothing more.

Because honestly, I don't know what it is. I know I'm completely in love with him, and I believe he loves me in return, but he runs so hot and cold, and I can't figure him out.

It's frustrating the hell out of me.

Caleb tenses even more beside me as a man I've never seen before approaches us.

"Excuse me, but are you Luke Williams?" The man asks Luke quietly.

"I am," Luke nods and turns to the older gentleman.

"I'm Roger, Jake's father," he responds with a grin, holding out his hand for Luke to shake. Jake is the guitarist for Nash. "My wife is a big fan. Would you mind saying hello?"

"Not at all," Luke responds with a smile and turns back to us. "I'll be right back."

"How did Luke hold up tonight, around all these people?" Stacy asks Natalie, referring to Luke's phobia of crowds and being recognized thanks to his movie star celebrity.

"He's fine," Nat assures us with a smile. "He does well when he's with all of us. It's when he's alone that it's difficult for him."

Will nods in understanding and rests his cheek on Meg's head as Sam and Leo come into the room, holding hands, sharing a smile.

"Did you guys enjoy the show?" Leo asks as he steps behind Sam and wraps his arms around her shoulders, pulling her back against his front and kissing the top of her head.

"It was great, Leo," I respond with a smile. "I love the new music."

"*Sunshine* is an excellent song," Jules agrees and winks at Sam.

I reach down and lace my fingers in Caleb's, hoping to anchor him and bring him into the conversation. He glances down at me quickly and squeezes my hand, but otherwise continues to watch and listen, not participating in the dialogue. Finally, I rise up on my toes and whisper into his ear, "Are you ready to go?"

"Yes," he answers immediately. "Brynna and I are going to take off," he announces, shaking hands with the guys and kissing the girls on their cheeks. "It was a great show, man."

"Thanks. I'll see you in a few weeks when I come home on our break." Leo smiles warmly at me and kisses my cheek, making my toes curl just a bit. "Give him hell," he whispers to me and winks as I pull away.

I wink back and trail behind Caleb, my hand still held firmly in his, out to the parking lot.

"Caleb?"

"Let's just get to the car, Bryn," he responds quietly, but I hear the edge in his voice. He's not mad.

He's scared.

And that just about brings me to my knees. Caleb is the strongest man I know, but being in this crowd, worried about my safety and dealing with his own demons simply because I wanted to come be a part of the concert speaks volumes for how he feels about me.

He'd sit through hell for me.

And he did.

We reach the car and he tucks me safely inside then moves around to the driver's side and lowers himself inside, shutting and locking the doors behind him.

He starts the car and white-knuckles the wheel, driving quickly and efficiently through the parking garage. His muscles aren't just tight, they're stretched and bunched under his black sweater, and every part of him is radiating sheer tension.

I reach over and lay my hand gently on his thigh and gasp. His thigh is flexed, and I can feel the outline of every muscle through his blue jeans.

"Are you okay?" I murmur.

He glances over at me, his blue eyes hot and tight, and nods. "Yeah."

"Babe, it's okay." He drops one hand off the wheel and covers mine on his leg, squeezing it reassuringly.

What can I do to help him?

As an idea forms in my head, I turn in my seat and brush my knuckles down his cheek and along his jaw.

"Caleb?" I ask softly.

"Hmm?" He responds.

"Talk to me, sailor."

He exhales deeply and concentrates on the road for a moment and just when I think he's not going to talk, he whispers, "I'm sorry."

"For what?" I ask, surprised.

"I know I wasn't a lot of fun this evening. I'm not good around a bunch of people, Bryn. It makes me nervous."

"We didn't have to come, Caleb."

"You wanted to be here. I wanted you to come and have a good time." He pushes his hand through his hair and I feel him start to relax, bit by bit.

"Thank you," I reply quietly and lean over to kiss his cheek. My fingertips move gently up and down his thigh, caressing him lightly. I drop a kiss on his shoulder and then his bicep.

"What are you up to, Legs?" He asks.

"Can I try something that I've never done before?"

He glances over at me and frowns slightly, curiously, and then finally offers me a half smile. "Okay."

"You're going to have to scoot back just a bit," I inform him and take my seat belt off and reach for his belt.

His eyes go wide.

"Bryn?"

"I'm gonna suck you off in your car," I say matter-of-factly and pull his zipper down, tug his underwear down and release his hard, hot cock. I pull my knees under me on the seat and brace myself on the center console and pull him into my mouth.

"Fuck," he whispers as he rests a hand on the back of my head, threading his fingers in my hair, as I rise and fall on him, sucking and licking and tugging on his gorgeous dick.

I lick a trail from his balls, up the under side along a thick, bulging vein, to the tip and trace the ridge of his head and the slit with my tongue.

"I love your cock," I murmur and sink down again, pulling him to the back of my throat. I hold him there, pressing with my lips and swallow, massaging the tip with my throat.

"Holy Jesus, Bryn, I'm going to crash this fucking car," he growls, but I don't let up. I suck harder and move faster, and grip what won't fit in my mouth with my hand, twisting and jacking him as I give him the best damn blowjob of his life.

He runs his hand from my head, down my spine, to my ass and grips hard, his fingertips brushing along the seam of my skinny jeans, setting my core on fire. I cup his balls in my hand and plant my tongue on the under side of his cock and tease him, knowing full well he's on his way to coming in my mouth.

I can't fucking wait.

"Stop, Bryn, I'm gonna come."

I shake my head and increase my efforts, and suddenly I can taste the salty essence of him filling my mouth, splashing against the back of my throat, and I swallow, taking all of him and licking him clean before I lean back, tuck him away and smile smugly from the passenger seat.

"I guess I got you to look at me now, didn't I?" I ask with a chuckle.

He's panting, his jaw dropped, and he looks over at me with a mixture of awe and lust and… *anger*?

I just sucked him dry. What the hell is he angry for?

He pulls up to the house, slams the car in park and before I know it, we're inside and I'm pinned against the front door and Caleb is pulling me out of my clothes.

"Caleb…"

"I've told you before, Legs," he begins and tosses my top and bra over his shoulder, then reaches for my jeans. "You always come first. *Always*. You want to play this game?" He pulls my jeans down my legs and tosses them aside, along with my thong and pulls one of my legs over his shoulder, spreading me wide. "I hope you're ready for what you just started."

And before I can form a coherent thought, he reaches up to clench a nipple between his thumb and forefinger and buries his face in my pussy, sucking and pulling on my lips, licking from my anus up to my clit in long, hard strokes.

"Holy shit!" I exclaim and grip his head in one hand, tugging his hair in my fist and holding on for dear life to the door handle, praying I don't fall.

"You think I didn't see you tonight, sweetheart?" He murmurs between long swipes up and down my pussy with his tongue. "You think I didn't notice how fucking hot your ass and legs looked in those jeans with these fuck-me heels on your feet?"

I squirm against the door as he pushes a finger inside me and pulls my clit through his lips with a loud *smack*.

"I can't see anything *but* you, Legs."

He presses his tongue against my clit and crooks his finger, sending me into a mind-numbing orgasm. My knee buckles, but he holds me strong, pressed against the door, as I cry out and circle my hips, pressing against Caleb's face.

He backs off for just a second, presses a second finger inside me and looks up to watch my face as he hits my sweet spot and sends more over into another screaming orgasm.

He stands and pulls me into the living room to the nearest surface, which happens to be a chair, bends me over the back of it and sinks to his knees again.

"Caleb, I need you inside me," I whimper.

"I'll get there eventually," he murmurs and bites each of my ass cheeks, hard enough to leave a mark.

"Ouch!"

He chuckles and pulls his hands down my back, over my ass and spreads me wide open.

"You love my cock?" He asks with a husky voice.

I nod vigorously.

"Well, I love this," he responds and plants his tongue on my clit and drags it slowly through my folds and up to my anus. "I love every inch of this. Do you know what this is?"

"Uh, it's my pussy, Caleb," I reply dryly. He slaps my ass, not hard, just enough to get my attention and I look back at him, shocked.

"No, it's your cunt, Brynna."

I scowl at him and he laughs, settling his eyes back on my wet, pulsing center.

"Yes, it's a dirty word, sweetheart. But this," he pulls his finger down my core and I shudder. "This is the sweetest cunt I've ever tasted."

He buries his face in me again, pushing his tongue inside me and pressing his thumb against my nub and I come apart for a third time, shuddering and jerking, leaning so far over the chair my feet leave the floor.

"Holy fuck!" I exclaim. "Caleb!"

"Yes, baby," he replies and kisses and licks the globes of my ass and up my spine, planting wet kisses between my shoulder blades.

"I want you inside me," I respond breathlessly. "Please."

He slaps my ass and then quickly turns me around and props me up on the back of the chair, wraps an arm around my waist to hold me steady and guides his long, hard cock inside me, but stops. His face is level with my own, millimeters from me, and as he speaks I can smell myself on him and can almost feel his lips move.

"You will learn," he begins and glides his free hand over my hip, between us, so he can press on my clit with his thumb. "That getting you off is my fucking *job*, Brynna." He moves his thumb, back and forth, over my already swollen and hyper-sensitive clit, making me clench around his cock.

"Please," I whisper.

"Please what?" He asks and sweeps his lips across mine.

"Please move, babe. I need you."

"Not until you come one more time," he informs me with a low growl. I feel him buried inside me, his balls against my ass, his thumb pressed to my clit, and he leans in and bites my neck, sending me over the edge once more.

I can't do this anymore!

I cry out as my body rocks and spasms against him. If it weren't for his arm anchoring me to him, I would have fallen into the chair.

Finally, he begins to move, slowly, with measured strokes, and I cry out again at the incredible sensation of his velvet-like cock dragging against my pussy.

He kisses me deeply, claiming me, *owning me*, and then rests his forehead against my own as he begins to move faster and harder, pumping my clit with his pubis with every thrust.

"You're so fucking sexy, Legs," he whispers and clenches his eyes shut as he comes, grinding and pushing against me as he releases inside me.

I hug him to me and bury my face in his neck, absorbing the shudders and trembling of his body as his orgasm works through him.

He's panting and sweaty, and clinging to me as though he's afraid to lose contact with me.

I kiss his shoulder and maintain my hold on him, comforting him, loving him.

Tell him you love him!

But before I can say a word, he lifts me from the chair, still inside me, and carries me up the stairs.

"I've never been carried by anyone before you," I murmur with a grin. "No one has ever been strong enough."

"I'll carry you anytime, sweetheart," he whispers as he lowers me to the bed and lays me down on my back, hovering over me on shaky arms. "You are beautiful."

I drag my fingers down his cheek and smile up at him. "Thank you."

"For what?" He asks with a frown.

"For tonight. I know you were miserable, but you were there because I wanted to be there. Thank you for that."

He shakes his head slightly and offers me a half smile, his sexy dimples flash and he whispers, "I think I would do just about anything for you."

"You haven't been yourself since the gym yesterday," I whisper, enjoying the dark and the quiet with him. "Wanna talk about it?"

He sighs and settles next to me, watching our hands link and unlink and finally, he whispers, "I was worried about tonight."

I stay quiet, just watching his face while he thinks and slowly relaxes, the muscles in his hard body finally releasing.

"I was afraid that one of two things, or both things, would happen. Either I'd have a panic attack in the middle of the concert or the whole damn experience tonight would trigger nightmares tonight, and I'm so fucking afraid of hurting you again." His voice is no louder than a whisper.

I climb over him and wrap myself around him, clenching my arms and legs around him and burying my face in his neck.

"I'm right here, Caleb Montgomery, and the nightmares aren't. Besides," I murmur and raise my hips, allowing him to slide inside me again. "You don't have nightmares when you're with me, and I'm not done making love to you."

"Is that so?" He asks with a soft grin and reverses our positions, tucking me under him. He begins to move slowly, braced on his elbows, staring down at me with bright blue eyes. He nuzzles my nose with his own and sighs softly as he slowly makes love to me.

"That's so," I confirm and moan when he shifts his hips to brush the tip of his cock over my G-spot. "I also plan to sleep naked tonight."

"Best plan you've had all day, sweetheart," he mutters.

162

Chapter Fifteen

Caleb's phone is ringing. I'm flat on my back and he's wrapped around me, clinging to me and breathing slow and steady, in a seemingly dreamless sleep.

Brynna – 1, Nightmares – 0.

"Caleb," I nudge his shoulder and try to reach his phone, but it's too far away. "Caleb, your phone."

He rubs his face against my breast and then looks up at me with sleep eyes. "Huh?"

"Your phone is ringing, babe."

He reaches for it and presses it to his ear, instantly awake and alert. "Montgomery."

A man on the other end is speaking. Caleb moves from the bed, naked as the day he was born, and I prop my head on my hand to watch him pace beside the bed.

"Just tell me what's going on," he barks, but the line goes dead. "Fuck."

"What's wrong?" I ask and sit up, glancing over at the clock. It's six in the morning.

"Matt's on his way over. We need to get dressed."

"What's going on?" I ask and move from the bed, only to be caught up in Caleb's arms and pulled against him.

"He wouldn't say. He'll be here in a few." He hugs me close and buries his face in my hair, breathing deeply. "You smell amazing."

I chuckle and kiss his chest before stepping away to pull on some clothes. Just as I pull my sweater over my head, there is a loud *bang bang bang* on the front door.

"That was fast," I mutter with a smile.

"He was already on his way when he called." Caleb pulls his jeans over his hips, grabs a shirt and flashes a grin at me before he turns and leaves the room. "Have I ever told you how fantastic you look first thing in the morning?"

"Uh, no."

"Well you do." He looks me up and down and then leaves me here in my bedroom, staring at the empty doorway.

I hear him answer the door and let Matt in, and I rush to pull on yoga pants and tie my hair up on top of my head. When I descend the stairs, Matt and Caleb are standing in the living room, Caleb with his arms folded over his massive chest, and Matt with his hands propped on his hips, both of them scowling.

"What's up, guys?" I ask. "And why are you in your scary cop attire?" I ask Matt, gesturing to his gun and badge.

"I'm on my way to work," he responds with a sigh. "Look, I got a call this morning from Chicago."

Every hair on my body stands on end and I automatically reach for Caleb's hand.

"Apparently, Will Montgomery getting engaged during a Nash concert is big news, and it has been splashed all over the morning news shows."

"So?" I ask and frown. "What's the big deal?"

"It wouldn't be, except several of the shots from last night include photos and video of the family, Brynna." He sighs and clenches his jaw, his eyes worried and trained on me as the implications of what he's said sinks in.

"I was in those pictures," I whisper and sit on the couch behind me. Caleb curses under his breath and sits next to me, drapes his arm around me and pulls me to his side.

"You were," Matt confirms. "One of the guys with Chicago PD called me this morning. We don't know that anyone else would notice, but it's only a matter of days before it hits national magazines as well, and it'll be all over the evening news tonight."

"Why did he have to propose like that?" Caleb asks softly and kisses my shoulder.

"He didn't know," I whisper and for the first time in more than a year, I regret my decision to keep the rest of the family in the dark. "He didn't know because I wouldn't let you guys tell them."

"We have to tell them now," Matt murmurs.

"I know." I nod and straighten my spine. "Today."

"I have to work a shift today," Matt says as he checks his watch and winces. "But let's have the family over here this evening and we'll talk to everyone, fill everyone in, and figure out where to go from there. I'll make some more calls today and keep an eye on the media. My contact in Chicago was going to try to contact one of the undercover guys to see what they know, but it can take a few days to hear back."

"Can your parents keep the girls one more night?" Caleb asks me. "I'd rather they weren't here when we talk with our families."

"Yeah," I nod. "I'm sure that's not a problem. I'd like to go spend time with them today, though." I swallow and glance up at Matt who nods and smiles reassuringly.

Caleb pulls his phone out and begins to text the family.

Family meeting, today, 6pm. Brynna's house. Mandatory.

***

"Hey, thanks for coming." I kiss Stacy's cheek as she and Isaac come inside my home. They are the last to arrive. "Do Luke's parents have all the kids?"

Stacy nods as Isaac leads us into the living room.

My house is bursting at the seams.

Isaac and Stacy's parents are all sitting at the dining room table, while all of the siblings are gathered in the living room. Luke and Natalie are sharing a chair while Jules and Nate and Mark and Sam are on the couch.

Will, Meg, Isaac and Stacy claim the remaining seats, and all eyes are on Caleb, Matt and myself.

Why do I suddenly feel so fucking guilty?

"So what's up?" Will asks. "Where are Bryn's parents and the girls?"

"My parents have the girls at home. It's best if they don't hear this." The last few words are said with a whisper, and everyone exchanges curious looks.

"Are you okay?" Steven Montgomery asks, and I have to blink furiously to keep tears at bay.

Geez, this conversation is just starting. Cut it out with the water works already.

I nod and look to Matt and Caleb for guidance.

"You all know," Matt begins and sighs, "that Brynna came home about a year ago rather abruptly."

Isaac scrubs his hands over his face and swears under his breath. He knows the story, and has kept my secret for all this time.

"You knew?" Stacy asks him, her voice full of hurt. He sighs deeply and wraps his arm around her shoulders, pulling her to him, and kisses her head while whispering to her.

"It's time you all know why," I announce and offer a wobbly smile to Caleb and Matt. "And you should hear it from me."

I swallow hard and look around the room at this beautiful group of people who have become my family and best friends.

"On Thanksgiving Day, just over a year ago, I was taking the girls to their father's to spend a few days with him. Just before we got there, Jeff was murdered by members of the drug cartel that he was working undercover with, and as I pulled up to his house, they were leaving."

There are mixed emotions from everyone in the room. Some gasp. Eyes widen. Mouths gape.

Nate's hands ball into fists.

"I couldn't identify any of them," I continue and wring my hands together. "But, they don't know that. I can't testify against them in court, so I don't qualify for the witness protection program, but they don't know that either."

"She was advised to leave town, and as long as she remained quiet and out of sight and out of mind, she should be safe," Matt announces.

"And I have been," I quickly assure them all. "The police in Chicago have kept their eyes and ears open, and for all I know, I've been forgotten."

"So what's going on now?" Luke asks, his voice hard.

"A few things have happened over the past few months to raise flags for us," Caleb begins, speaking for the first time. "First, Matt received a call from a P.I. at the station, asking all kinds of nosy questions about the family."

Matt nods and picks up where Caleb left off. "Then there was an employee at Isaac's company who seemed…"

"Creepy as hell," I finish for him. "He made comments about me being tied to a cop, and kept finding reasons to hit on me. Turns out he was just a creepy guy with a crush, but…"

"But I didn't like it," Caleb adds. "Then, the girls noticed someone poking around the house, looking in the mailbox up by the road after they got off the school bus one day."

"Why are you telling us this now?" Jules asks. "We've been trying to figure out what's going on with Brynna for months. So why now?"

"I'm sorry, guys," I begin and close my eyes with a sigh. "I just didn't want you all to worry and I figured the less you knew the less likely you could be a target, especially given how high profile some of you are."

"But, our baby brother decided to grow a romantic side, and proposed to his girlfriend in a very public way last night," Matt mutters and rubs his forehead with his hand. "It was on the news this morning, and I got a call from Chicago."

"I was in the photos," I add, and light bulbs go off above everyone's heads.

"Are you in danger again?" Gail asks.

"We don't know," Caleb answers her. "But it's only a matter of days before the images spread to papers and rag magazines, and as time progresses, chances improve that the wrong people will notice where Brynna is, and *who* she's with."

"Fuck," Will mutters. "I'm sorry, guys."

"You didn't know," I rush to assure him. "This is *not* your fault, Will."

"We want you all to know so you can pay attention," Matt informs everyone. "Keep your eyes open to anything that seems off. Someone's already been asking around about the family, and we want to make sure that you all know what's happening so you are sure to set your alarms and watch your backs. Whether we like it or not, we're a high profile family."

Suddenly, we notice that Gail is whispering feverishly at Steven, who is adamantly shaking his head.

"You have to tell them," she insists, louder now. "They have the right to know. You can set their minds at ease, at least about this."

"Mom?" Jules asks with a frown. "What's going on?"

Steven stares at his wife for several long seconds and the tension is so thick in the room you could cut it with a knife.

"Dad."

Isaac's voice is calm but firm and Steven turns his gaze to him, and then to each of his children, one by one. His face is completely sober as he moves his eyes about the room and back to his wife who nods reassuringly.

Finally, he stands and moves next to Matt.

"I don't really know how to say this," he mutters, his eyes never leaving his wife. Finally, she stands and joins him, linking her hand with his and tilts her head to kiss his shoulder.

"You're scaring me," Jules whispers with wide eyes.

"Right after Caleb was born," Gail begins and rubs her free hand up and down Steven's arm, as though he's cold. "Your father and I split."

"What?" Matt exclaims.

"Let me finish the story," Gail scolds him and keeps talking. "We went through a rough patch, like most marriages do. I had three little boys at home, and he worked more than I liked, and we decided to split. So, he moved out."

"You moved out?!" Jules scoots forward in her seat, leaning forward, listening carefully.

"I did," Steven confirms. "Worst fucking three months of my life."

"Okay, this is surprising, but what does it have to do with what's happening now?" Matt asks.

"The P.I. was looking for me," Steven announces and meets Matt's gaze. "While I was separated from your mother, I had a very brief affair with a woman while I was on a business trip. I didn't know it then, but she became pregnant."

"You have *got* to be kidding me," Isaac growls.

"No," Steven shakes his head. "I'm not kidding. The boy has been trying to find me since his mother passed away several months ago. He is the person who hired the P.I."

The room is dead silent for several seconds while everyone processes what has just been said. I look up at Caleb's face, and his jaw is clenched, muscles flexed and eyes narrowed on his father.

"You have an illegitimate son," Matt clarifies.

"I do," Steven nods with tears in his eyes. "His name is Dominic."

"Holy shit," Nate whispers and clenches his eyes closed. "We met him."

"You *met him?*" Isaac exclaims, jumping to his feet.

"Yes, the day we took the girls shopping." Nate nods. "He was having lunch with your parents."

"You've been having lunch with him?"

"I can't fucking believe this," Caleb mutters, speaking for the first time.

"Look," Steven holds his hands up, as if surrendering. "I was waiting for DNA tests to come back before I told the family. What if he was some asshole trying to get to my high profile children?"

"Your father was protecting you," Gail tells them all with a stern voice.

"But the DNA confirms it," Caleb states coldly.

"Yes."

Matt swears, long and loud and paces around the room while Isaac just glares at his father. Jules and Will look shell-shocked, and Caleb is scowling, a tense ball of anger and frustration.

"I have something to say," Caleb begins with a hard, yet deceptively calm, voice.

"Go ahead," Steven says.

"You taught us what it is to be a man. A partner. A father." Caleb inhales deeply and a muscle in his jaw ticks as he grinds his teeth together. "I feel like everything you've ever taught us has been a lie."

"It's not a lie," Gail interrupts angrily.

"He fucked around on you behind your back! What kind of a man does that?"

"He did not!" Gail storms over to Caleb and stares up into his eyes. "We were not together, Caleb. And he told me about it when he came home, begging me to take him back."

"He was fucking married!" Isaac interrupts. "I don't give a shit if you were on a *break*." Isaac laughs humorlessly. "This isn't *Friends*. He was married to you, whether he lived in the same house as you or not."

"We were taught to respect women," Will adds with a husky voice. He looks up and pins his father in his blue gaze. "*You* taught us to protect the women we love. To take care of them. To never hurt them."

Steven sighs deeply and hangs his head, staring at his shoes. "It was a horrible mistake, and something I've regretted every day of my life. Your mother was more forgiving than I deserved, and I'm thankful every day that she loved me enough to take me back and mend our marriage with me."

"Where is he?" Caleb asks quietly.

"He lives not far from here," Gail responds with tears in her eyes. "He grew up mostly in Italy with his mother's family."

"Were you ever going to tell us?" Jules asks. Tears are rolling down her cheeks.

"Yes, I just didn't know how," Steven whispers.

"But not if there hadn't been a kid," Isaac adds.

"If Dom hadn't been born, there would be no reason to tell you," Gail informs them all. "What happens in our marriage is between your father and me, and no one else."

"How can you protect him?" Caleb asks his mother angrily. "After what he did to you?"

"Honey," Gail takes Caleb's hands in her own. "You need to remember, this happened more than thirty years ago. We've had more children since then, grandchildren. *Thirty years* of life." She turns and looks at all of us as a tear falls from her eye unheeded. "This is fresh for you. For you, it happened today, but for us, it's so far in the past it was a lifetime ago."

"Do you have any more information for us?" Isaac asks Matt and pulls his wife to her feet.

"No," Matt shakes his head.

"I'm out of here."

Isaac leads Stacy out the door and we hear him start his truck and peel out of the driveway.

Jules is crying in earnest now and Nate pulls her into his lap, rubbing his big hand up and down her back and whispering in her ear, trying to calm her. Natalie's face is pressed to Luke's chest, where tears run silently down her cheeks.

Will stands and crosses to his father, his eyes full of anger and disgust and stops, toe to toe with the older man.

"I want to deck you right now. But out of respect for my mother, I'll say this: I never expected to be this disappointed in you. Not you."

Will shakes his head and turns away, striding quickly to the front door. Meg brushes tears from her cheeks and follows behind him.

Caleb's gaze hasn't left his father since he began speaking. He hasn't moved. His face is white and his body is tight, and I can feel the anguish rolling off of him.

Tears are rolling down my own face, though I barely feel them. I don't know what the fuck to do, so I do what feels right. I wrap my arms around Caleb and hold him. He unfolds his arms and wraps them around me tightly, pulling me against him. His body is practically humming with agitation.

"I think…" Matt begins but pauses and swallows hard. "I think this meeting is over. Just keep your eyes and ears open, everyone."

As he passes by Caleb and me, he pats my shoulder reassuringly and walks out the front door, closing it quietly behind him.

"Come on," Steven says to Gail. "Let's go and let them process all of this." He looks about the room, to his friends sitting shell-shocked at the dining table, his children, Luke's siblings. "I love you all very much. I can't tell you how sorry I am that you had to find out about Dom this way."

He stops in front of Jules, his face in absolute torment, as he gazes down at his daughter. "Jules," he whispers.

Jules jumps up out of Nate's arms and launches herself at her father, holding him tightly. "I love you so much, Daddy."

"I love you too, baby girl."

Jules hugs her mother and sniffs loudly as she pulls back and we all watch them walk out the front door.

"Fucking-A," Caleb whispers.

Chapter Sixteen

~Caleb~

"He fucked around on my mother!" I yell and pace the living room, still mad as hell an hour after everyone has left after the meeting.

"Caleb…" Brynna begins but I cut her off.

"Do not try to defend him."

"I'm not," she shakes her head. "But honestly, your mom is right. It happened a long time ago."

"Everything he taught us was a fucking lie." I push my hand through my hair and stare out the front window into the dark yard. The sun set a long time ago.

"No it wasn't, Caleb. Did you ever stop to think that that man was teaching you based on his own mistakes? He didn't want you to make the same ones he did."

I exhale and close my eyes.

Damn her for making sense.

"Your dad loves your mom fiercely. It's obvious to anyone who sees them."

"I have a brother I didn't even know about!" I exclaim and pace the room again.

"He didn't know either. There's no way that if Steven knew he'd fathered a child he would have abandoned him, Caleb. You know that." She watches me pace, her face calm and eyes watchful, and I suddenly feel like a dick.

"You're right," I mutter and pull my hand down my face. "He wouldn't have. But it's fucking bullshit that he left my mom right after I was born."

"It's called being human. Frankly, I'm relieved that the Montgomerys aren't as perfect as they all look from the outside." She chuckles and I scowl at her.

"What is that supposed to mean?"

"Oh, come on, Caleb. Your parents are still happily married, all of you are super-model gorgeous, you all get along with each other." She ticks off each point with her fingers. "You have one brother who is a freaking professional football player, you're a SEAL…"

"Was," I interrupt, but she keeps going.

"You're all successful. It's like none of you could do any wrong, and you're this cookie cutter perfect family. Well, surprise, you're all human after all." She shrugs and watches me carefully, as I stand here and just stare at her.

"Matt likes kinky sex, there is nothing perfect about him," I inform her, trying to keep a straight face.

"Oh, get real, you like the kinky shit too," she waves me off, but I smile wolfishly at her.

"Not that kinky, but I wouldn't mind tying you up sometime, Legs."

She laughs and shakes her head, then stands and crosses to me.

"Give it some time," she urges and wraps her arms around my waist. "You might find that Dominic is a nice guy."

"He could be a homicidal maniac. An asshole. A *Denver fan*," I cringe and shudder at the thought, making Bryn laugh and for the first time all day, I feel my body relax.

"He might just be a regular guy who wants to know what his biological father is like," she counters with a grin. "From what I remember when we met him at lunch, he's handsome."

"You met him too?" I ask, surprised.

"Briefly, yeah. Your dad was trying to get them out of there fast when he saw us. He seemed normal." She fiddles with the button on my shirt, but before I can ask more questions, there's a knock on the door.

"Expecting anyone?" I ask her with a raised eyebrow.

"I called my mom and asked her to bring the kids home. I miss

174

them." She grins shyly and I kiss her soft forehead before opening the front door. Two small girls and an eager dog come bounding inside, with Brynna's parents close behind them.

"Thanks for bringing them home." Brynna smiles at her parents and hugs both girls close.

"No problem. They were ready to come home anyway."

"Grandpa says we're bad for his high pressure," Josie informs her mother with a serious face.

"He says we'll give him vagina," Maddie joins in and I snort before catching the laugh that wants to come out of me.

"Angina," he corrects them and rolls his eyes. "You'll give me angina."

"That's what I said," Maddie counters.

"We'll head out, honey." Eloise hugs Brynna close and kisses my cheek as she passes by.

"Thanks again, Mom. And don't forget that Monday night is our monthly night out with the gang, so the kids will be back with you that night."

"No problem," Eloise smiles.

"I don't think we'll be going to that, Bryn," I begin but am met with a glare from Brynna.

"I will have a cop, a SEAL, a professional football player and a former UFC fighter with me, Caleb. I will be well taken care of." She props her fists on her hips and looks at me like I'm nuts.

"I guess when she puts it like that," I shrug and smile. Her parents laugh as they leave and the girls immediately start chatting about their night with their grandparents.

Bix wanders over to me and I settle on the couch with him half in my lap and half on the couch. With all of his training, he still hasn't figured out that he's not a lap dog. I'm content to scratch his belly and gently massage around his bad ear, earning moans of pleasure from the big goof as the girls talk excitedly to their mother.

She's such a good mom.

She smiles happily at the girls and gestures for them to join her on the loveseat adjacent to where I'm sitting, settling one on each side of her, wrapping her arms around them and kissing their heads.

I wish I'd seen her with them when they were babies. What a sight it must have been to watch her soothe them, cuddle them.

Nurse them.

"My tooth is loose!" Josie tells her excitedly.

"It is?" Brynna asks. "Let me see."

Josie shows her mother her loose top front tooth and then turns around to show me. "See, Caleb?"

"I see. Let me go get my pliers, I'll take it out for you."

"No!" Josie giggles and covers her mouth with her little hand.

"My tooth isn't loose," Maddie pouts with a long face.

"Don't worry, baby," Brynna chuckles and kisses her cheek. "It will be soon."

"Can we watch a movie, mama?" Josie asks with a yawn.

"I think it's time for bed, sweetheart."

"I want Caleb to tuck me in," Maddie responds and turns her big brown eyes on me, gazing at me hopefully.

"Come on," I snap my fingers and Bix jumps off my lap, happy to head upstairs to bed. I scoop both girls up and carry them, one under each arm, like they're sacks of potatoes, making them giggle like crazy. "I'll dump you in bed!"

"Mom! Help!"

"You're on your own," Brynna laughs as I climb the stairs. "I have a kitchen to clean."

"I'll be down to help in a while!" I call down to her as I toss the girls on their beds.

Time to put them to bed and have some quiet time with their sexy mother.

***

"Yellow stripe, corner pocket," Will calls out and takes his shot, easily sinking the ball.

The pub is loud thanks to an old jukebox in the corner playing *Livin' On a Prayer* and the girls at a nearby table laughing their mostly drunk asses off.

"You know," I mention to Nate who's sitting on a stool next to me, watching Will shoot. "Your wife is the loudest one over there and she isn't drinking anything other than water."

Nate laughs and looks over at my sister with humor and love. "She likes to have fun with her friends," he murmurs.

"They all do," Will agrees as he joins us after missing his last shot.

"Woot! Woot!" Meg chirps and the whole group collapses into a fit of giggles just as a waitress arrives with plates of food for them all.

"Our girls can eat," Luke remarks and motions with his chin as heaping plates of ribs and nachos and chicken in baskets with fries are laid out on the table before them.

"I'd rather that than Stacy starving herself," Isaac mutters and circles the table, looking for the best shot.

I silently agree. I love watching a woman eat.

"Nat's sexy when she eats," Luke mutters, almost to himself, mirroring my thoughts.

"Hey, ace!" Jules calls from the table, waving the dessert menu about. "They have chocolate cheesecake! I'm getting two slices!" She holds up two fingers and laughs, turning back to the girls.

"Nope, not afraid to eat, those girls," Will laughs and pats a laughing Nate on the shoulder.

"Where's Matt?" Isaac asks, checking his watch. "We've been here for almost an hour."

"We've only been here an hour and Meg is already that drunk?" Will asks, a horrified expression on his face, making us laugh.

Just then we all go quiet as we see Matt walk through the door with a tall, dark-haired man with him. As we watch, the stranger smiles, listening intently to what Matt is telling him as he leads him to the girl's table.

I don't have to ask to know who the stranger is. It's like looking at a darker version of my father thirty years ago.

"Oh, hell no," Isaac growls but Will stops him with a hand on his chest.

"Chill out, man," he murmurs to him softly. "This is no more his fault than it is ours."

Isaac scowls over at Will and then back to where the girls are smiling and giggling at something Dom has said. He shakes each of their hands respectfully, but when he gets to Jules, he stops and holds her hand in his for a moment, his face sober and watchful. Jules' eyes are glued to him in awe, and finally, she hops off her stool and hugs him close and smiles up at him happily. He smiles back, pats her shoulder if somewhat awkwardly and Jules takes her seat and digs into her nachos. Natalie also offers him a hug and a smile before he and Matt begin to walk this way.

Three siblings down.

"I have someone for you guys to meet," Matt begins as he and Dom approach. Dom's blue eyes are wary and reserved.

Nervous.

Luke steps forward and offers his hand. "I'm Luke Williams, Natalie's husband," he gestures to his beautiful brunette wife and shakes Dom's hand.

"Dom Salvadore," he responds.

"Nate," Nate stands and offers his hand. "Jules' husband."

"Will, the youngest brother." Will approaches Dom and shakes his hand, holding his gaze. "Do you like football?" he asks, making us all smirk.

"I don't watch much of it, I admit," Dom responds with a half smile. "But I hear you play."

"That's right," Will confirms, still holding Dom's hand tightly. "Don't tell me you play *European football*," he sneers.

"Some," Dom says with a slight nod. "Europeans don't wear pads to protect them like the American pussies do."

We all hold our breath and watch for Will's reaction. He stares at Dom, blinks twice, and then busts out laughing.

"Fuck you, man."

Dom turns to me and I shake his hand, pleased that his own grip is firm and strong. Mom always said, you can tell a lot about a person by their handshake.

So far, I don't have any complaints.

"I'm Caleb," I tell him.

"You're the one in the military?" He asks.

"I was, yes."

He nods and leans in to murmur to me, "Thank you for your service, man. It's an honor to meet you."

Well fuck.

I just nod as Isaac approaches, still scowling.

"I'm Isaac."

"The oldest," Dominic responds.

"That's right," Isaac confirms and shakes Dom's hand. "I'm not sure how I feel about you yet."

"Well, that makes two of us, I guess," Dom nods and steps back, eyeing us all. "I wasn't expecting to discover that Steven Montgomery has such a large family. I had no idea what I'd find, to be honest."

"Let's get some food and more beer over here," Luke suggests and motions for a waitress whose eyes light up and she scrambles to come take our order.

"What made you come looking for him now?" I ask as he takes a seat and a beer from the waitress.

"My mom died last fall," he begins and takes a swig of beer then grimaces as he looks at the label. "She never told me about my biological father."

"Did she ever marry?" Matt asks.

"No," Dom shakes his head and I can't help but feel for the guy. Growing up without a father would suck.

"After she passed, I was going through her things, and I found a letter from her." He shrugs and clears his throat. "She explained who he was, and what she could remember about him, in case I wanted to try to find him."

"Steven said you grew up in Italy?" Nate asks.

"Partly, yes," he nods and shifts in his chair. "My mom's family was still there, and when I was about five she moved us there so she would have her family nearby. We moved back to the states when I was fifteen. I went back in the summer and I studied there for a while. My grandparents died a few years ago, and I inherited their property there."

"Do you visit often?" Will asks. "I've been dying to get Meg over there, we just haven't had time to go."

"I don't go as often as I'd like because I own a business here, but you and Meg are welcome to use the house there whenever you want." He shrugs like it's the most natural thing in the world to offer his Italian home to his newly found brother to use whenever the mood strikes him.

Maybe Bryn's right; he's just a normal guy.

"Are you married?" Isaac asks him and crosses his arms over his chest.

"No," Dom shakes his head and smiles ruefully. "Too busy for that. But I met your lovely wife."

"What do you do?" Nate asks him calmly.

"I run two vineyards. One here in Washington and one in Italy, although a cousin of mine runs the one in Italy for the most part these days."

As he continues to tell the guys about the wines he makes here in Washington, I notice the girls are laughing hysterically and suddenly, Jules yells over to us all, "Hey! Brynna can suck the fuck out of a bone!"

Chapter Seventeen

~Brynna~

"Caleb! Did you know that Brynna can suck the fuck out of a bone?" Jules yells in the general direction of the guys, earning snorts of laughter from the other girls.

"Of course he does," Natalie giggles and points at me as she reaches for another hand full of fries. "Hello! She probably blows him all the damn time."

"Oh yeah!" Jules exclaims and laughs her ass off.

"Um, hello!" I spread my arms out to my sides and stare at the girls, my mind just a little cloudy from the liquor. "I'm right here."

"Dude, do you blow him a lot?" Stacy asks me and sucks on a rib.

I blink at her and look over at Meg, Jules and Nat, but they're all staring at me, waiting for my answer.

"Of course," I reply with a shrug.

Meh, if you can't beat 'em, join 'em.

"I knew it!" Nat yells and pumps her fist.

"Ew!" Jules exclaims and laughs. "So don't want to know this."

"I think I've found someone new I'd blow," Stacy murmurs and wiggles her eyebrows, her eyes pinned to Dom.

"I know, right?" I exclaim and take a sip of my sex on the beach before reaching for another rib, much to Jules' delight. "Jules, I have to tell you, your new brother is hot as hell."

"It's the Montgomery genes," Meg agrees and stuffs nachos in her mouth. "They're like, super-human or something."

We all turn and stare at him, taking in the gorgeous. Where the

Montgomery brothers are fair, with varying shades of blonde hair, Dom is olive-skinned with black hair, but his eyes match theirs to a T. They're perfectly blue, and when he smiles, he has one dimple, in his left cheek.

"I wonder if he has dimples above his ass," Nat observes.

"Oh, those are sexy!" Meg agrees. "Will has them."

"You know," Stacy leans in with a knowing smile. "If he grew up in Italy, he speaks Italian."

"I wonder if he'd teach Will Italian," Meg ponders. "Just the naughty words."

"Okay, we really need to bring in more hot guys that I'm not related to," Jules pouts and sips her water. "I want to talk about naked body parts and sexy foreign languages."

"Just pretend," Stacy suggests with a drunk wave.

I work on cleaning all the meat off the rib, making sure there's nothing left before I throw it in the basket.

"Seriously," Nat mutters while watching me. "That's impressive."

"I bet you guys leave a whole bunch of meat on the bone," I snicker and sip my drink.

"I'm done," Meg announces and throws her napkin on the table. "Let's take our drinks and go sit with the guys. I want to hear what they're saying to Dom."

We all agree and join the boys, drinks in hand.

"Brynna has some mad oral skills, man," Jules informs Caleb as we approach, and I want to simply die.

"Jules!" I exclaim and glare at her.

"What?"

"She's not even drunk," Stacy smirks and leans on her husband. "But I have mad oral skills too, don't I?"

"You do, babe," Isaac grins down at her.

"Enough of this. We'll scare Dom off," Meg announces and grins at the handsome Italian. "I'm sorry for their adolescent behavior."

"I'm fine." He chuckles and shakes his head. "I went to college. I know how girls are when they get together."

"So," I begin and sip my drink. Delicious. "You are Italian."

He nods and grins at me, showing off that dimple that's so similar to Caleb's, and my panties may have just flooded.

"Which means you naturally *speak* Italian."

He nods again and chuckles, his smile spreading across his face. Caleb wraps his arms around me from behind and pulls me against him, tucking me close to him, and while I should feel guilty for blatantly flirting with his half brother right in front of him, I don't.

I think it's funny as hell.

"I think what she's getting at," Meg begins, "is that it's kinda hot that you speak Italian."

"Oh please," Will rolls his eyes and scowls at Meg.

"It's true!" She insists.

"*Avete un bellissimo fidanzato, fratello,*" Dom murmurs, his eyes light with mischief as he speaks.

"Sweet Jesus, what did you say?" Stacy asks.

"I said," Dom laughs, "you have a very beautiful fiancé, brother."

Stacy sighs dreamily and I giggle despite myself. The guys roll their eyes again and Nate chuckles.

"Dude, stop flirting with the girls. Your brothers will kill you," Nate urges him with a laugh.

"I'm not flirting," Dom holds his hands up and laughs. "Although I think it's funny that women like foreign languages."

"Yeah, what's up with that?" Isaac asks.

"You don't think that a woman speaking a foreign language that you don't understand is sexy?" I ask Isaac with a grin.

"Never thought about it," he replies with a shrug.

"Liar," I respond.

He glares at me, so I walk over to him and hold my hand out for him to take. He does and I glance at Stacy, who nods and grins and I lean into him and say, "*Vous êtes un sacré menteur. Vous savez que c'est sexy et je pourrais dire vous manger de la nourriture pour chien pour le petit déjeuner et il serait toujours le son chaud.*"

Isaac swallows hard and then shrugs, as though it didn't affect him at all.

"Okay, that was fucking hot, what did you say?" Luke asks with a grin.

"I told him how hot he is in French," I smirk and walk back to Caleb, who's eyes are molten and he's looking at me like he wants to throw me down and fuck the hell out of me right here in this pub.

"Liar," Dom responds softly. "I speak French."

I throw my head back and laugh and wink over at him. "Well, they don't, so we'll leave it at that."

"I think it's time to go," Caleb growls and grabs my hand in his. "Have fun, guys. Dom, it was nicer to meet you than I thought it would be."

Dom nods and winks at me as we walk past. Caleb pulls me through the pub and all of a sudden, I hear our group bust out in laughter.

"Hey!" Isaac calls out. "I do not eat dog food for breakfast!"

I giggle and try to keep up with Caleb as he pulls me along through the parking lot to his car.

"Slow down!"

"You did that on purpose," he whispers and presses me against his car, leaning in to me, his arms caging me on either side. He lowers his head and brushes his lips over mine gently, barely tasting me.

"Did what?" I breathe.

"Taunted me by flirting with my brothers and speaking French. I didn't know you could do that, by the way."

"I took French in school and then spent a summer in Paris after I graduated," I whisper when he slides his lips down my jawline to my neck. I run my hands up his arms, over his shoulders and up into his hair. "Caleb?"

"Mmm…"

"Please take me home now."

With just fifteen seconds of kisses and the feel of his hands on me in the cold night air, I'm ready to climb him. My skin is on fire, my nipples hard, and my pussy already swollen and wet with need.

He guides me in the car and drives me the few minutes down

184

the street to my house. We could have walked the short distance to our favorite pub, *The Celtic Swell*, but Caleb said it wasn't safe.

Now I'm just happy it was so close to the house.

He leads me inside and up the stairs to the bedroom where he quickly disrobes us both and gently pulls me into the bed.

He's never been this gentle, and it's throwing me off a little.

He pushes me onto my back and braces himself over me, kissing me alternatively fast and hard and slow and soft, each time I get used to his rhythm, he switches it up on me.

Finally, he slows his pace and leans his forehead against my neck, breathing heavily. "You astound me, Bryn. You're so fucking *amazing.*"

I frown and pull back so I can see his face. He cups my cheeks in his hands and brushes his thumbs over my skin.

"You're so damn funny, and sweet, and smart." He swallows and kisses me again, still softly. "You could make the devil himself fall in love with you," he whispers.

"Did you know I also have mad oral skills?" I ask him with a grin. He chuckles softly and sweeps his lips across mine again, nibbling on the corner of my mouth and sending goosebumps over my body. I tilt my pelvis, silently inviting him to push himself inside me, but he pulls away.

"Caleb," I moan and drag my teeth down his stubbled jawline.

"Yes, baby," he whispers, kissing the top of my shoulder.

"I really want you to fuck me now."

He pulls back and stares down at me, brushing tendrils of my hair off my face. "I can't fuck you tonight, baby." He shakes his head and clenches his eyes shut, then opens them and pins me in his bright blue gaze once more. "I need to make love to you tonight."

Before I can respond, he lowers his head and kisses me again. I brush my hand up his naked arm and frown when I feel scrapes on his smooth skin.

"Caleb, what happened to your arm?" I ask

"Work," he mumbles and continues to kiss his way down my throat.

"These scrapes are nasty," I respond.

"No big deal." He wraps his lips around my nipple and sucks softly, making my back arch against him.

"I don't like seeing you hurt," I whisper. "Ever."

"I'm fine, Legs." He pulls his big hand over my hip and down my thigh to my calf and back up again, hitching my knee around his hip and opening me up to him even more. His hard cock nudges my clit and I about come undone.

"Ah, Caleb, that feels so good."

He grins against my breast and repeats the motion on the other side, sucking and tugging my nipple with his lips. He moves his hips, just enough to cause friction between the head of his cock and my clit and I groan his name.

"Gonna make this last, sweetheart," he whispers.

"I need you, Caleb."

"I'm right here," he replies softly. My body is on fire for this man. I can't stop moving beneath him, can't stop my hands from roaming over every damn amazing inch of his smooth skin.

Finally, he slips just the very tip of his cock inside me and stops, pulls his face back up to my own, kissing me deeply and passionately, sliding his tongue along my own, cupping my face in his large hands.

He's worshipping my body, and it's the most amazing fucking thing I've ever felt in my entire life.

He slowly slides the rest of his cock in my pussy and then swears under his breath as he holds himself there, sheathed in me.

"So damn amazing," he whispers. The room is quiet, the house still, as he makes soft sweet love to me. Our breathing is labored, but we hardly make any sound at all as he moves above me and I raise and lower my hips to meet him, relishing in the way his hardness feels inside me.

It's as though he's home.

"Love you so much," I whisper into his shoulder as his pubis presses against my clit, sending me into a rolling orgasm, gentle as a calm ocean wave, but no less staggering than the wild choppy seas of a hurricane as he follows me over the edge and into his own climax. He shudders above me, not making any noise as he collapses beside me and pulls me into his arms.

If he heard my declaration seconds ago, he doesn't say. He simply tucks me up against him, pushes his fingers through my hair and kisses my forehead before falling into a deep sleep.

After several minutes, I untangle myself from his embrace to go to the restroom and clean myself up, pull on some clothes, and mentally pull myself together.

Did he not hear me?

Possible.

When I return to the bedroom, he's turned onto his side, facing away from my side of the bed. I climb in behind him and lay on my side, several inches from him, watching him as he breathes in sleep. The light from the moon casts a shadow of light over his back, illuminating his tattoo.

I can't resist lifting my hand and tracing the letters and numbers with the tip of my finger. He's so much more than what's written in these four lines.

He's everything I've ever wanted.

Chapter Eighteen

~Caleb~

I've avoided her all day. All fucking day. And that's not easy to do when the person you're avoiding is the one you're living with and doing your damndest to protect.

It's not easy.

But for my own sanity, it's necessary.

I heard her last night when she whispered that she loved me while I was buried inside her and couldn't tell where I ended and she began. She didn't have to say the words aloud, I could fucking *feel* her, and to say it scared the shit out of me is an understatement.

So I did the only thing I knew and ignored it.

Because somewhere along the line I fell in love with her too, and now I'm too much of a pussy to admit it.

I slide out from under the sink in the kitchen, throw my wrench in my toolbox and wipe my hands on a towel. I've managed to work out twice, repair a loose board on the deck, re-caulk the bathtub in the kids' bathroom, and repair a leak under the kitchen faucet, all since we all returned home from work and school this afternoon.

I even opted out of eating dinner with Brynna and the girls, insisting that I'd eaten a big lunch at work.

I'm fucking starving.

I frown as Bix saunters around the kitchen island, sniffing for any scraps that may have fallen while Brynna made dinner and comes to me for an ear rub.

"Hey, boy," I whisper and kiss his cheek while I rub him down.

"How are you feeling?"

Bix nudges my chin with his head and sits next to me on the floor, enjoying the attention.

"You're such a faker," I mumble with a laugh. "You get more attention from those two little girls than you have in your whole life."

He grins up at me and moans as I rub the sensitive area around his injured ear.

"Does that still give you problems, boy?" I ask with a whisper and gently massage the tender area.

"What's wrong with him?"

I glance up, surprised to see Maddie standing in the kitchen and I didn't hear her approach. She's in a long nightgown, her dark hair is still wet from her bath, but it's been combed to hang over her shoulders. She's barefoot and is holding her doll close to her chest.

She's all fresh and clean and just about the sweetest thing I've ever seen.

"Nothing, buttercup," I respond and smile. "Sometimes his ear just hurts."

"Oh," She frowns and watches me rub Bix's face. "Poor Bix."

"He's okay," I reassure her. "What are you up to?"

"I want you to read us a story and tuck us in, so Mom said I should come find you."

She watches me with wide sleepy eyes.

"Shall we take Bix up and read a story?" I ask her with a smile.

"Yes, please," she responds happily.

I rise from my seat on the floor and motion for Bix to follow us up the stairs. Brynna is just coming out of the girls' room as we approach and she hugs Maddie tight and grins at her.

"Good night, baby girl," Brynna croons to her daughter.

"'Night, Mama," Maddie responds and jumps up into her bed. Bix happily curls up on his bed between the two, but he's not fooling me.

He'll be up on one of their beds as soon as I turn the light out and leave.

"You and I need to talk," Brynna murmurs to me before turning and walking down the stairs.

Yeah, we do, Legs.

"Come over here with us, jellybean, and we'll read a story."

Josie climbs into Maddie's bed and the two little girls curl up together. "I want Ferdinand," Josie informs me.

"Ferdinand it is, then," I grin and find the book about the bull on their bookshelf before sitting on the edge of the bed to read.

Bix sighs as I begin the story about a bull who is content to just sit and smell the flowers under his favorite cork tree. The girls settle in and watch the pictures as I read, making my voice different for the different characters. They yawn, their eyes growing heavy.

By the time I reach the end, they both have their eyes closed and are breathing deeply with sleep. Rather than wake Josie and make her get up out of Maddie's bed to get into her own, I lift her carefully and carry her to her bed, tucking her in.

Before I can pull away, she tightens her arms around my neck in a hug and whispers, "Love you, Daddy."

My heart stops as she wiggles away, turns on her side, and sighs as she falls back to sleep.

Suddenly, I feel a sheen of sweat form on my forehead and pulling air in and out of my lungs is a struggle.

I need out of here.

I back out of the girls' room, turn out the light and walk quickly down the hall through Brynna's bedroom to the bathroom and turn the faucet on cold, briskly splashing it over my face, over and over again, not caring that I'm splashing water all over the floor, the sink, down my shirt.

I stop and lean my hands on the countertop, staring at my own refection, water dripping, panting, trying to drag enough air into my lungs.

Rat tat tat tat tat!

"Move, move, move! Retreat!" I called to my men in the wilderness of Afghanistan. "Get the fuck out of here!"

"Marshall is down!" Lewis yelled at me from twenty yards away, shooting with precise calm at the Taliban that ambushed

us.

"Fuck!"

"I'm going up the hill to try to call for help," Bates, the fourth on our team informed me.

"No, we stay together," I shook my head and aimed my rifle, taking out another of the enemy.

"We need backup, man," Lewis called over.

"You'll get hit," I call to Bates as we make our way through the trees. "There are at least fifty of them!"

"We need backup," Bates repeats and looked me square in the eye. "I'm going up."

Before I could respond, he ducked and ran back up the hill to get to high ground for the communication unit to work and Lewis and I opened fire, covering him.

"Three O'clock!" Lewis screamed and I turned to my right, firing, taking out three more Taliban.

My eyes searched for Bates and found him, still making his way up the mountain.

Suddenly, I heard Lewis grunt and as I looked his way, he dropped to one knee, but kept firing.

"Are you hit?" I asked.

"Affirmative, sir," he called back and continued to fire.

"How bad?"

He didn't answer. Looking up, Bates had reached the top and was setting up the comm unit when suddenly a bullet caught him in the right shoulder, knocking him back. He grimaced, but pushed on, raised the CB to his mouth, calling for help. Another bullet pierced the hand holding the mouthpiece, but damn if he didn't pick it up with his other hand and kept talking.

"Lewis! Bates is calling for help!" I called out. Lewis was on his stomach now, still shooting and taking down men.

My own rifle continued to fire as well, and for a moment, I thought we might survive it, just one man down.

Until a fucking sniper landed a shot in Lewis' forehead, killing him instantly.

"Motherfucker," I growled and continued to fire in earnest, sure that all four of us would die here on this mountain, and I'd

be damned if we went out without a fight.

"Back up is coming!" Bates called down to me, just before another bullet caught him in the left shoulder and he slumped to the ground.

"You hold on!" I called out to him, my heart beating errati-cally. "Get down, Bates!"

"Roger, sir," he responded and watched me with glassy eyes as I continued to take out the enemy around us.

A flash of light came straight for us and landed several yards away, knocking me out cold.

What am I doing?

I shake my head, pulling myself back into the here and now and splash more water on my face with shaking hands.

I've wanted Brynna since the first time I laid eyes on her. She's fucking gorgeous, who wouldn't want to fuck her?

But goddamn it, she's more than that. Why did I think I could just have her in my bed, and not fall in love with her?

Why couldn't I keep my fucking hands off her?

I stare at the hollow, broken man in the mirror, knowing the answer already.

Because Brynna Vincent is it for me. There will never be an-other woman who can make me feel safe, make me feel happy.

Make me feel loved.

And her daughters are two little beacons of light in this dark hell I call a life that I just can't resist.

And God knows I don't deserve them.

Any of them.

Just the thought of Josie and Maddie calling me Daddy fills me with so much pride and so much fear I don't know what to do with myself.

Things have gotten so far out of hand. We have to stop playing house. If not for my own sanity, for the sake of the girls because only heartache can come of this.

I couldn't protect my men. What in the name of Christ made me ever think I could protect these precious women?

I stomp out of the bathroom and into the bedroom, punching

the keys on my phone as I move, yank my bag out of the closet and throw the few articles of clothing and toiletries I have into it, zip it, and jog down the stairs, preparing myself to go toe-to-toe with the best thing that's ever happened to me.

Because I'll never be the best thing for her.

"What are you doing?" She asks with a scowl, rising from the couch when she sees me.

"I've texted Matt to come be with you and the girls. It's time I go, Bryn." *Dear God, don't look at me like that.* She blinks and her eyes turn sad, but she crosses her arms over her chest and thrusts her chin in the air.

"Why?"

I shrug and pull my jacket over my arms.

"It's time. I think I'll take a job I've been offered in San Diego. You'll be fine with Matt." Every word is like a knife stabbing through my heart.

"So, I tell you I love you, my girls fall in love with you, and all you can do is *run away?*" She asks, her soft voice full of anger.

Betrayal.

"Look," I begin and wipe my fingers over my mouth, not able to look her in the eye. "I can't help it if you mistook me fucking you for anything more than that."

She gasps and I turn my back on her, my chest heaving, hating myself.

How can I do this to her?

"I figured I'd have some fun with you while I was here, but…"

"But what?" She growls between clenched teeth.

"But I don't love you back," I can't turn around and look her in the face. *God, I love you so fucking much I can't stand it.*

I hear her breathing hard behind me and pray she doesn't cry. Doesn't beg.

But this is Brynna we're talking about, and she doesn't beg for anything.

"I'm telling you right now, Caleb Montgomery, if you leave you will not be welcome to come back." Her voice wavers on the very last word and it's a kick in my gut.

I nod stiffly. "I've already texted Matt."

"Am I supposed to fuck him too, since he'll be filling in for you?" She asks, her voice full of venom and anger, and she does exactly what she's aiming for.

Stabs me right through the heart.

I'll fucking kill him if he puts a hand on you.

I clench my jaw and my fists and turn to look her in the eye. I do my best to keep my face impassive, but I know I'm failing horribly.

I'd never crack under pressure if I were being interrogated by the enemy, but this is breaking me, and I need to get the fuck out.

"Fuck whomever you want," I reply.

Her jaw drops and eyes widen, filling with tears, but she pulls herself together and narrows her eyes on me again.

"You're a fucking pussy," she growls.

"I told you I'm done and I'm leaving, Brynna. What do you want?" I ask in anger, raising my voice for the first time.

"I want to be someone's fucking first choice, goddamn it!" She yells back at me. "I want someone to *want* to stay with me. To choose me!" Her eyes are wide and pissed as she stomps her foot and glares at me. "I thought you were that man."

"You thought wrong."

You are my every *choice, Legs.*

She turns away just as I hear Bix jump off the girls' bed and begin barking. One bark, about every three seconds.

"I'm so fucking…"

"Stop." I hold up a hand, making her stop mid-sentence and listen. The house is quiet, except for Bix's measured bark.

"Why is he…"

"I said stop talking," I interrupt and she covers her mouth with both hands, watching me with wide eyes. Suddenly something shatters the back picture window, next to the sliding glass door, and I spring into action. I pull the pistol from my waistband and push it into Brynna's hands.

"Take this and get upstairs with the girls," my voice is low and hard. "Get all of you, including Bix, into the bathroom and lock the door. Do not open it unless I say to. Do you hear me?"

She shakes her head, eyes wide with fear and just stares at me.

"Go!"

"I love you," she whispers and runs up the stairs.

***

~Brynna~

Get the girls. Get the girls. Get the girls.

I repeat it to myself, over and over, as I climb the stairs two at a time and race to their bedroom. Bix is standing at attention at the foot of their beds, hackles raised, teeth bared. He whines when he sees me.

"Mommy!" Maddie cries and launches herself at me just as I hear Caleb's hard voice downstairs, swearing and grunting.

Someone's in my fucking house!

I quickly grab both girls and pull the comforter off the bed as I hurry into the bathroom. Bix joins us and I shut and lock the door.

"What's happening?" Josie cries.

"There's a bad man downstairs," I say as calmly as I can. *There could be more than one!*

I throw the blanket into the tub and lift the girls inside, then join them. Bix stands a few feet from the door, growling, hackles still raised and teeth bared, standing guard.

I fucking love that dog.

I pull my cell out of my pocket and dial Matt.

"Yeah," he answers.

"Matt, we need you here," I begin and Maddie lets out a loud wail, scared to death.

"What's wrong?" he asks.

"Someone broke in. Caleb's downstairs alone. We're in the upstairs bathroom."

"I'll be there in thirty seconds."

He hangs up and I dial 911, fill them in on the situation and set the phone on the side of the tub, still connected to the operator, as we wait.

The girls huddle against my sides and I grip Caleb's pistol in my hands, aimed at the door, and wait, panting and shaking in fear.

Oh, God, what is happening down there?

More glass breaks, and I hear furniture being toppled over.

I can hear muffled voices and more grunting in pain, and I pray with everything in me that Caleb is whole and safe.

After several seconds of no noise at all, there are two gunshots, and then a third, and then silence.

Tears run down my cheeks. I wipe them on the arms of my shirt and keep the gun trained on the door. Bix is still growling and barking, but suddenly, he stops and tips his head to the side, as though he's listening carefully.

"Bryn?" Caleb calls from the other side of the door.

"Caleb!" Maddie cries as I stand and reach over to unlock the door and let Caleb in.

"Where is he?" I ask through my sobs.

Caleb simply shakes his head and pulls us all into his arms, squeezing us hard.

I pull away, and the girls cling to him, crying, afraid, and I want to follow suit, but the words he spoke moments before our world came falling in are still here between us.

He's leaving us.

I'm not who he wants.

When the girls are calm, he whispers for them to hug Bix, and as they do, he pulls me against him, buries his face in my neck and holds on tight, but I still don't wrap my arms around him.

I hold still and wait for him to finish.

"Brynna," he whispers.

"Where are you?" Matt calls out frantically.

"We're in here!" I call back.

Matt rushes into the room, other cops following close behind him, spreading through the house to be sure there is no further threat.

"You're hit," he announces to Caleb, his eyes hard, and I glance down to find blood running down Caleb's arm.

"Oh my God, I missed this!"

"It's just a graze," Caleb shakes his head, his eyes still on me, full of worry and fear, but I ignore him and launch myself at Matt, hugging him tight.

"Are you okay, honey?" He asks me.

I nod, and turn back to Caleb. "You need to go to the hospital."

"No, I'm fine," he shakes his head and pats Josie's back, who has latched herself around his waist, hanging on with dear life.

"The ambulance is on the way," Matt informs us just as sirens come from the driveway. "They can patch you up."

We finally all move downstairs after the coroner comes in and removes the body. The girls and Bix huddle together on the couch while Caleb is cleaned up by a paramedic and I give my statement to Matt and his partner, distracted by the mess surrounding us; broken furniture, glass littered on the carpet. Even the loveseat is sitting on its back. Blood is pooled on the hardwood floor in the dining room.

The process is long and exhausting, and as we all come down off the adrenaline from the break in, it's all the girls and I can do to keep our eyes open.

"We can't stay here until the window is fixed and this place is cleaned up," I murmur to Matt.

"I'll take you to a hotel," he responds with a smile.

"They can stay at my place," Caleb replies as he joins us.

"We'll take the hotel," I mutter, not meeting Caleb's gaze with my own.

"I think…" Caleb begins but I cut him off.

"I don't want to be at your house, Caleb. We'll go to the hotel."

His blue eyes harden, but I look away and swallow as Matt watches us both closely.

"I'll take them," Caleb murmurs softly.

"I…"

"I'll take you," he repeats, his voice hard and leaving no room for argument.

I turn away without responding and kiss the girls. "I'll be right back, okay? I'm just going upstairs to pack our bags. You stay here with Bix and Matt and Caleb."

They nod sleepily as I turn to Matt. "Make sure the hotel takes dogs. He goes where we go from now on."

Matt smiles and nods. "Good girl."

Once our bags are packed, Caleb loads us into his car. Matt has offered to stay behind and oversee the cleanup and make sure the window is boarded up.

"Bryn…" Caleb begins but I sigh and cut him off.

"You've already said all you need to say, Caleb. We'll be fine."

Although I don't know if we'll be fine. I don't know that we're out of danger. Who was that guy that broke in and tried to hurt us?

The check-in process is blurry and I feel like my feet are filled with led as Caleb leads us to our room. He's carrying both girls, and I'm pulling our one suitcase behind me. Bix is at my side, even without a leash.

I think I forgot the leash.

The room has one giant king sized bed, but I requested that. I want my girls with me tonight.

Caleb tucks the kids in the large bed and motions for Bix to join them. I pull my own pajamas out of my suitcase and move into the bathroom to change.

"You don't have to do that on my account," he whispers.

"You never get to see me naked again," I reply, noticing the way his jaw tightens and his eyes harden at my words. I can hear the sadness in my voice and I don't have the energy to try to be brave.

He's leaving us.

When I return to the room, I join the girls in the bed. Josie has begun crying again, and is clinging to Caleb.

"Where is the bad man now?" She cries softly.

"He's gone, sweetheart," Caleb croons to her. "He can't hurt you."

But he hurt you. I glance at his arm and frantically temper down the need to crawl to him and kiss his wound, to fuss over him and make sure he's okay.

He doesn't want me.

Finally Josie's cries disappear and Caleb lowers her back into the bed. He's stretched out on his side, on the other side of the girls, watching them sleep. Bix is curled up at their feet, and I'm lying opposite to Caleb, also on my side, but I'm watching him.

Memorizing every line of his body, every hair on his head.

Finally, he brushes their hair back and leans in to lay a soft kiss on each of their foreheads. He lifts his gaze to mine, and in his bright blue eyes is sadness and regret. He reaches across the girls and cups my cheek in his hand, wipes a tear with his thumb and takes in every inch of my face with his eyes. He sighs deeply and releases me, rolls away from the girls and stands, turns off the light and walks to the door.

As he pulls it open, he looks back at me and whispers, "I'm sorry, Legs," just before he walks out and quietly pulls the door closed behind him.

For several long seconds I stare unseeing where Caleb left, then I roll away from my babies and bury my face in the pillow, letting my tears and grief flow out of me in violent sobs.

Caleb is gone.

Chapter Nineteen

Three months later.

~Caleb~

"Your usual?"

I nod at the redheaded bartender and keep my head down, staring at the scarred bar top in front of me.

"Isn't your contract up?" She asks me as she reaches for a tumbler and a bottle of Jack Daniels.

"How do you know that?" I ask and slam back the amber liquid and push it forward in a silent request for more.

"I've been tending this bar for more than fifteen years," she informs me and pours me another. "I know the comings and goings of the military guys on this base. And I can tell by looking at you that you're not active duty anymore."

I glare at her and take a sip of the Jack, not confirming or denying her assumption.

"So why are you here and not back home fighting for your girl?" She asks with a sympathetic smile.

Fuck off and let me drink.

"You don't know anything about it," I growl and slam my drink.

"I know plenty." She grabs a white bar towel and wipes off the bar, clearly not ready to leave me in peace. "I know you've been coming here three nights a week like clock work for the past three months. You drink whiskey until you stagger out of here and walk back wherever you came from. You're drinking to forget something, and my bet is it's a woman."

"Maybe it's a man," I smirk.

"Nah, I've seen you check out some of the SEAL bunnies' asses, but if they approach you, you growl and scare them away."

"Ain't nothing wrong with looking," I sulk. I just want to drink until I'm so drunk that it dulls the mile-wide ache in my chest and I forget the look in Brynna's face as I walked out of her hotel room three months ago.

"No," she agrees and shakes her head thoughtfully. "But you look guilty as hell after you do."

"What do you want?" I ask and push my empty glass forward for another.

"Just thought I'd talk to you is all," she replies with a smile. "You don't scare me with that glare, by the way. Been married to a SEAL for ten years, and his glare doesn't scare me either."

"Congratulations," I mutter and swig my whiskey.

"Oh, it hasn't been a walk through the park, trust me. The fool actually left me for a while. Claimed he didn't deserve me." She shrugs and chuckles as I whip my head up and stare at her with narrowed eyes.

"What did you say?" I ask.

"Said he didn't deserve me," she repeats and watches me for several seconds. "Ah, there it is." She shakes her head again and rolls her eyes. "So, when they're teaching you guys to bench press a pine tree and hold your breath for forty-five minutes…"

"Four minutes," I correct her with a growl.

"Do you they also teach you to be stubborn asses?"

"They taught me to ignore nosy fucking bartenders," I reply and pop a pretzel in my mouth.

"Okay, don't talk, then, moron and listen to me."

"Why are you talking to me?" I ask incredulously.

"Because you're gonna ruin your fucking life, and you're too damn hot for that, so shut up and listen to me." She crosses her arms over her chest and glares at me, and for a minute I'd swear I'm talking to my mother.

"Fine," I sigh and keep my eyes on the bar.

"He didn't come back to me until we found out I was pregnant," she begins and then sighs. "Lost that baby, though."

"I'm sorry," I whisper.

"I've had three more," she responds and I can hear the smile in her voice and I can't help but hate her just a little. She's a nice, if not way too nosy, woman, but I don't give a rat's ass about her kids.

"But I'm going to tell you what I told him, and then I'll go pay attention to the other customers."

"Oh, goody," I respond sarcastically.

"That *American Dream* that y'all fight so hard for over there? The freedoms that you would die to protect? They're yours too, you know."

My head jerks up and I stare at her as she continues.

"You've earned the right to be happy, more than most of us." She swallows and lays her hand over my arm. "You have *earned her*, Sergeant."

"How did you know?" I ask but she cuts me off.

"You scream Sergeant. Or Lieutenant."

"Sergeant," I whisper.

She nods and glances down the bar. "Before you go home and claim her before someone else does, you need to get some help for the PTSD and get your head on straight."

"What are you a fucking shrink?" I sneer.

"No," she shakes her head and smiles softly. "But I know a good one." She pulls a card out of her back pocket and slides it across the bar to me before she winks and saunters down the bar to help other customers.

What the fuck does she know, anyway?

I suddenly don't want any more whiskey, and can't stand the stale smell of liquor in this bar, so I throw some bills on the bar and walk away, through the crowd beginning to gather and out the door. This particular joint isn't far from the apartment the Navy put me up in during my contract. I've been training SEALs near San Diego, California for the better part of three months, and the pretty bartender was right.

The contract is over.

I have an open invitation at the mercenary training center I left near Seattle, but living in Seattle means living near Brynna and the girls, and I don't know that I could survive that.

Look how well you're surviving down here, asshole.

I slam into my apartment and flop onto the couch, staring at the ceiling and listening to the air conditioning unit click on. It's only May, but it's already warm in southern California, even late in the evening.

I wonder what the weather is like back home.

I pull my iPhone out of my pocket and bring up the weather app. It's already set to Seattle.

Sunny and mid-sixties.

Nice weather. My girls would like to go to the park in that kind of weather.

My girls.

God, I'm such a fucking mess. I chose to leave, knowing that they loved me.

I chose.

Because staying would only end up hurting them.

You've earned her.

I scrub my hands down my face with a long sigh and squeeze my eyes shut. I miss them. I thought it would get better with time, but the truth is, it only gets worse. Every day is it's own special sadistic kind of torture and I'd give anything to be with them.

All of them.

I fucked up big time.

I stare down at the phone and bring her number up, along with her photo and stare down at it, my thumb hovering over the number and debate about calling her.

I need to hear her voice.

More than that, I need to feel her. Hold her close and breathe her in.

I need it so bad it hurts.

Instead of pressing the button to call, I lay back on the couch and stare at her sweet face, her big brown eyes, long dark hair, and remember what it's like to feel her close to me while I sleep.

How safe it feels to fall asleep near her, where the nightmares stay far away, and pray it's enough to keep them at bay because I didn't get drunk enough to numb myself tonight.

Liquor is the only thing that numbs my brain of thoughts of

Bryn and the nightmares.

***

Where are they?

"Brynna!" I scream and run through her house, up the stairs and back down again, room to room, trying to find them.

They're screaming and crying for me.

"Daddy!" Maddie cries hysterically.

"Caleb, help us!" Brynna calls out.

Bix is barking frantically, not his alert bark, but a full out attack bark.

Glass shatters.

Gunshots.

"Daddy!"

I can't fucking find them!

I run back up the stairs, but when I get there, I'm somehow in the kitchen. I need to get upstairs. That's where the crying is coming from.

"I'm coming!" I yell and run for the stairs again, but when I try to climb them, I'm moving in super slow-motion, not able to move fast enough to get upstairs.

"Daddy!"

Now their cries are coming from the kitchen, but I can't turn around to get back there.

Fuck!

Suddenly, everything is dead quiet. Even Bix has stopped barking, and I can hear quiet sobs coming from somewhere, although I can't tell where, I just know that I can't move fast enough to reach them.

"Daddy," Josie whispers.

I wake with a start, gasping for breath, sweat running down my face.

Sonofamotherfucker.

I jump from the couch and run through the apartment, frantically searching, before it occurs to me that it was a dream and the girls aren't here.

"That American Dream that y'all fight so hard for over there? The freedoms that you would die to protect? They're yours too, you know."

Damn right they're mine.

They're mine.

I pull the business card from the redheaded bartender out of my back pocket and dial the number.

It's time to fix this shit and go home.

***

"How have the nightmares been in the week since you've been coming to me?" Dr. Reese asks calmly.

"I've only had one," I reply and lean forward in my chair, resting my elbows on my knees.

"That's an improvement."

I nod and sigh. "Still not great in crowds."

"Have you been in a large crowd of people lately?" He asks with a raised brow.

"I was at the grocery store on a Saturday. It was crowded." I shrug.

"And what happened?"

"I left."

"The crowds may always bother you, Caleb. Post Traumatic Stress Disorder never really goes away, you just learn to manage and live with it."

"PTSD is another term for pussy, doc. Let's not sugar coat it."

His eyes narrow on me for a moment before he frowns and sits back in his chair.

"Are you saying that if any of your teammates…"

"Brothers," I correct him.

"Brothers had survived that day on that mountain, and were currently going through what you are, you'd call them a pussy?" He tilts his head, watching me carefully.

"They didn't survive because I couldn't keep them safe!"

"Caleb, it was the four of you against more than fifty heavily armed men. How in the world do you think you could all survive that?"

"It was a fucked up mission," I mutter and scrub my hand over my mouth.

"Agreed," he nods. "But your lack of intel didn't kill your men, Caleb. The enemy killed them. You know this."

"I know." It's the first time I've admitted it. "But why did I survive? I'm the cursed one, doc."

"It doesn't sound like you're living a cursed life, Caleb. You have a great family, a woman who loves you, a strong career."

"And when will the other shoe drop?"

"Why does it have to?" He leans forward in his chair and pins me in his gaze. "You did your job, Caleb. You saved Brynna and her daughters from an intruder. You did what you were there to do. You kept them safe."

I stare at him as images from that night race through my mind. Telling Bryn I was leaving. The shattering of the window. Fighting that motherfucker who came to hurt them, and aiming my pistol at his head and pulling the trigger.

"I would die to keep them safe," I whisper. "But I was so horrible to her. The things I said, telling her I don't love her. It was the only way I could think of to push her away."

"Don't you think she'll understand that when you explain it to her? From what you've told me, she sounds like a reasonable woman. And you're facing your demons to keep them in your life. You're making progress."

"Well, the first step is admitting there's a problem, right?" I ask sarcastically.

He smirks and shakes his head. "Have you spoken to the family members of the men you lost that day?"

I sober and blink at him slowly. "Not since their funerals."

"Maybe you should."

"Call and talk to Bates' and Marshall's wives and Lewis's mom, just to hear them tell me it should have been me and hang up on me?" I ask incredulously.

He shakes his head. "No. Call them. That's your last lesson from me, and then I'm sending you home. You will need to continue to see someone for a while, but you're going to be fine, Caleb."

Home.

I stand and stare down at the doctor, uncertain about this last task. The talking and rehashing of the mission was hard enough.

Talking to the family members?

Fuck.

"You'll be fine," he repeats.

I nod and leave his office and walk briskly to my car, slam the door and pull my phone out. If this is what I have to do to get home, so be it.

I firm my jaw and dial the first number.

***

The drive back to Seattle has been too long. Another week has passed since I made those calls. A week to pack up my shit, sit through a few more sessions with the good doctor and get on the road.

Jesus, what if she doesn't take me back?

I pull to a stop in front of her house and jump from the car, leaving the door wide open, and race to the front door, banging with my fist.

No answer.

The house is calm.

I run around to the back and notice with satisfaction that the back window has been replaced. My workout gear is gone.

I'll have to replace that.

I bang on the sliding glass door, but there is still no answer and no movement inside. Even Bix doesn't come running to see who is knocking.

Please let them be at her mom and dad's.

I climb back into the car and race to Bryn's parents, but am faced with another quiet, still house.

Where is everybody?

It's Sunday morning, for Christsake.

With a frown, I head north of Seattle toward my parent's house. I haven't spoken to them, or anyone, in almost two months. I need to clear the air and apologize.

To everyone.

Just as I pull up to the house and step from the car, Matt pulls in behind me with Pop and Isaac with him.

Before I can get a word out, Matt storms from his car, his eyes pissed and teeth bared and grips me by the collar of my shirt and slams me against my car.

"You fucking cocksucker!" He yells and pulls his fist back and plants it firmly in my jaw.

"What the fuck?" I yell and reverse our positions, pinning Matt to the car. "What the fuck is wrong with you?"

Instead of answering, he swings again, planting his fist in my eye and I reel back, landing flat on my ass.

He's a strong fucker.

Before Matt can continue with his ass-beating, Isaac and Pop grab both his arms and hold him back.

"I said stop!" Pop yells.

"Jesus Christ, man!" Isaac cries.

"It's his fault!" Matt points at me and spits to the side, blood lands on the concrete from the jab I managed to get in.

"What the fuck is my fault?" I demand and press the heel of my hand to my eye. Christ, that hurts. "I haven't even been here!"

"Exactly!" Matt shrugs Isaac and Pop off and gets in my face again, but doesn't touch me. His nose is inches from mine, his eyes wide and dark in anger, jar clenched. "You weren't fucking here. I told you before you left she wasn't safe yet. We didn't know enough to pull her security."

"What are you saying?" I ask as my heart stutters into over-drive.

"They've been hurt, son," Pop murmurs from behind Matt.

"What?" My eyes find Isaac and Pop's only to find them full of sadness and fear. "What?" I ask Matt.

"Someone cut her brake line," Isaac informs me. "She and the girls were in a pretty nasty accident last night."

I back away from them all, my feet moving without any direction from my head. I shove my hands up into my hair and stare at my brothers and father.

"*What?*"

"The kids aren't banged up too badly. Mostly bruises, although Maddie needed stitches in her hand," Isaac informs me.

"Brynna?" I ask.

"She's unconscious," Pop replies softly. "Concussion. Dislocated shoulder. They're keeping her to watch the head injury and to make sure there's nothing internal."

"Oh my God."

"There was video surveillance in the parking lot of the mall she was parked in, so we know who did it, and we have already arrested him," Matt mutters, still glaring at me. "But you weren't here, Caleb."

"Why was she alone?" I ask.

"You weren't fucking here!"

"So what!" I scream back. "You're here! You're all here! She's as safe with you as she was with me!"

"She wouldn't allow it," Pop inserts with a sigh. "She said she could take care of her and the girls on her own, she'd been doing it for years, and she wouldn't let us move her in with us or stay with her."

I'm pacing around the driveway, not believing my ears.

"You have got to be kidding me."

"You messed her up, man," Isaac says. "She's been a mess. The girls cry a lot."

Direct hit, right to the gut.

"I left because I thought it was the right thing to do."

"You left," Matt interrupts, "because you're a fucking pussy."

"Where are they?"

None of them will answer me, and it tears me apart that they don't trust me. That they think that I'll hurt Brynna and the babies.

"Where are they?" I repeat. "Dad, I love them. That's why I'm here."

Pop sighs and rubs his eyes with his hands.

"They're at Harborview."

Without answering I jump in my car and peel out of my parent's driveway.

My girls are hurt!

I race down to Harborview, not paying attention to the posted speed limits or traffic laws, find parking and run inside.

"Brynna Vincent," I bark at the woman behind the registration desk. "I need to find her."

"One moment," she murmurs and types on her keyboard. "Looks like she's up on the fourth floor, room four-oh-nine."

I bypass the elevator and climb the stairs, three at a time, until I reach the fourth floor. As I stomp past the waiting room, I hear, "Caleb!"

I stop dead in my tracks at the sound of that little voice.

"Hey, buttercup," I fall to my knees as Maddie throws herself in my arms, crying and clinging to me. "Hey, are you okay?"

"I have stitches," she pouts and leans back to show me her little hand wrapped in gauze. I kiss it gently and offer her a smile.

"Where is Josie?"

"Caleb!"

Josie jumps on my back, hugging me around the neck. "I had to pee!"

I tug her around and wrap my arms around both girls, breathing them in. Josie has a black eye, and Maddie's lip is split.

I'm going to fucking kill whoever got their hands on Brynna's brakes.

"Are you sure you're both okay?" I ask with a rough voice. They nod and Josie snuggles close to me.

"Where did you go?" She whispers.

"I had a job," I respond and clench my eyes shut. "I'm home now."

"Brynna won't be happy to see you."

I glance up to find Luke and Nat, Meg, Nate and Brynna's parents watching me. Even Leo and Sam are here, along with Dominic.

Of course the whole family is here.

"I have to see her," I respond and kiss the girls' heads softly. "You stay here, okay? I'm gonna go see your mama."

"She's sleeping," Maddie informs me with tears. "I wanna see her too, but she keeps sleeping."

"You'll get to see her soon, sweetheart."

"Jules and Will are with her now," Sam calls to me with a sympathetic smile. "Welcome home."

I wave and hurry to Bryn's room and approach just as Jules and Will are coming out.

"Oh, my God," Jules mutters with wide eyes. "Who called you?"

"No one," I scowl. *Why didn't anyone call me?*

"She's not your woman," Will counters and crosses his arms over his chest, blocking my entrance to the room. "And you're not going in there."

"Yeah, I am." My gaze bounces between my brother and sister. "I love her. More than anything. I know I fucked everything up, but I have to make it right. I have to see her to make sure she's okay."

"She's okay," Jules assures me. "But I don't think you should go in there either, Caleb. She won't want to see you."

"For the few minutes she was lucid, she insisted we not call you," Will tells me and for the first time, what looks like sympathy moves across his face.

"So, here's the thing," I cross my arms, mirroring Will's stance. "I'm going in there. You can both either move, or I can move you. It's your choice."

Jules rolls her eyes. "Fine, stubborn ass," she mutters and stomps off toward the waiting room. Will doesn't move.

"Well?" I ask him.

"You've already hurt her enough."

I stare at him for what feels like minutes. Finally, I sigh and drop my head. "I know."

"She deserves to be treated with respect."

"I know." I nod and pace away in a circle, right here in the hallway of the hospital.

"She deserves to be loved unconditionally."

"Look, I know I'm not good enough…"

"That's not what I said, asshole," Will interrupts. "You are exactly what she needs, but she needs you to love her and her girls. To stay, Caleb. So if you're going to puss out and run again, I need to know now so I can throw you out of here on your sorry ass."

"I'm never leaving her again. I promise you that." I sigh again and prop my hands on my hips. "I've been seeing a shrink. Working my shit out. I'm here to get my girl back, Will."

He watches me carefully and then a slow smile spreads across his face.

"I'll be in the waiting room." He slaps my shoulder and pauses next to me. "And I'm warning you now, she won't be happy to see you when she wakes up. You've got some work to do."

I nod and push her door open, step inside and feel my stomach fall to my knees.

There are monitors beeping and wires running under her hospital gown to her body. Her face is white and scratched. Her hair is matted with dried blood.

Her left arm is in a sling and on her right index finger is a clip with a red light on it that seems to monitor her temperature.

She looks small and frail and it brings me to my knees.

I lower myself into the chair at the side of her bed, lean over and grip her uninjured hand in my own, bring it to my lips, and kiss her knuckles. Her skin is soft and I can smell her lavender and vanilla body wash.

I press her hand against my cheek and gaze into her face.

"Hey, Legs." I clear my throat and glance up at the heart monitor, mesmerized by the blip, blip, blip of the machine. "I'm so sorry, baby."

She doesn't stir. I kiss her palm and lay my head on her stomach and for the first time in as long as I can remember, I let tears come.

Please, baby, forgive me.

Chapter Twenty

~Brynna~

Everything hurts.

Everything.

I'm fighting against the heavy weight of sleep. I want to wake up and see my babies. My eyes are so heavy, but I blink them open and then slam them shut against the light in the room.

It feels super bright, although I know it probably isn't. My head is killing me.

My shoulder is on fire.

I try to move my head, but it just aches and I feel myself moan in protest.

"Bryn?"

My eyes open again at the sound of his voice, and I stare at him in awe.

"Am I dreaming?" I ask, my voice unrecognizable.

He shakes his head and kisses my hand, then leans forward and kisses my forehead, making me moan again.

"Head hurts," I whisper.

"I know, baby. I'll call the nurse."

When I look up at him again, I frown at the worry in his eyes. What's wrong?

"Kids?" I whisper.

"They're fine. Your parents took them home a little while ago, but they'll come see you tomorrow."

My mouth is dry, and now the room is starting to spin. I whimper.

"Ms. Vincent, you're awake." A nurse bustles in and checks

the monitors.

"Hurts," I mutter softly.

"I'm going to give you some more medicine. You'll sleep for a while."

She pushes some buttons and my veins feel warm and I sleep folds around me again.

"Love you," I hear Caleb whisper, but I can't make my mouth move as sleep claims me.

***

Someone is holding my hand. It's probably Stacy or my mom. I wish I didn't have to take so many meds that make me sleep so much.

My head has gone from a hard, pounding throb to just an ache. My shoulder is still screaming.

"Had a dream," I whisper, keeping my eyes closed. It feels so much better when I just keep them closed.

Mom or Stacy gently brushes my hair off my forehead.

"I dreamed he was here," I whisper and feel a tear fall. "Why do I keep dreaming about him? When is it going to stop?"

"I'm so sorry, baby."

I open my eyes and gasp when I see Caleb sitting beside me, leaning his elbows on my bed. I cry out in pain at the abrupt movement and he curses.

"Don't move, Bryn."

"What are you doing here?" *And why did I just say that in front of you?*

"You're hurt," he responds, as if that explains everything.

"You're not supposed to be here." My voice is gravel and the dull ache has returned to a pounding throb in my head.

"Brynna, I didn't know you were hurt until I got here. I was coming home for you, baby."

I frown and stare at him.

"Who said I wanted you?"

He clenches his eyes shut and kisses my hand, but I tug it out of his grasp.

"I don't want you here, Caleb."

"Look, Brynna."

"Shut up," I mutter and close my eyes, turning my head away from him, embarrassed and hurt and not ready or willing to trust him. "Go away."

"Please," he whispers.

"Go away!" I yell and wince as I wrench my shoulder with the movement and reduce myself to tears. "Just go."

"I don't want to leave you."

"Get the hell out of here!"

"Mr. Montgomery, you need to leave," the nurse insists as she comes in my room. "She's in too much pain to be this upset."

"Let me just sit with you," he pleads, his voice rough with pain, but all I can do is cry and shake my head.

"Go," I whisper around my tears.

"Please, Mr. Montgomery. Your family is still in the waiting room."

"I want my mom," I cry.

"I'll send her in, sweetheart." He stands and kisses my forehead. "I'm so sorry, baby."

"Go," I whisper again.

He leaves the room. I lay and cry in silence, trying not to jar my body too much, but unable to stop the flow of tears. Finally after several long minutes, my mom pushes through the door and hurries to my side.

"I'm so sorry, sweet girl." She kisses my cheek and gently strokes my hand in hers. "He loves you, honey."

"I don't want him," I whisper.

"Your tears say something different."

"He left me, Mom."

"I know. He's just a stupid man, Brynna."

I gingerly turn my head and look at my mom through swollen eyes.

"I can't have him hurt my girls again, Mom," I whisper.

"I know. Don't worry about it now. Rest and get strong so you can go home and take care of your girls."

"Are they really okay?" I ask her.

"They are fine. Nothing that time won't heal." She offers me a reassuring smile. "Your father just took them home to bed."

"Good," I sigh. "I'm thirsty."

"I'll get you some fresh water," the nurse replies and hurries out of the room.

"Did they find him?" I ask my mom.

"Yes. He's been arrested and from what Matt said, he's ratting out the others in Chicago." She squeezes my hand I am reduced to tears once again. "You're safe, darling girl."

The nightmare is over.

***

"I don't see any reason that you can't go home this morning," the doctor remarks the next morning as he looks in my eyes with a bright light. "You'll just need to take it easy with that shoulder for about a week. It's going to hurt. Take your pain meds."

"I have small children," I remind him. "I can't be loopy."

"You'll need help with them," he tells me sternly. "And I can give you meds that won't make you too loopy. If you take them when you're supposed to, you should stay ahead of the pain. But if you faint, get dizzy, or have any concerns at all, come back to the hospital right away."

"Okay," I agree. "Can you send my mom in?" I ask the nurse.

"Oh, she left last night."

I frown at her and then look about the room for my phone. "I guess I'll call her."

"You sure are a lucky woman," she remarks as she helps me get dressed.

"What do you mean?" I ask.

"That handsome guy you threw out of here? He sent the family home and camped out right by your door all night." She grins at me and I just stare at her.

"He did *what*?"

"He insisted he wouldn't leave you, so I took pity on him

around midnight and got him a chair. He stayed put all night."

"I suppose he's still there?" I ask, already knowing the answer.

"I'm right here," Caleb responds softly behind me. The nurse has just finished helping me dress, and I close my eyes, not quite ready to face him yet.

"Will you please call my mom and ask her to come get me and take me home?" I ask him quietly.

"No," he responds. "I'm taking you home."

"Caleb..."

"I have some things to say, Brynna. I'm not trying to upset you. You need a ride, and I need to talk, so there you have it."

I turn to face him and have to pull in a sharp breath when I see him. His dark blonde hair is a messy riot from his fingers combing through it over and over. He's in a black t-shirt and faded blue jeans.

His eyes are shadowed and his chin is stubbled.

He looks like shit.

He looks amazing.

I shrug like I don't care either way and glance around the room. "Suit yourself."

"What are you looking for, dear?" The nurse asks.

"My purse and... things."

"Oh, you don't have anything with you, honey."

"Oh." I frown and look down at my empty hands. It feels weird.

"Can I take her home now?" Caleb asks her.

"Yes, you're good to go," she responds with a smile. "Remember; take your meds when you're supposed to, and take it easy."

"Thank you," I murmur and follow Caleb out of the room where a wheelchair is waiting for me. He helps me into the chair and pushes me slowly to the elevator and out to his car.

He gently takes my uninjured hand and helps me from the chair to the car, scowling when I wince. After I'm settled, he shuts my door and joins me in the car.

"Are you okay?"

"I'm sore," I admit. "Tired."

"Brynna, I'm so fucking sorry. For everything."

I settle back against the seat and close my eyes.

"Can we talk when we get to my house?" I ask. "I want to be able to see you when you answer my questions."

"Sure," he responds and reaches over to lay his hand on my thigh, but I pull it away. "Can I fix this, Bryn?" He asks with a whisper.

"I don't know," I reply.

We ride in silence to the house, and when we pull into the driveway, he goes through the motions again of helping me from the car and inside.

"Couch or bed?" He asks.

"Couch. I don't have the energy to climb the stairs."

"I'll carry you."

"Couch," I repeat, ignoring his scowl. I lower myself into the corner of the sofa and adjust the pillows until I'm as comfortable as can be.

Until I need to readjust everything in about four minutes.

"Sit on the ottoman," I order him. I want to see him square on when we're talking. I need to see his face. His eyes.

He complies and leans forward, his elbows on his knees and watches my face.

"I hate that you're hurt," he mutters.

"I'm not enjoying it myself," I reply dryly.

"I want to kill him," he growls, and I can see that he means every single word.

"I understand he's in jail," I respond and watch him for a moment. "Where did you go?"

"You don't know?" He asks with surprise.

"No. I wouldn't let anyone talk about you around me."

He flinches. "I was in San Diego, on a training contract with the Navy."

"SEALs," I guess.

"Yeah," he nods. "The contract is over now. I'm going back to work at the old job."

"You hurt my kids," I blurt, unable to keep it in anymore. "You hurt me too, but the most important thing is that you hurt them, and they didn't deserve that."

"I know," he sighs. "I'm so sorry I said the things I did. I didn't mean any of it, I swear. I just didn't know how to make you let me go. I got scared, Bryn."

"Why?" I demand. "What is it about the three of us that's so fucking scary to a Navy SEAL, Caleb?"

"I didn't know how to handle the way I felt about you," he begins and swallows. "How I *feel*."

"And how is that?"

"I love you so much it hurts," he responds immediately, his eyes holding mine.

I will not cry!

"So you think you can come waltzing back in here and profess your love for me and that makes it all better?"

He swears under his breath and shakes his head.

"I'm here to apologize, first and foremost. I had a long talk with the girls last night before you kicked me out of your room and before your dad took them home."

"You did?" I ask, surprised, and worried that he's got their hopes up again.

"I apologized to them, and hugged them, and we got some things worked out."

"What, exactly, did you get worked out with two six-year-olds?" I ask with a laugh.

"I'll get to that," he responds with a grin, showing me his dimples, and I want to cave right then.

Those damn dimples get me every time.

I try to move in the sofa to find a comfortable position and cry out when I bump my shoulder.

"Hey, easy," he croons and helps me rearrange the pillows behind me. "Easy, baby."

"Don't call me baby," I whisper.

"Why not?" He whispers back.

"It hurts," I admit and close my eyes. "Having you here hurts far worse than these injuries, Caleb."

"I'm sorry," he repeats, and I'm just sick of hearing it.

"You know what, I think I will go up to my bedroom." I stand, wincing but proud of myself for not crying out.

"Let me help you, damn it!" He stands next to me, ready to wrap his arms around me, but I move away.

"I can do this on my own. My legs aren't hurt."

Without another word, I slowly walk to the stairway and up the steps, one at a time, gripping the handrail for balance.

Getting onto the bed and into a comfortable position is pure hell. I don't bother to try to change my clothes or get under the covers.

I just want to sleep.

I want to sleep with Caleb's arms holding me, but that's not going to happen.

Tears fall down my face as I lean my head back against the headboard and pray for a dreamless sleep to claim me.

***

I wake with a start, gasping for breath. It's still light out, and glancing at the clock, I see I've only been asleep for an hour.

But the dream was chasing me again, the one where I can't find my girls or Caleb, and panic seizes me.

Did I dream him?

Is he really here?

I need to see him. I struggle from the bed, swearing at the dull throb in my shoulder, and slowly move down the stairs to the living room.

There he is.

Caleb is sitting on the couch, his elbows on his knees and head propped in his hands. He looks defeated and broken, and despite my resolve to tell him to go to hell, I can't stop myself from going to him.

I push my fingers into his soft hair and he quickly sits up, his eyes wide as he looks up into my face.

"Bryn?"

"I thought I dreamed you." I voice catches as tears fill my eyes. "I needed to see you."

KRISTEN PROBY

"Ah, baby," he murmurs and stands, lifts me gently into his arms and lowers us effortlessly onto the couch, cradling me close to him, kissing my forehead and cheek. "I'm sorry baby."

"I know. You can stop saying it. But I do need you to talk to me." I tip my head back so I can look him in the eye. "The past three months have been horrible for me and the girls, Caleb. They miss you. They kept asking if they did something wrong to make you go away."

His eyes fill with tears but I keep talking. "We love you so much, and you just left us. After everything we'd been through together."

"I know," he whispers, his voice raw. "I was pretty fucked up, Bryn. You saw the nightmares. I couldn't bear the thought of hurting you again, and I convinced myself that I wasn't good enough for you."

"What are the nightmares about?" I ask and watch as his face goes white. "You can tell me."

"It's classified," he replies, but I cup his cheek in my hand and make him meet my gaze.

"Who the hell am I gonna tell, Caleb?"

He sighs and leans his forehead against mine.

"I was on a mission in Afghanistan about seven months ago with three other men. It was just supposed to be a recon mission…"

I raise my eyes at him as if to say, "English, please."

"We were just supposed to go in and gather information," he continues. "We knew there were armed Taliban in the area, but we didn't know if there were ten or a hundred. Our intel wasn't the best."

I frown and watch his face as it tightens as he continues the story.

"Turned out there were roughly fifty of them, and they were waiting for us."

"How did they know you'd be there?" I ask.

"Good question," he responds. "I'll spare you the details, but I lost all three of my teammates that day."

I gasp and drag my hand down his cheek, comforting him.

"Oh, I'm so sorry. How did you make it out?"

He swallows hard and licks his lips. "I was knocked unconscious and they thought I was dead. Just as they began to retreat, our Special Forces guys came in to help. It was too late for the other guys on my team, but they pulled me out of there."

I stare at him, processing all he's telling me, and I can't stop touching him, his hair, his face.

I almost lost him before I even had him

"Was that the last mission?" I ask.

"Yeah," he confirms. "I was up for re-enlistment, and I decided against it. I put enough years in."

"Caleb, there are people you can talk to about the nightmares."

"I already have been," he replies, his gaze sober. "I started seeing a shrink in San Diego, and I'll keep seeing one up here. I'm working my shit out, Brynna. I even called my guys' families, at the direction of my shrink." He blinks, as though he's surprised.

"How did that go?" I ask softly.

"Not like I expected."

"What did you expect?"

"I thought they'd say it was my fault. Yell at me. Hell, I would have." He shakes his head and clears his throat. "But they all said that they knew it wasn't my fault, and that they wished me nothing but happiness and peace."

"They sound like good people," I whisper.

He nods and glides his knuckles down my, watching my lips as I lick them.

"I'm so sorry I ran, Legs." He exhales and leans in to rest his forehead against mine. "I was so afraid."

"Why?" I ask.

"Because I was afraid that I would eventually disappoint you. I figured that you and the girls deserved someone who hasn't been to hell and back and has the baggage to prove it."

"Oh, Caleb," I murmur and drag my fingertips down his cheek. "It's *us* who doesn't deserve *you.*"

He shakes his head but I cover his lips with my fingers before he can interrupt.

"I'm so proud of you. From the minute I met you, I've been proud of you. Not many can do what you've done, Caleb. I'm sorry that you have demons, that you lost your men in that mission, but that doesn't make you less of a man, any more than my baggage from my first marriage makes me less of a woman."

I sigh as he sweeps his hand up and down my back, soothing us both.

"You need to know, we're a package deal, Caleb. My girls and I are a team, and if you want to be a part of my life, you have to join the team, not just me."

He frowns and stares at me like I've lost my mind.

"Brynna, you don't have to remind me of that. I've never given you any reason to think that I don't want your girls." He kisses my forehead before smiling softly down at me. "They asked me if I was gonna come home where I belong. I told them that was up to you."

"They love you, you know," I murmur. "They were devastated after you left. Maddie cried for days. Even Bix couldn't console her. We adopted him permanently, by the way."

He nuzzles my nose with his own and then backs away before kissing me, watching me closely.

"I love the three of you with all my heart, Brynna. Your girls may not have come from me, but no one will ever love them more. Let me give all of you my name. Marry me."

I swallow and my jaw drops in shock. My damn eyes are leaking again, but I can't move to brush the tears away.

"I want to adopt them," he continues. "Seeing you there in that hospital made everything crystal clear for me. The thought of ever losing you is like a knife twisting in my soul. I want more babies with you. I want to give you everything you've ever wanted."

I continue to silently cry and watch his handsome face, his deep blue eyes are moist and full of emotion, and I know without a doubt, he is meant for my girls and me.

He's ours, and we are his.

"You are my happy, Legs. Marry me."

I smile slowly and cup his face with my hand. "We would be

honored to marry you, Caleb Montgomery."

He smiles widely and leans in to kiss me. Gently. Tenderly. Lovingly.

"Love you so much," he whispers against my lips, sending tingles through me.

"Love you too, stubborn man," I whisper back and kiss him, sweeping my lips over his, enjoying the way his stubble feels against my face.

"Keep kissing me like this," he murmurs and kisses a trail down my jawline to my neck. "And I'll forget that you were in an accident the other night and have a concussion."

"I missed kissing you," I mutter.

He pulls back and cups my face tenderly in his hand, staring down at me longingly. "God, I missed it too. I missed you."

"Thank you for coming home."

"You're gonna marry me." He smiles proudly.

"We are," I nod and smile back. "When?"

"As soon as possible. There's no need to wait." He shrugs and frowns. "How big of a wedding do you want?"

"I'd love it if it was just our family," I confess with a shy smile. "Something small and intimate with the people closest to us sounds perfect to me."

"Hell, we can do that tomorrow."

"Well, I would like to buy a dress, and the girls will want pretty dresses too," I remind him.

"Two weeks?"

"I guess I'd better call Alecia the Montgomery party planner extraordinaire and start making plans."

"Tomorrow," he agrees. "For right now, I just want to hold you."

"Good plan."

Chapter Twenty-One

"Mommy! Look how pretty I am!"

I turn from the mirror where my mom is zipping me into my own dress to admire my daughters in their little ivory dresses with pink sashes and pink roses in their dark hair, both smiling so proudly.

"You are both beautiful," I announce and kiss both of their cheeks. "Caleb is going to be so excited when he sees you."

"He's wearing a suit," Josie informs me with a giggle. "He looks really big in it."

"The man has the broadest shoulders I've ever seen," Mom agrees with a chuckle.

"I think they're ready," Stacy announces as she walks into Steven and Gail's formal living room, which has been dubbed the bride's dressing room for today's event. "Oh, honey, you're so beautiful." Her eyes fill with tears and I shake my head adamantly.

"No! No, no, no! No tears today. My makeup is done and I'll look all red and stupid if I cry, and if you start I will too." I pull my sweet cousin into a tight hug and fight tears.

"You know, this means we're really sisters now. Who knew we'd end up marrying brothers?" She giggles as she pulls away and smiles happily. "I'm so happy for both of you."

"Thank you."

"Come on!" My dad calls as he steps in the room. "They're not going to wait forever."

"Oh please," Mom waves him off with a roll of the eyes. "She's the bride. They'll wait as long as she wants. Where are they going to go?"

"I'm ready," I assure them as I turn to take one more look in the mirror. The dress I chose is a simple ivory gown. It's strapless and form-fitting, but has rouching all the way down to my feet, which are in pink satin Louboutin's, a gift from Natalie and Jules.

Those girls and their shoes.

My hair is up in a twist at the base of my neck, and I've decided to forgo the veil.

I want to see him clear as day when I walk out there before our family and pledge myself and my children to him.

"Okay, I'll see you out there." Mom kisses my cheek and smiles wide before leaving the room.

"Here we go."

Stacy leads us to the back door, and I take a moment to peek out at the beautiful back yard I'm about to get married in. Steven Montgomery's yard is always lovely, especially in the spring. The fresh scent of lilacs fills the air. Seattle weather had mercy on me today and the sun is out with a light breeze floating through, making it perfect.

Alecia has outdone herself, as usual. She managed to get my favorite restaurant to cater, and they are set up and ready to go under the cover of the patio. Steven's sound system has been wirelessly piped outside and *At Last* by Etta James has just started to play.

The family is seated in white folding chairs in the center of the yard in a semi-circle, and everyone is here. Leo Nash even returned late last night from his tour schedule so he could attend.

"Okay, girls, follow me." Stacy winks at me and clenches her pink-rose bouquet in front of her as she sets off down the yard, and the girls follow, side by side, also clutching small bouquets rather than baskets of petals. When Caleb sees them, his face breaks out in a wide smile and he winks at the girls as they stand off to the side.

"Ready, baby girl?" Daddy smiles down at me.

"Absolutely. Let's go."

We step outside as everyone stands and smiles at us, but I only have eyes for my handsome man. His gorgeous blue eyes are soft and happy as he watches us approach.

"Nervous?" Dad whispers to me.

"Not a bit," I whisper back.

"You may be seated," The justice of the peace, Brian Parker, announces.

"Beena!" Olivia announces from Luke's lap, making us chuckle.

"Yes, Brynna is pretty," Luke murmurs.

"Who presents Brynna to Caleb?" Mr. Parker asks.

"Her mother and I do," Dad answers, kisses my cheek and joins my hand with Caleb's before taking his seat.

I pass my bouquet to Stacy and stand facing Caleb. He winks at me, making me chuckle.

"We are gathered here to celebrate the union of Caleb and Brynna in marriage, but we are also here to celebrate the union of a family."

I swallow hard as I watch Caleb's eyes.

"The sacred vows about to be exchanged are not just between Brynna and Caleb because you will not only be a new couple, you will be a new family. So, Madeline and Joseline, will you please join us now for the special family rites of this wedding?"

Caleb and I step back as Josie and Maddie approach, standing between us. Caleb pulls two necklaces out of his jacket pocket. They are platinum chains with heart pendants that have today's date inscribed on the back.

As he drapes the first necklace over Maddie's neck, his strong voice fills the air with the vows he's written for each of them.

"I love you, Maddie, and I am devoted to making your life full of happiness and accomplishments, nurturing your creativity, encouraging your independence and making sure you always know what a gift you are to this world." He kisses her forehead and she smiles up at him happily before admiring her pretty new necklace.

My eyes fill with tears as he turns to Josie.

"I love you, Josie, and I am devoted to making your life full of happiness and accomplishments, ensuring that you thrive to your fullest potential and that while you reach for the sky, you remain grounded by the love of our family and our home."

There are many sniffles coming from our family now as Caleb kisses Josie's forehead and then turns back to me.

"Girls," Mr. Parker begins, "Please come stand by me as we marry Mommy and Caleb. We want you to have a front row seat."

Maddie tugs on the hem of his jacket, and Mr. Parker looks down at her with a smile. "Yes, sweetie?"

"His name is Daddy now," She whispers loudly so everyone can hear, making us all laugh.

"Of course," Mr. Parker laughs. "Excuse me."

"Caleb and Brynna, please join hands and face each other. Josie, do you have the ring for Daddy?"

Josie hops up and down and opens her hand so Caleb can have my ring. I gasp when I see it. We picked the rings out together, but seeing my ring, with the two bands that twist together, signifying our girls, coming together at the center with a beautiful princess-cut diamond takes my breath away.

"Caleb, please place the ring on Brynna's finger and repeat after me."

Caleb looks into my eyes as he repeats our vows. His own eyes moisten and it's enough to send a tear falling down my own cheek.

"I give you my promise to be by your side forevermore. I promise to love, to honor, and to listen as you tell me your thoughts, your hopes, your fears and your dreams. I promise to love you deeply and truly because it is your heart that moves me, your head that challenges me, your humor that delights me and your hands I wish to hold until the end of my days."

He brings my hand to his lips and gently kisses my knuckle, just above my ring.

"Maddie, do you have the ring for your Mom?"

Maddie grins and opens her hand, revealing Caleb's ring, a simple thick platinum band, that has my name inscribed inside.

"Brynna, please place this ring on Caleb's finger and repeat after me."

Holding Caleb's hand in my own, I repeat my vows to him, the same he just spoke to me.

As I step back, Mr. Parker finishes our short ceremony.

"May all your days be filled with joy and happiness. It is my honor and great pleasure by the power vested in me by the state of Washington, that I now pronounce you husband and wife. You may kiss your beautiful bride."

Caleb steps forward, cradles my cheek in one hand and wraps his other arm around my waist and pulls me to him.

"I love you, Mrs. Montgomery."

He slips his lips over mine, and he kisses me softly, sinking into me slowly and nibbling my lips thoroughly, not caring that our nearest and dearest are all looking on.

Finally, Mr. Parker clears his throat loudly and Caleb laughs as he pulls back and kisses my forehead.

"It's my pleasure to be the first to introduce Caleb, Brynna, Maddie and Josie Montgomery!"

"Yay!" Josie exclaims and our family jumps to their feet, applauding. Jules and Natalie are wiping tears. Leo is whispering in Sam's ear and then places a sweet kiss on her neck, making her grin softly.

"Let's eat!" Will announces right before he gathers me up in a big hug and twirls me about. "It's about time," he mutters with a wink.

Before I know it, I'm passed about from brother to brother, caught up in hugs and kisses.

"Congratulations, sweetheart," Luke murmurs and kisses my cheek.

"Thank you," I reply with a grin.

This is more male attention than I've ever had in my life.

Dominic gathers me close for a hug. In the three months that Caleb was gone, Dom has worked hard to get to know all of us and he's been a welcome addition to the family.

"You deserve to be this happy," he whispers to me.

"Hey, get your own girl," Caleb growls and pulls me out of Dom's arms with a mock glare.

"You're the one who left your new wife all alone minutes after marrying her," Dom taunts him and I can't help but smirk.

"I will cut you. Wedding or not," Caleb threatens but Dom throws his head back and laughs hard.

"Yeah. You scare me, brother." He pats Caleb's arm and smiles warmly. "Congratulations. Oh, I brought this." He raises a bottle of wine from next to his chair and smiles. "For you."

"Oh, thank you so much!" I accept the heavy bottle and admire the pretty label. "Yours?"

"Of course," he smirks.

"Alecia," I catch the event planner's attention as she passes by. "Dominic brought this. I'd like to use it for the toast, please."

The pretty blonde takes the bottle from me and her eyes go wide when she reads the label. Her wide brown gaze find Dom's.

"This is a rare bottle of wine. You have good taste." She smiles at me and walks off toward the house. "I'll see to it."

"I love her," I sigh as I watch her walk away. I would never have been able to pull this wedding off without her.

Suddenly, *When The Stars Go Blue* begins to play through the sound system and Caleb kisses my hand and then searches the yard. "Well, Maddie and Josie Montgomery, I think it's time we dance."

The girls giggle as Caleb lifts them both, one on each arm, and takes them out into the grass where he sways around, talking and laughing with our daughters.

"I've never seen him this happy," Jules murmurs as she and Natalie join me, one on either side of me.

I grin and continue to watch the three most important people in my world.

"He's gonna be an amazing dad," Natalie agrees. Suddenly it occurs to me that they're both sniffling, and I look back and forth between them, laughing.

"You two are so sappy!"

"I can't help it!" Jules wails and wipes her cheeks. "It's these damn hormones."

"I hate being pregnant," Natalie grumbles, but smiles when she rubs her round belly. "He's making me all emotional."

"It's a boy?" I ask excitedly.

Natalie smiles and nods happily. "We just found out yesterday."

"Oh my God, that's so exciting!" I wrap my arms around her

in a big hug.

"I need a hug too!" Jules exclaims and hugs us both.

"What is happening over here?"

We pull apart to find Nate, Luke, Will, Matt and Dom watching us with confused looks.

"We're happy," I respond with a shrug.

"Why do girls always cry when they're happy?" Mark asks as he approaches with a loaded plate.

"Dude, you got food?" Will asks and takes off running toward the house.

"We won't see him for a while," Meg smirks and hands me a glass of champagne. "Have you seen your cake?"

"Yes, it's so pretty!"

"Did the owner of *Succulent Sweets* in downtown do it?" Sam asks, her blue eyes excited. "Cause if she did, I may eat it all."

Leo laughs at her and shakes his head. "We just had cupcakes from there this morning."

"Don't judge me," she responds with a scowl. "That woman is really talented. Baking is an art form, you know."

"What's your favorite flavor?" I ask her and glace over to where Caleb is still laughing and dancing with the girls. Now Bix is barking and bouncing around them in his black bowtie, getting in on the action.

That dog is never far from the girls.

"Chocolate," Sam responds automatically.

"I went with chocolate in one tier and lemon in the other," I respond.

"Yes!" Leo pumps his fist and high fives Sam. "That's our other favorite."

"You guys are a hot mess," Jules shakes her head at them and then seems to reconsider. "Wait. There's chocolate? You can't hide chocolate from the pregnant chicks!"

"It's over there," I point to the table under the patio where our beautiful two-tiered cake is set up and the baker, Nicole Dolan, is fussing over it. "Have you guys met Nic?"

"No, get her genius self over here," Sam responds.

I wave to Nic and she grins and joins us in the grass. She's a petite brunette with her hair in a short asymmetrical bob. Her eyes are bright green.

"Congratulations, friend!" She raises on her tip-toes and wraps her arms around me to hug me tight. "Where is your man?"

"Right here," Caleb murmurs and grins at us as we pull apart. "The cake is beautiful, thank you."

"My pleasure," Nic beams.

"You make the best cake in the whole world," Sam gushes, but Nic's gaze is stuck on Matt. She's gone pale and takes a step back.

"Holy shit," she whispers.

"Do you know each other?" Caleb asks.

Nic recovers with a shake of the head and forces a fake smile. "I'm so happy that you like the cake. It's ready to go for you. Congratulations again." She turns to go but Matt interrupts her.

"Stop," Matt commands, his voice deceptively soft. Everyone watches in awe as Nic immediately stops talking and folds her hands in front of her, watching Matt warily.

I glance at the men and all of their eyebrows are high on their foreheads as they watch the exchange.

Matt walks forward and gently takes Nic by the elbow and leads her a few feet away where he leans in and whispers something in her ear. She blushes furiously, but her eyes flash in anger as she pulls her arm out of his grasp. She says nothing as she turns her back on him and stomps away.

"Spank her ass," he whispers angrily and marches after her.

"I guess they know each other," Will observes while stuffing a dinner roll in his mouth.

"Do you know anything about this?" Isaac asks Caleb, who shakes his head in bewilderment.

"Not a clue."

"You know, I know it's hard for you all to believe this, but you don't know everything there is to know about each other," Meg reminds them with a smug grin.

The brothers frown at Meg as Nate smirks.

"Don't know why you're smirking," Will elbows Nate. "We know you have your cock…"

"Daddy dance with us again!" Josie interrupts as she skips up to Caleb.

"I will in a little while, sugar." Caleb smiles at her as she skips away and then scowls at Will. "Dude, watch your language."

"It's true," Will shrugs.

Dom scowls at all of us. "What am I missing?"

"Nothing," Nate hurries to assure him and glares at Jules. "You're getting a spanking of your own later."

"Don't tease me now, ace," Jules purrs.

I laugh as I lean my head on Caleb's arm and gaze lovingly at the people surrounding me.

"I love this family," I chuckle.

"I love you," Caleb whispers in my ear and kisses my temple. "Mrs. Montgomery."

Epilogue

~Caleb~

I pour some cream in Bryn's coffee and carry it out onto the patio. She's lounging in one of the many plush lounge chairs that sit on the massive space just outside my brother, Dominic's home in Tuscany.

This is the last day of our honeymoon, and I'm determined that she relaxes and I make love to her at least a hundred times today before we head back to real life tomorrow.

Although, I admit, I'm excited to see our girls. Two weeks away from them has been too much.

"Thank you, babe," she mutters and sips her coffee as I sit in the chair beside her. It's very early morning. There are rows and rows of grape vines, for as far as the eye can see, covering green and brown hills that are just waking up under the soft light of the morning sun.

"It's beautiful here," I murmur.

"Mmm," she agrees and concentrates on her phone.

"It was nice of the family to pitch in and charter the plane for us to come here. I had no idea when Dom said he has a house in Italy that it's this huge mansion with a few thousand acres of vines."

"Mmm," she agrees again, not looking up from her phone.

"What are you doing?" I ask with a laugh.

She lowers her phone to her lap, tucks her hair behind her ear and takes a sip of coffee, then looks over at me. "I'm late."

"We're on vacation, Legs. We're not late for anything."

"No," she shakes her head and giggles and then gives me a

pointed look with those big brown eyes. "I'm *late.*"

I stare at her for a long moment and then it hits me.

She's late!

"You mean…?"

"I think so," she smirks and nods. "I went off the pill a month ago, and here we are." She shakes her head and shrugs. "Crazy."

"We need a test!" I jump up out of the chair and pat my body down. "Where's my wallet?"

"In your pocket," she replies dryly.

"I'll be back!" I race out of the house and drive the short distance between Dom's estate and the nearest village. After I find a drug store and buy one of each kind of pregnancy test they have, I race back to my hopefully pregnant wife.

"That was fast," she murmurs with a grin. She's still sitting in the lounge chair, sipping her coffee.

"Should you be drinking coffee?" I ask.

"Let's not get crazy," she responds. "I need coffee."

"I got one of each kind," I announce and upend the bag, sending small white and blue boxes scattering.

"Uh, Caleb, we only need one."

"What if we can't figure them out?" I ask and pick one up to examine it. "All of the instructions are in Italian."

She laughs hysterically and then stands, wiping her eyes.

"It's not funny."

"Yes, it is. Pregnancy tests are pretty universal, Caleb. You pee on it and a line either appears or it doesn't." She rubs my arm sweetly and kisses my shoulder before plucking the box out of my fingers. "I'll be back."

"I'm coming with you." I begin to follow her but she turns quickly with her hand out to stop me.

"Oh no, you aren't. You are not going to watch me pee on this stick."

I scowl down at her and cross my arms over my chest. "I've helped you bathe and dress and every other damn thing when you were hurt. I can handle watching you pee."

"Absolutely not." She shakes her head but then leans in and kisses my chin. "But thank you for helping me when I was hurt."

She turns and runs for the bathroom and it feels like an eternity before she comes back out, white stick in hand.

"Well?" I ask.

"It takes about three minutes, babe." She sits in the lounge chair and stares out over the vineyard. "Are you sure about this whole having another baby thing?"

I lean down and pick her up, sit in her chair and settle her on my lap.

"I want more babies," I whisper and kiss her cheek.

"Okay," she whispers back and smiles shyly. God, she can destroy me with just a look. I've faced horrors that no man or woman should have to see and faced them without qualms, but this woman and her two daughters bring me to my knees.

"I love you, Legs."

"I love you, too, sailor." She grins and kisses me, wraps her arms around my neck and turns her body until she's straddling my lap.

"Hold up. Check the stick," I interrupt before we're both naked and sweaty and the stick is a distant memory.

She glances down. "It's not ready yet."

"Go pee on another one," I instruct her. "This one is taking too long."

"I don't have to pee anymore!" She laughs. "*You* pee on one! They say *we're* pregnant, so it should work just fine."

"Smart ass," I mutter and pull her face to mine so I can kiss the fuck out of her. God, she's so amazing.

Finally, she pulls back and offers me a lazy smile.

"Look again," I whisper and lean my forehead against hers.

"Its positive, babe."

My heart stops as I gaze into her deep chocolate eyes.

We're having a baby.

"Really?" I ask.

She nods as tears gather in her eyes.

"Oh, baby," I sigh and gather her to me, rocking us back and forth and clinging to her. "Thank you."

"You're such a good daddy," she murmurs.

I grin and tip her chin back so I can see her face.

"I'm so honored to be your husband, my love. To be the father of our kids. When I left the Navy, I thought I was losing everything that mattered to me, but now I know that it was leading me to you. I wouldn't change anything. I love you."

She grins and pulls my face down to hers, presses her body closer to mine and nuzzles my nose. "I love you too."

The End

The With Me In Seattle series continues with book six, TIED WITH ME, Matt and Nic's story, in the spring of 2014.

A note from the author:

Every book I write is personal to me on some level, but Caleb and Brynna's story is one that I hold dear to my heart. My own husband is a soldier in the Army National Guard, and has deployed to Iraq twice, each for one-year deployments. I know what it is to live with a war veteran who lives with and fights the inner battles he brings home with him. Many, many brave men and women return home from war with internal scars that we can't see. PTSD is a wound these proud men and women may struggle with for many years to come, often to a debilitating degree.

According to statistics, more soldiers lost their lives by suicide (averaging one every day) than on the battlefield in 2012. This statistic is heartbreaking.

Our men and women in uniform fight battles we can't or won't to keep us safe in our homes. They know what they sign up for when they take their oath to protect our country, and they do so willingly and bravely.

There are many programs out there to help men and women who have been injured, including those who suffer from PTSD. If you would like to learn more about how you can help, please consider looking into the Wounded Warrior Project. www.woundedwarriorproject.org You can start there.

Like Brynna, I am proud to be married to a soldier who has bravely served his country, and I am proud of every person who wears a uniform and courageously serves our country so that we may live free.

I never take that for granted.

Acknowledgements:

A huge thanks goes out to my husband and kids for being so patient with me when I'm "in the cave." Thank you for your love and support. I love you guys!

To my Naughty Mafia sisters, Emily Snow, Michelle Valentine and Kelli Maine. You girls have become more to me than friends. Thank you for your unending support, loyalty and love. You rock my world.

To my agent, Kevan Lyon, for believing in me and working your rear off for me. I appreciate you more than you know!

To KP Simmon of InkSlinger PR, my publicist. You're not only my publicist, but also my friend, and I love you.

Thank you to my assistant, Taryn, for keeping me in line and on task! And for being a great friend. Love you, girl.

To my beta readers. You know who you are, and how much I value every single word of feedback you give me. This book would not be possible without you. Thank you.

To the many authors who I am blessed to call my friends, and proud to call colleagues; I'm humbled and honored to be a part of this community!

To Pamela Carrion and all of the members of my street team, thank you so much for keeping me laughing and the "inspirational photos" on hand! You guys are awesome.

To the scores of bloggers who support me every single day, THANK YOU!! I know that I would not be where I am in this industry without you, and I am beyond thankful for you!

And as always, to you, the reader. Thank you for loving this family as much as I do.

Happy Reading,
Kristen

Made in the USA
Charleston, SC
24 July 2014